About the Author

Ben Griffiths grew up in the Welsh countryside, wandering woodland trails with a head full of stories. With a father who's a librarian, it's no surprise he grew up a bookworm. After reading *The Inheritance Cycle* series at age thirteen, he was hooked on fantasy for life. Very unoriginally, Tolkien and Terry Pratchett are his favourite authors. He hopes to write books that combine the best of both of those authors and, of course, fails miserably. He doesn't think they're half bad, though. You should give them a read, and judge for yourself. Maybe you'll be surprised.

A Thread of Fate

Ben Griffiths

A Thread of Fate

Olympia Publishers
London

www.olympiapublishers.com
OLYMPIA PAPERBACK EDITION

Copyright © Ben Griffiths 2026

The right of Ben Griffiths to be identified as author of
this work has been asserted in accordance with sections 77 and 78 of
the Copyright, Designs and Patents Act 1988.

All Rights Reserved

No reproduction, copy or transmission of this publication
may be made without written permission.
No paragraph of this publication may be reproduced,
copied or transmitted save with the written permission of the publisher,
or in accordance with the provisions
of the Copyright Act 1956 (as amended).

Any person who commits any unauthorised act in relation to
this publication may be liable to criminal
prosecution and civil claims for damage.

A CIP catalogue record for this title is
available from the British Library.

ISBN: 978-1-83543-805-3

This is a work of fiction.
Names, characters, places and incidents originate from the writer's
imagination. Any resemblance to actual persons, living or dead, is
purely coincidental.

First Published in 2026

Olympia Publishers
Tallis House
2 Tallis Street
London
EC4Y 0AB

Printed in Great Britain

Dedication

This book is dedicated to Helena, the love of my life.

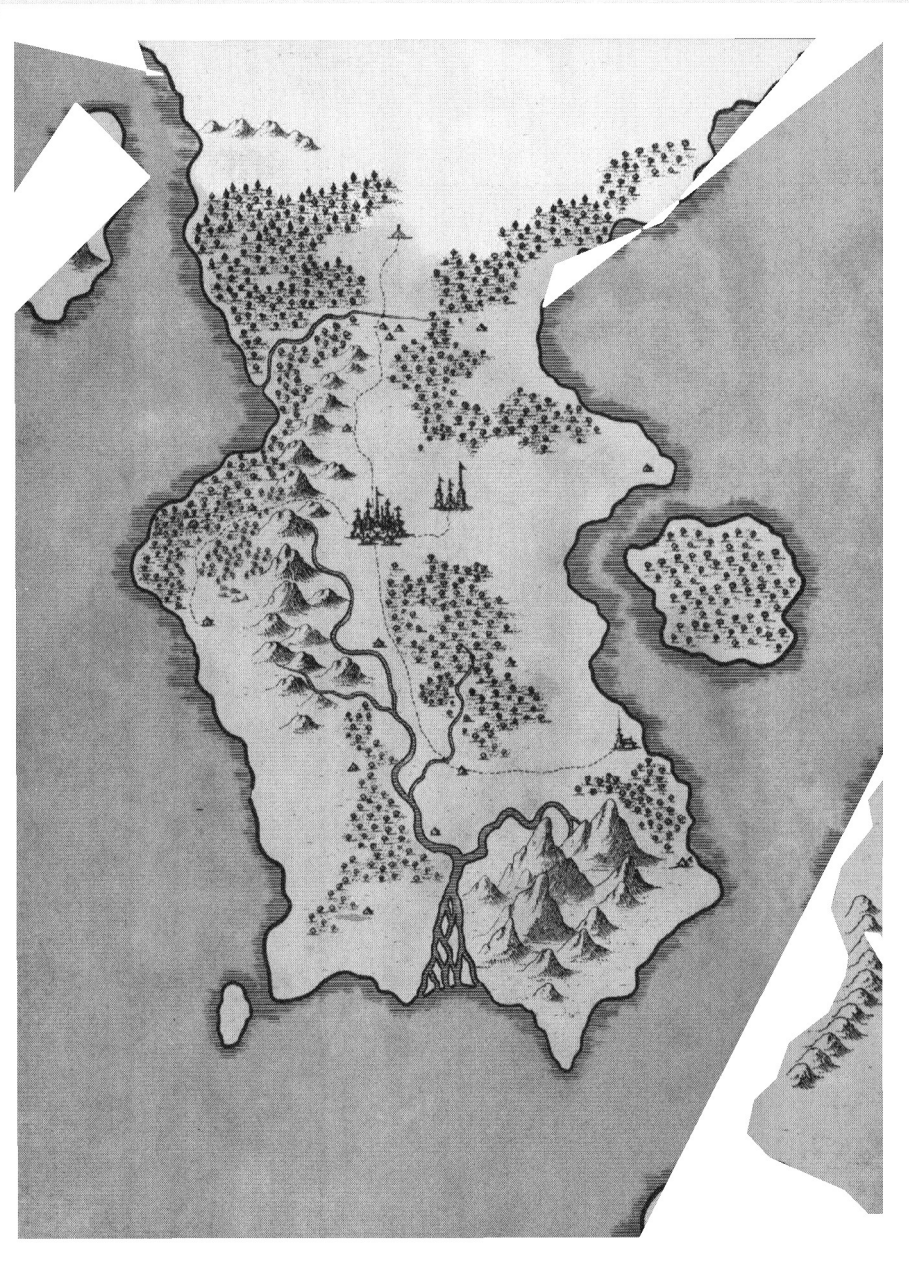

Intro

It's hard to follow a thread of fate. They are, at the best of times, temperamental. This one in particular is adventurous. It twists and turns in all sorts of unexpected directions, winding through the lives of the mighty and the low, the brilliant and the dim, the sinners and the saints. Dragons, bakers, goblins, squirrels, wizards and gods all play their part. Some moments are grand, era defining; others are banal. All are important.

As the thread flies through the ages, people come and go, but a quiet humanity, common to us all, persists. Read on and you may recognise yourself in this thread, in a distant time and place.

Dinner and a Story

The Royal Palace, 3210

The hall was exquisite, and William felt out of place. A man walking past raised an eyebrow. He said nothing, of course, but the message was quite clear. The man was dressed in an elegantly tailored suit. His own clothes could only be described as practical. William's gaze fell downwards to shabby shoes. Even after spending all morning scrubbing, they were dirty. It's hard to make up for years of negligence in a few hours. Mary stood with an affected nonchalance, but her eyes flitted around the room nervously. They made their way through the hall with no small amount of trepidation.

As he caught sight of the doors to the royal chamber, William gasped, momentarily forgetting his embarrassment. He gawked – thirty-feet high of mahogany, every inch intricately carved with fantastical creatures and motifs. He stepped forward to take a closer look, tracing his finger along the wing of a dragon. The doors immediately swung open, and he took a startled step back. William found himself positioned behind the door and awkwardly scrambled around towards his sister. Mary chuckled. The attendant gave him a quizzical look but remained professional as he led them through.

The murmur of high society faded into a silence, broken only by the rhythmic steps of the attendant's dress shoes against the marble. The corridor was warm and smelled of lavender. William took deep breaths and steeled himself. They turned the corner, and the sense of calm he'd collected disappeared. The corridor opened into a giant room, resplendent in colour. His heartbeat boomed in his ears. There he was, sat at the table – the Dragon King.

The stories and the stolen glimpses didn't do him justice. To see him in person and up close was remarkable. His age was undeniable. Ancience was etched into every scale – if you looked closely, you could almost see the hundred lifetimes they'd lived play out in front of you. The dancing shadows from the warm candlelight gave him a grand, majestic air.

William stood up a little straighter. As he met the king's steady gaze, he was once again painfully aware of his dirty shoes.

"Welcome," said the king with a warm, sharp-toothed smile. "I hear you two are quite remarkable, that your quick thinking saved many lives during a barn fire. I, and the kingdom, thank you for your bravery. I'm honoured to have you here."

"Thank you, my liege," said William, bowing deeply.

"It's about time that I was recognised," snorted Mary.

William's cheeks turned red.

"I am remarkable." She pointed at her brother. "I don't know about him, though."

"You remind me of my sister," said the king, chuckling. He gave William a wink. "Don't listen to her. Please, both of you, sit."

The siblings sat opposite the dragon. The table had been specially built to accommodate his inhuman proportions, and the two felt very small. William sat sheepishly, while Mary unhesitatingly grabbed at the appetisers. A bottle of wine caught her eye, and waiting until the king looked away, she reached for it. It didn't escape his notice, though.

"How old are you?" he asked with a smile.

"Eighteen," stated Mary confidently.

"You're a bad liar," replied the king. "You can have one glass."

She didn't need to be told twice and eagerly filled hers to the brim.

"Don't tell your parents, though," the king added quickly under the questioning eye of his attendant. He didn't miss William's unvoiced appeal. "You can have one too," he said, smiling.

"How old are you, anyway?" asked Mary through a mouthful of food.

"I'm afraid my life has been longer than my memory," said the king, laughing. "I don't actually know how old I am. The other dragons and I, we've been around for a very long time."

"It's really true that the dragon gods created the world?" asked Mary. She didn't waste any time in getting to the questions she really wanted to ask. It wasn't every day you got to speak to the Dragon King, after all.

"It is."

"Can you tell us about it?" asked Mary.

"What was it like before?" asked William eagerly. "It must have been lonely," he mused, "before the world existed."

"Oh, no," said the king. "We weren't alone."

"You weren't alone?" repeated William, a little confused. He put down his knife and fork.

"There were" – the king paused, considering how to phrase it – "others."

William's eyes widened. "More dragons?"

The king shook his head.

"Then what were they?"

"They were…" The dragon paused. "I'm not quite sure," he admitted.

"You don't know?" asked Mary.

"There's a lot I don't know," said the king. His ancient, weary eyes met hers, young, bright and full of life. "And there's even more you don't know," he added good-humouredly.

"Then tell me."

The king cocked his head, a little surprised but amused by her forthrightness. "Okay, then," he said, after a pause. "Let me tell you about life before."

A hush fell over the room. Shadows flew up the wall as the candle flames grew longer. The king took a deep breath, and his voice took on a new grandeur. No longer jovial, it was a voice that demanded you listen – the voice of a king.

"Before this world, there was only the void. Empty darkness, forever. In this darkness there burned just one flame – the God of the Sun. All of the light and all of the warmth that existed, it existed within Her.

"The others wanted the flame for themselves. We fought, in a space that existed outside of time, for what felt like a thousand lifetimes, the Sun, the Moon, the Earth, the Stars and I, against the numberless forms born from the void.

"We fought with tooth and claw and magic, and we became strong. Before long, the creatures posed no real threat to us, save one. It was mad with desire for the flame. We couldn't defeat it, no matter how hard we fought, and we couldn't escape it, no matter how hard we ran. We were in an endless plane, but we were trapped.

"In an act of pure desperation, the God of the Stars poured her soul into erecting a barrier to keep us safe – a giant sphere, which, by the work of the gods, later became the creation you know. You all exist within it."

"The God of the Stars' magic is strong, and as long as that strength endures, we're safe. Maintaining the barrier takes its toll on her body and her mind, though." His voice hushed. "While you listen to me speak, sat comfortably in this warm hall, it is outside, trying everything it can to get in. If the barrier fails for even a moment…" The king didn't need to finish that thought.

The children shuddered.

"But for now," he continued, "we're safe. Finally free from danger." He gestured all around. "The dragons worked together to build all of this."

"That's…" began William, struggling to find the right words. In the end he settled on just one. "Terrifying."

"The barrier will stand well beyond your lifetime, don't worry. You—"

"You're a dragon?" interrupted Mary.

"Yes," replied the king, slightly bemused. He scratched his scaly chin with a sharp claw. "I am."

"You've had too much wine, Mary," said William, laughing. "Your cheeks are shiny."

As she'd become well accustomed to doing, Mary ignored her brother. "The other four dragons are gods. But you're… just a king? Without any magic?"

"She didn't mean that, my liege!" William quickly interjected. "She means no disrespect!"

"It's okay, William," assured the king. "I quite like being king. I think I do a good job of it."

"You do!" cried William.

"You do," admitted Mary.

"I've always been the most grounded of the dragons, and I think that's needed to be a good king." He was more talking to himself than to the siblings now. "Sun would do a terrible job." He laughed gently, his wings shuffling slightly as he did. "She's always been the special one, and it hasn't half gone to her head." He gestured with his hand at the food on his plate, and it lifted itself up and into his mouth. "And who says I don't have any divine power?"

"Everyone knows you don't have any powers," said Mary. The little display of magic was completely lost on the inebriated young woman. "Even little kids know that."

The king laughed, louder this time. "You got me, Mary. You're right; I don't." He winked at William, who looked back at him quizzically. The king continued, "You know, what I've told you two tonight is only known by a small handful of people. You can't go around telling everyone."

William was quick to reply. "I won't, I promise!"

Mary was slower to reply. While the king was focused on William, she was trying to top up her glass. She suddenly froze, not exactly seeing the king look but feeling it. "Well, look at that," she said, without turning to face him, "my hand slipped." She put the bottle back down quite a bit harder than she intended to. "Oops," she added, with her sweetest smile.

The king nodded to his attendant, who, much to Mary's dismay, took away both the bottle and the glass.

He decided to steer the conversation back towards the mundane. "You're two interesting people," said the king. "Do you know what you'd like to be when you're older?"

"I'd like to work with the University of Magic," said William shyly. "It's always been my dream. Maybe I could be a professor." He put his hand to the back of his neck and laughed awkwardly. "But I don't know if I'm good enough."

"It's an admirable goal," said the king. "And you should never discount yourself. I hold a lot of sway at the university. Maybe when you're older I could put you in front of the right people for an application. I'm sure you have a bright future."

William bowed over the table, almost putting his face in his food. "Thank you so, so much, my liege."

"You're very welcome." Smiled the king. "And you, Mary, what would you like to be when you're older?"

She shrugged. "I dunno," she said, a little defensively.

"A perfectly valid answer."

"Live a life full of existential dread now, probably," she mumbled.

"She does know," said William, "she just doesn't want to say."

"Shut up," said Mary.

The king raised an eyebrow. "Oh?"

Mary turned red. "It's nothing."

"She wants to work in the court," spilled William. "She always talks about how she wants to work here, with you."

"No, I don't!" shouted Mary, giving William an I'll-punch-you-later kind of look. "The court is stupid."

"Well, you're definitely not a yes-man," said the king, laughing. "You're a bright young woman. If you work hard for the next few years, sharpening your quick wit and blunting your quick temper, there may well be room for you amongst my advisors."

Mary's red face turned a shade deeper. "You really think so?" she asked apprehensively.

"I make no promises," said the king. "I only ever hire the best person for the job. But I see no reason why that couldn't be you, one day."

"Thank you," said Mary, and she really meant it. "People don't usually take me seriously."

William rolled his eyes. "I wonder why?"

Before Mary could retort, the attendant laid dessert in front of her. The scent of apple crumble derailed her train of thought, as it often did. "That smells incredible," she said.

"Doesn't it?" agreed the king. "The best in the land." He tucked into his own portion enthusiastically.

As the king was finishing off his plate, a woman came to whisper in his ear. The king nodded along gravely as the woman talked for some time. His brow furrowed. "This, I'm afraid, marks the end of our evening," he said, turning to the children. "I must excuse myself."

"It's been an honour, your majesty," blurted out William who turned red as soon as he said it.

"It's been a pleasure," agreed Mary.

"Likewise," said the king, rising to his full height. He towered over the children "I hope we meet again," he said fondly. "Good luck, William, Mary."

They smiled to themselves as the attendant unceremoniously ushered them out, through the lavender-scented corridor and the amazing doors. Just like that, it was over. They left chattering endlessly, getting along a lot better than they had just a few minutes previously.

As they walked through the gate of the castle, and back towards the streets they called home, their happiness was replaced with something a little more complex which neither could really elucidate. It wasn't necessarily a negative emotion, but it sort of felt like one. Emptiness may have been one part of it. Their foray into a different life was over, for now. They'd had a glimpse at how other people lived, and now they were back in the cold. Aspiration burned inside of them both.

Necromancer Supreme

University of Magic, 3236

The woman left, and the next person in line walked up to the desk. "Name please?" asked the clerk, without looking up.

"Morsdecanus the Vile, Necromancer Supreme!" said Morsdecanus the Vile, Necromancer Supreme, with a real theatrical flourish.

The clerk glanced up from his papers, obviously unimpressed. Once, he would have been amused, but he'd worked the job too many years now. "I want your real name," he said, with a scathing look.

Morsdecanus the Vile, Necromancer Supreme cleared his throat awkwardly. "Morris," he said.

"Morris…?" prompted the clerk.

"Morris Thompson."

"Thank you," said the clerk with a sigh. He began searching through the papers for the right name.

"I'm here for the trials," added Morris, feeling the need to fill the silence. "I'm trying to join the university. Hence the—"

The clerk stopped rifling through the papers. "Hence the 'Necromancer Supreme'?"

"Yeah," said Morris sheepishly.

"You know how many people have come through here just today?"

"No."

"A lot. You know how many of those people have called themselves 'the supreme' or 'the great' or 'the brilliant'?" He held up his hand to prevent Morris from replying. "It's also a lot. You people are so naive. You gotta earn a title like that; you can't give it to yourself."

Morris' cheeks turned red. "Oh, and I suppose you…" he paused, squinting to see the clerk's name badge.

"William," offered the clerk.

"Oh, and I suppose you," continued Morris, with a raised voice, "William, are the gatekeeper of greatness?"

William rolled his eyes. The egos were the worst part of the job. "No," he said calmly. "I'm just a clerk. I apologise for any offence caused."

"I'm going to be the greatest necromancer the world has ever seen! Watch this." Morris motioned madly with his hands in a gesture that, if you were feeling generous, could be called esoteric. He began to chant in an unfamiliar language.

"Hey!" shouted the clerk, tapping a sign on the front of the desk, which read: 'No magic allowed in the office'. "No magic in here!"

Morris paid no heed. The floor cracked into a bottomless chasm, and he cackled madly. A bony hand emerged from the chasm, and a skeleton pulled itself out of the earth. Morris looked around, swelling with pride. He didn't get the reaction he was hoping for.

"No magic in here," repeated William sternly.

"Hello there," said the skeleton with a wave. "Nice to meet you."

"Be quiet," hissed Morris. "You're not intimidating when you talk."

"Are you even hearing what I'm saying?" asked William. He motioned over to the guard, who came over. "No Magic!"

"Behold," shouted Morris, bringing back that theatrical flourish, "my undead minion!"

The guard laid a strong hand on Morris' shoulder. His deep, commanding voice was in stark contrast to Morris'. "No magic in here, son."

The necromancer spun around, finding himself faced with a broad, heavily armoured chest. He looked up to the guard's face. It was, Morris thought, very mean. "Yes, Sir," he mumbled. He chanted some more, and de-summoned the skeleton.

William finally found the correct sheet and checked a few boxes. "Through there, Morris," he said, pointing down the hall. "They'll call you when they're ready."

Morris nodded and left quietly.

William looked at the guard. "Henry," he said with a smirk, "you just defeated the Necromancer Supreme."

Henry laughed. "That's my third Necromancer Supreme," he said. "I keep a list."

"He had one whole skeleton," remarked William.

"You know how it goes" – Henry shrugged – "guy comes from a village where he's the only magic user, thinks he's hot stuff. We see them every day, so it's easy to forget that people like him are actually pretty rare."

"I suppose," agreed William, "but he's in for a harsh dose of reality in there."

Henry nodded his agreement, and William called for the next person in line.

Re-reborn

A Cave 30 Miles Due West of the Capital, 3241

The skeleton rose from the grave. Bound by dark magic, its bones took their original configuration suspended in the air. It took one shaking step, followed by another, feeling the cold air of the living world.

"You're worthless."

"Master," said the skeleton, "that's not very nice."

"I hate you. If you weren't such a disappointment, I might actually have made something of myself." The master snatched the skeleton's humerus from its place and hit it against the wall. The skeleton screamed, and the master stared at it blankly. "You don't even feel pain, you imbecile."

"No," said the skeleton, rushing to grab its missing bone, "but words can hurt too, you know."

"It's your fault that I'm in a cave right now and not in a palace. You deserve everything you get."

The skeleton reattached his upper arm. The rest of its arm had held its place, despite the missing bone. "Why do you summon me, master? How can I do your bidding?"

"I need some fungus."

"Need it removed?" asked the skeleton.

"Did I say that?" he cried. "Idiot! I need them for a ritual."

"Exciting! More necromancy?" suggested the skeleton. It paused for a moment, then added tentatively. "Maybe you're going to finish my body?"

"No," said the master. "And it's none of your business what I'm doing. Bring me veiled lady, bleeding tooth, and the amethyst deceiver."

"Aren't mushroom names wonderful?" mused the skeleton.

"No," snapped the master. "Go and collect them."

"And what about you, master?"

"I'm going to the tavern," the master replied. The skeleton looked about to say something, but the master spoke before it could. "Do you have a problem with that?"

"No, master," said the skeleton quickly.

"You exist to serve me, remember?"

"Yes, master."

"Oh, and don't forget – you're worthless."

"Yes, master."

"Say it."

"Master—"

"Say it."

The skull dropped dejectedly. "I'm worthless."

"That's right," said the master. "You'd better have those mushrooms by the time I get back." He put on his coat and left without another word.

The skeleton stood in the cave. It looked out over the forest, and the freedom it represented. It could just keep walking and never go back. It couldn't, though; it knew it couldn't. Its chains weren't physical or even magical.

Veiled lady, it thought. "Veiled lady, bleeding tooth, and the amethyst deceiver. I don't know what any of those look like. Maybe I am worthless. But I need to try, for the master." It took the first step, out of the cave, and down the mountain. "He cares about me, really," it figured. "He just has a strange way of showing it. When I bring back these mushrooms, he'll be happy."

It entered the forest and stooped down in front of the stream. It washed its face, removing the layer of dust that had accumulated there. In a stroke of good fortune, a cluster of mushrooms was growing right on the banks. The skeleton stared at them intensely. It cocked its skull and made as if to squint its non-existent eyes. "If you look at it from this angle," it mused, "that could be a veiled lady. That bit's the veil, and that bit's the… lady? A very funny looking lady," it admitted, "but who am I to judge?" It picked it gently and laid it down in the basket. "What good luck! One down already."

The skeleton continued on its way. "Amethyst deceiver… that one's probably purple. Unless it deceives you by not being purple at all. That would make a lot of sense." Its head was in the clouds as it waded through the brush towards a dead log. It spotted a mushroom straight away *Okay,* it thought. *This is a bleeding tooth if I've ever seen one.* The white, tooth-shaped mushroom grew from the log, and deep red globules oozed from the top. "That makes two." It smiled to itself. "The master is going to be so happy."

As the sun was falling from its zenith, the skeleton had made no further progress. It looked nervously at the sky. "He'll be back soon. I need to hurry up."

As it made its way back, it made a last-ditch search under a rotten log. There was a very plain white mushroom growing from it. It hesitantly placed it in the basket. "It's called the deceiver because it's not really purple," it muttered out loud. "It's deceiving. It's not really amethyst coloured or amethyst shaped." It tapped its phalanges against its femur nervously. The motion helped relieve some anxiety. The sound was grating. It got back just before the sun set but still ended up waiting several hours for the master to return, who was, of course, late.

Eventually, he stumbled in, under a star-filled sky. He had a smile on his face, which instantly faded when he saw the skeleton. "What are you doing?" he asked.

The skeleton nervously held out the basket containing the three mushrooms.

"You actually did something right for once," snorted the master.

If the skeleton had a nose, it would have smelt the whisky on his breath. The master didn't know what the mushrooms were supposed to look like any more than the skeleton did.

"Well done," he said sarcastically.

"Thank you, master!" The skeleton beamed. It had all been worth it to hear those two words. "I tried my best. It was hard work, but—"

The master took the basket, then slapped the skeleton's skull, sending it flying across the cave. "You talk too much," he muttered.

"Sorry, master," mumbled the dislocated skull.

The master threw the mushrooms into his cauldron and flipped some pages in his grimoire. Then he paused. "Why am I not wearing my robe?" he asked expectantly.

The decapitated skeleton rushed to grab the robe. It draped it over the master, gently. The master gave it a look of disgust, and the skeleton stepped back.

The writing in the grimoire was small, and the master had to squint to read it in the candlelight. He muttered to himself as he made the preparations for his spell. The skeleton saw that his work was sloppy but held his tongue. The master went to grab some water and stumbled. It suddenly became incredibly apparent to the skeleton how drunk he really was.

He shouted angrily and kicked the wall. "You!" he shouted at the skeleton. "What are you looking at?"

"I'm sorry, master—"

"Sorry! Oh, you're sorry? Well, that fixes everything!" shouted the master. "You were a mistake!" The master grabbed the bridge of his nose, before he swung his arm wildly. Vials crashed to the floor.

"Master, I'm so sorry!"

The master breathed loudly and irregularly. He curled his hand into a fist. The skeleton shrunk as much as it could. The master opened his hand. "Clean this up," he said quietly. "Quickly."

Wordlessly, the skeleton complied. The master fetched the bottle of liquor he always kept hidden in the back cupboard and took a swig. "Veiled lady, bleeding tooth, and the amethyst deceiver," he read. "An ounce of powdered chalk." He threw in all he had, figuring it was about an ounce. It wasn't. He continued with the rest of the ingredients in a similar fashion, while the skeleton swept. Soon the cauldron began to bubble and boil. It became hot and putrid.

The skeleton stopped sweeping and watched nervously. The master had a look in his eye that it didn't like.

"Yes!" shouted the master. "Yes! Ha, ha, ha!"

The skeleton recognised the look of the mixture in a way not many had the misfortune to. It was death. "Master," it asked nervously, "what are you making?"

He didn't reply.

"Master, I think that's a dangerous spell."

The master didn't look away from his cauldron. "Shut up."

The skeleton stepped towards the master. It made to say something, but the words wouldn't come out. It steeled itself and tried again. "I can't let you cast this spell," it said quietly.

The master spun around. "What was that?"

"I can't let you cast that spell," repeated the skeleton, louder, and with more confidence.

The master stepped towards the skeleton. Red face and pale skull were just an inch apart. The master spat as he spoke. "You can't stop me." He reached to grab the skeleton's skull, but this time he was met with resistance. The skeleton grabbed his arm, with a strength much greater than his own.

"Let go of me, you worthless pile of bones!"

"No."

"I will grind you into dust!" The master's face was contorted with shaking rage. "You ruined my life! You're only here because I pity you."

"It wasn't my fault!" shouted the skeleton, squeezing tighter. "You brought your failure upon yourself!"

The master began to chant in his dark, guttural language. The skeleton began to lose consciousness. The bones that were suspended in the air began to fall, collapsing into a pile. Before he could finish his incantation, though, the master retched. He went to lean against the wall and vomited. He spat onto the pile of bones to get the taste of sick out of his mouth, before returning to his cauldron. He resumed chanting over the bubbling mixture.

One small flicker of consciousness still remained in the skeleton. Suddenly, a realisation swept over it. One that, in hindsight, it should have had a long time ago. With all of its willpower, it concentrated on pulling itself together.

Soon she stood at her full height. She strode forwards, and snatched the grimoire from the master's hands, pushing him out of the way. A putrid smoke began to leave the cauldron. While he looked on, dumbstruck, she kicked it over and its contents spilled all over the floor.

"You wretch!" the dark wizard shouted, finding his words. He began to chant the same words as before, but this time they had no effect. The skeleton stood strong.

She looked at him with a newfound sense of disgust. "You're pathetic," she spat, "absolutely pathetic." She turned and, without a second look, began to walk out of the cave.

"Wait!" shouted the wizard. "Come back!"

She didn't even turn her head.

"Come back! You're not a wretch! You're not worthless! I never meant it!"

She kept on walking.

"Go then!" He shouted after her. "I'll be better off without you anyway, you waste of space! Yeah, keep walking!" After she was gone, his voice dropped from a shout to a whisper, and he said something quite to the contrary.

As she stepped into the forest, she felt the cold air of the living world. It felt good. Invigorating. As she threw the grimoire in the stream, she didn't notice the small bit of purple smoke behind her, that snaked up through the air and caught a gust of wind.

Fickleness

Little Maybury, 3241

I put my hand on Salie's cheek.

Hilda yanked me back. "What are you doing?" she hissed. "Do you want to get sick too?" I thought that was a rhetorical question – it wasn't. "Well," she shouted, "do you?"

"No, ma'am."

"No! I didn't think so," she said as she shooed me out of the door. "Now stop getting in my way." I obviously looked worried. She put her gnarled hand on my shoulder, and the almost ever-present grimace softened a little. "Salie will be right as rain before you know it, Loran, don't you worry. I know what I'm doing." Her eyes were sincere, and it put my mind at ease. Soon enough the softness was replaced again with that characteristic hardness, and the brief moment was over. "Now for the sake of the gods, leave me to my work!"

The next day someone else got sick. The day after that, six more. The day after that, they stopped counting. There wasn't enough time for it. My mother, my father, and my friends were among them.

I rushed to Hilda. "Here you go," I said, breathing heavily. "All the angelica I could find."

She snatched the basket from my hands. "Rosemary," she barked, before turning back to the patients.

I rushed out again, without waiting to catch my breath. Eric passed by and gave me a grim nod, on the way back from his own mission. My mind was full of a dozen floating thoughts, but seeing him brought one of them to the forefront. The overwhelming smell of rosemary, as he and I crouched to hide behind the bush. It had been years…

It had been Eric's idea. You tell two ten-year-olds to avoid the 'haunted' graveyard enough times, and they're bound to eventually go.

It was a long summer's day, the sun was shining in the sky, and we were finished with all of our work. Eric told his parents he was coming round to mine. I told my parents I was going round to his. Foolproof.

We knew the way well enough – it was over Cooper's Hill. The mood was that of the inimitable excitement of children doing something they shouldn't be doing.

As we saw it for the first time, Eric shouted. "Come on," he cried, and I didn't need telling twice. We sure-footedly ran down the hill, and soon enough we were stood by the rusty, weather-beaten gates.

Eric rattled them dejectedly. "Damn!" he said. They were locked. I hopped the fence. What was the point in a big, locked gate when your fence was only a few feet tall?

I distinctly remember my initial disappointment. I was promised ghosts, ghouls and gremlins. What I saw was just a graveyard – an old, uncared for graveyard. The inscriptions on the headstones had faded beyond readability, and everything was overgrown with weeds. The only semi-interesting thing was a large mausoleum in the centre. The facade was full of cracks.

Seeing my disappointment, Eric, ever the voice of reason, said with complete confidence, "The ghosts are in the mausoleum." Of course! Where else would they be?

We approached it cautiously. I picked up a stick, just to be safe. In hindsight, I don't know what I would have done to a ghost with a stick. Thankfully, we didn't see a ghost. But we did experience something we still can't quite explain.

As we got close to the mausoleum, we heard a shout. "Oi!" We ducked down behind the nearest bush. That was the moment I'd just remembered – ducked down behind that rosemary bush. Despite the impending danger, I was distracted for a moment by the bold, pleasant smell. Sometimes the strongest memories are some of the least consequential.

I desperately looked at Eric. "What do we do?" I whispered.

He poked his head above the bush, just for a second. "I don't see anyone," he whispered back.

"Well, someone just shouted."

He poked his head up again. "There's no one there." He looked expectantly at me, like he was expecting me to poke my head up too. I didn't. He called me a chicken, which instantly had the desired effect.

"I'm not chicken!" I shouted, standing up tall. "I'm not scared of ghosts!" I was, of course. He was too.

He stood up next to me, eager to prove his bravery. I cast a nervous glance over my shoulder and was reassured by the fact no one was there. Undeterred, we continued towards the mausoleum. A crow cawed, and Eric jumped.

"You're the chicken!" I shouted. "You're scared of a crow."

"Shut up, Loran. I'm not chicken," he replied. He picked up a mossy stone. "If I was chicken, would I do this?" He threw it as hard as he could at the mausoleum. It clunked as it collided with the old walls, and he looked at me smugly. His face dropped when the second shout came. "Scram! Get out of here, Loran!"

Without another word, we both turned to run. We jumped back over the fence, scrambled all the way up Cooper's Hill, and sprinted to the village. We didn't stop until we were panting in my front room.

The strange part of it, though, was that I swore the voice had said my name, and that the voice sounded just like my mother's. Eric swore that the voice said his name, and that it sounded exactly like his father. We knew that neither of them had been there. My mum had been waiting for us when we got in (and really made her presence known), and Eric's father couldn't walk, let alone climb Cooper's Hill.

I'd always told myself some passerby who just happened to be there was having some fun at our expense.

I told myself that again, as I reached the top of Cooper's Hill and looked down at the graveyard. There were no ghosts, but there was rosemary.

As I got closer, I noticed the gates stood wide open. *It's been almost a decade,* I thought, *it's not weird that things have changed.* I strode through with an affected confidence. Spotting the rosemary bush, I wasted no time in walking over. My pocketknife was always kept sharp, and it cut easily through the sprigs. I threw them into the basket, and the familiar smell filled my nostrils.

I glanced up at the mausoleum and immediately forgot about the rosemary. I felt a sudden beckoning. We never did go inside, Eric and I. There was an air about it. It was mysterious, enticing. I felt, in the back of my mind, there was something I needed to do, but I no longer cared. My feet walked themselves towards it.

Inside was nothing but cobwebs and a set of stairs leading down. I took them.

At the bottom was a tunnel. It was dark, but with my hand against the wall, I kept walking. I didn't know why, but I felt I had to see what was at the end of it. A cool breeze hit my face. The tunnel had opened into an impossibly large cavern. I felt very small and then remembered the rosemary.

What on Earth am I doing? I turned to leave, then a rumbling shook the cavern. Spots of light began to shine in the dark. It lit up, like the night sky when it was clear.

A vivid image flashed in my head. I recognised it as my own memory. *Me and my brother had been fighting, and he came bursting into my room. Instantly, full of anger, I shouted, "What the hell are you doing here?"*

Why am I thinking of that now?

"What the hell are you doing here?"

The rosemary—

"What the hell are you doing here!"

I experienced the memory so strongly, it overwhelmed my senses. "I don't know!" I shouted out loud. "I just took the stairs. I—"

"What the hell are you doing here!"

I felt the all-encompassing presence in front of me, and I felt a ray of hope. I suddenly understood the compulsion to visit. "Can you help me? Can you save my village?"

Eric had just told a joke. I threw my head back and laughed like I hadn't in a very long time.

"Hilda's doing her best, but I don't think it's enough. The sickness isn't like anything she's seen before. It—" Tears were forming in the corners of my eyes.

"Stop it, Eric, you're cracking me up!"

Hope turned into anger. "My people are dying!"

Cherry, my dog, lay motionless. My father turned me away, held his arm around me. I cried and hugged him. I don't think he knew what to say. He just told me that death was a part of life.

"Just because death is inevitable, doesn't mean it needs to happen now! In this arbitrary way!"

I'm stepping on an ant. Annoyed, I'm flicking a fly off my jacket. I'm grabbing a wriggling worm and putting it on a fishing hook. I'm slaughtering a chicken.

"Those are just animals, it's not the same."

My mother's asking if I want chicken soup or potato soup. I shrug. "It's all the same to me." I'm wringing the neck of a chicken, and another, and another, and another. Dozens.

"Human beings are dying! And you're worried about chickens?"

I shrug. "It's all the same to me."

"It's all the same to you, if people live or die?"

"Death is a part of life, son."

"It's all the same to me."

"Then I promise to never hurt another living thing. Is that your price? Anything, please, just stop it!"

I wrap my pinkie finger around Susie-Jane's pinkie finger. "Together forever?" she asks tentatively.

"For ever and ever." I nod enthusiastically. "Even when we're all grown up! I promise."

Pain coursed through my body as the memory engulfed me. I broke that promise.

"Promise you'll clean the dishes before I get home?"

"Yes, Mum," I replied. "I promise."

Pain coursed through my body again. I fell to my knees as every promise I'd ever broken played in my head on a loop, each one sending jolts of pain splitting through my body. It seemed as if nothing else existed but the loop of broken promises and the pain. I didn't know how long it had been. Eventually, I managed just one thought, one idea. I put all of my energy into picturing one memory – focusing on it as hard as I could through the pain, broadcasting it outwards.

I'm hugging Salie. She moves to let go, but I squeeze her tighter. She smiles and squeezes me even tighter still. "I love you," she whispers.

I smile into her shoulder. "I love you too."

The pain was unbearable, but I kept my focus on that one moment.

"I love you," she whispers.

I smile into her shoulder. "I love you too."

The pain stopped, as did the barrage of memories.

I'm hugging Salie. She moves to let go, but I squeeze her tighter. She smiles and squeezes me even tighter still.

I thought back to all of the memories I cherished the most, the memories I had with the people of the village.

The sun is shining. The sky is clear. I'm walking along the trail. "Hey, Loran!" shouts old man Marley. He stops ploughing.

"Marley!" I cry. We shake hands warmly. We talk for a few moments and part ways smiling.

My mother kisses my forehead and tends to the scrape on my knee. It's cold outside, but warm by the fire. My dad ruffles my hair, and my brother brings over a bowl of warm stew.

I walk with Salie through the orchard, hand in hand. We talk about everything and nothing in the warm evening.

"I promise to never hurt another living thing," I cried. "They're good people," I sobbed, "please."

There was a moment of silence, and for the first time I felt how cold the cave was. I heard an unfamiliar voice booming in my head. It said, simply, "The bargain is struck." A new, unfamiliar image entered my head.

Salie sits up from her bed, face shining. My mum and dad hug each other, smiles on their faces. All around her, the people of the village are getting better. Hilda is overcome with relief.

"Do not break your promise, Loran." Every word dripped with threat.

A man I don't recognise, wearing a black cloak, collapses to the ground. I know he's dead.

"I won't," I shouted, wiping away my tears. "Thank you."

I stood for a while, waiting for some reply. When I was sure there'd be none, I turned, and ran up the stairs, out of the mausoleum. The graveyard gates were shut, but I didn't stop. I hopped the fence, like I did all those years ago. I ran all the way up Cooper's Hill, kept running until I had Salie in my arms. Tears rolled down my cheeks again. "I'm so glad you're okay," is what I intended to say, but really the only sounds I made were muffled sobs.

After a while, I moved to let go, and she squeezed me tight. I smiled and couldn't help laughing an ugly laugh through my tears. I squeezed her even tighter. "I love you," I said.

"I love you too." She smiled.

In the end, Hilda got all the credit for stopping the plague. I was happy for that to be the case – she deserved it. The look she gave me, though – as I rushed back into the village completely empty-handed, at the exact moment everyone miraculously got better at once – that look told me she knew more than she was letting on. What was that look? It was a grateful smile. I wonder if she knew about that rosemary bush, too.

I sat that evening with Salie and my parents, watching the sun set. As we were talking, my mum interrupted. "You have an ant on your leg," she said.

I lifted my hand, instinctively ready to squash it. I stopped myself as soon as my brain caught up to what my body was doing. I knew that the death of that ant would be the death of everyone I cared about. I gently guided it onto my hand and put it down in the grass.

The significance of the moment was lost on the others. They were listening to my mother, who asked what I wanted for dinner the next day. "You two should come round," she said, "a little celebration. I could do soup. What do you think, Loran, potato, or chicken?"

"I'd really like potato," I replied.

Pie

Littlewood, 3241

I quickly turned away from the front page. What absolute rubbish. I sighed and went back to the Classifieds. I re-read the ad and smiled. 'Chef wanted.' I surveyed the ingredients laid out on the stump in front of me. Everything I needed. Perfect.

I took a pile of flour and made a little well in the middle. I'd gone into the village to buy it. The miller's a good man – he doesn't care that I'm a goblin. He treats me just like anyone else.

I poured some sunflower oil into the well, slowly. Using just my fingertips, I rubbed it all together, which made my fingers very sticky. It's messy work, but I don't mind. I needed to fetch some water anyway. Holding my hands out in front of me, and being careful not to touch anything, I ducked under one branch and hopped over another. Bending down at the bank of the stream, I rubbed my hands together in the water. One piece of dough was being really stubborn around my thumb. I had to scrub really hard to get it off.

I realised I forgot my bowl, sighed, and went back to get it. I filled it and went back. Little by little I added the water, until the dough was just right. I prodded it with my finger. It didn't stick, but it was still plenty moist. Perfect.

While leaving it to rest, I went to see Millie. We laid down in the sun and held hands. We talked, as we do, about nothing much of significance. She always laughs at my silly jokes. When cooking, I do my best to remember the love I have for her, and put some of it in the food – there's definitely enough to go around. I think it makes all the difference, putting care into the things you do.

I split my dough into two uneven parts, took my rolling pin, and began to roll them out into two circles. I'm really proud of the rolling pin. I made it, myself, from a maple branch. It wasn't very fancy looking, sure, but it was very smooth and very round. It works like a charm – rolls like it's nobody's business. I carefully trimmed the edges of each circle so they were tidy.

Then it was time for the special touch. I ever-so-carefully pressed nettle leaves into what was going to be the lid of the pie. They were arranged in a spiral pattern, going out from the middle. It looked pretty. I took the larger circle, and carefully laid it into the pan, pushing it carefully into shape.

I'd already made the filling. Mushrooms, nettles, and roast acorns cooked in vegetable stock and white wine. It smelled delicious. Wine was a real luxury, but worth every penny. I took a sip from the bottle. Hey, I'd earned it.

I carefully spooned the filling into the pie. It had taken some trial and error to find the perfect level, but now I knew it instinctively. As full as possible without being overfull. It's a delicate balance.

I wetted the edges of the pastry and carefully placed the lid on top. I crimped the edges, making sure it'd all hold fast. I very carefully scored the top, so steam could escape as the pie cooked.

I gently pushed the pan into my little clay oven and shut the door behind it. I double checked my little sundial. Just past noon, so it'd be ready at two o'clock. I sat on the log I'd dragged there especially for the purpose and read the rest of the newspaper – or tried to, at least. I couldn't focus and kept skipping back to the classifieds. A chef! I could be a chef. My hands were shaking slightly as I cut out the ad.

After a very fidgety two hours, I took out the pie and left it to cool. There was a slight breeze in the air. Perfect. Once it was cool enough, I gently placed the pan on my gingham blanket. I grabbed each corner, pulled them together in the middle, and tied an – admittedly slightly messy – four-way knot.

I left the next day, after giving Millie a kiss goodbye. She was going to join me in the capital later, if I got the job – fingers crossed. It was a long way, so I had to leave bright and early. The first part of the journey was nice. It took me through the forest I knew and loved. I passed by old acquaintances and made small talk. I learned that Mizzy, who I went to school with, had become an actress with a travelling theatre! Good for her. I always hoped she'd make it.

It was after I left the forest that I really started to become anxious. I didn't leave very often. It was a big world outside of it, a big, intimidating, not-always-friendly world. The road was busy and loud. There were huge carts full to the brim pulled by great big oxen, and there were countless people carrying baskets and crates.

"Market day," grumbled a man, obviously catching my look of awe and confusion. He kept walking and shouted to no one in particular as he did. "I hate market day!" It seemed a very cathartic shout.

I joined the reluctant convoy and was immediately jostled by a woman carrying carrots. "Watch where you're going!" she snapped – quite unkindly, I thought.

"Sorry, ma'am," I apologised quickly. "I meant no offence."

Taking a good look at me, she laughed. "I guess I can't blame someone who's only up to my knees! Ha! You're tiny!"

I smiled, on the outside. "It won't happen again, ma'am."

It wasn't long until I was jostled again. It was a crowded road, sure, but it wasn't that crowded. I tried to make myself as small as I could and gripped onto the pie tightly.

A shout came from behind me. "On your right, greeny." I stepped to the left, and a cart came careening past, just missing me. It didn't miss the puddle of mud, though, and I got splattered. I stopped to rub the muck out of my eyes, and someone walked into the back of me. I fell onto my face, and the pie went flying from my grip.

"Watch it!" shouted the man behind me. "You can't just stop like that!"

"Sorry, Sir!" I shouted. I scrambled forward to grab my pie. It had landed the right way up, thank the gods.

"What's that then?" he asked.

"It's a pie," I replied, taking it as friendly curiosity.

It wasn't.

"A pie? Well, well, well," he said, smiling. "I'm pretty hungry; isn't this convenient?"

"I'm sorry," I said, "this is a special pie. You can't have a slice this time, but you'd be more than welcome to come round and—"

"Oh," said the man, "I wasn't asking." He reached forward and grabbed a hold of the pie tin. I didn't let go. He snarled. "Give me the pie, greeny."

I clutched it even tighter. "No!"

"Give. Me. The. Pie."

"No!"

He yanked. He was much stronger than me. He took the pie, and I stumbled forwards.

"Hey!" I shouted. "Give that back!"

He began working on the knot, but the messiness of it worked in my favour. While he struggled, a cart passing by stopped and an old lady hobbled out. "Haddon!" she chastised. "Give that greeny back its pie."

He looked down at her. She was barely taller than me. "It can have the pie back," he said, "if it can reach it." He waved it above his head and laughed as if it was incredibly funny. She rapped him across the shins with her cane. "Ow!" he shouted.

She enunciated her words very clearly. "Give it back."

"Whatever," said Haddon, rubbing his shin. "I didn't want your grubby pie anyway." He threw it on the ground and walked away. I rushed to pick up the pie.

"Thank you," I said. "I don't know what I would have done."

"You folk should stay in your forest," she said, in a tone of voice suggesting that she believed she was saying something kind. "You don't belong out here." My heart sank, and she obviously noticed my dismay. "Need a ride?" she asked, with a voice full of pity. "We're going to the capital."

I didn't have enough pride to refuse. There was still a very long way to go.

"I'm Judra. This is my grandson, Mark," she said, pointing to the driver as she clambered back up onto the cart. I clambered after her. "What are you doing out here anyway?" she asked.

I was embarrassed to answer, after what she'd said, and after what had happened. I'd only been out of the forest for fifteen minutes. Maybe she was right. Maybe I should stay there, where I belonged. I hugged my pie tightly. The blanket was muddy, but miraculously, the pie seemed okay. It was a good pie! A damn good pie. "I'm going to be a chef," I exclaimed, suddenly full of defiance. I pulled the newspaper clipping from my pocket. "I'm going to apply for this job, and this delicious pie will get it for me."

"I'm sure you will," said the amused lady, patting my head patronisingly. My bubble of enthusiasm burst.

"The city is very diverse," said Mark, more sincerely. "They're more tolerant than some people out here are."

"They do have all sorts of queer folk there," agreed Judra.

"She's quite old fashioned," whispered Mark, coming in close. "Don't take her too seriously. If that pie really is as good as you say it is, I think you're in with a good chance."

I smiled.

"What are you two whispering about?" barked the old lady.

"Nothing, Grandma," said Mark quickly.

I arrived in the capital way ahead of schedule. By the look of the sun, it was around noon. I thanked them both earnestly, and we went our separate ways – them to the market, me to… I wasn't exactly sure. The ad had an address written at the bottom, but I had no idea where it was. Uphill road. I started my search by taking the road up the hill. I guess it wasn't all difficult – I found the restaurant quite easily.

Before I stepped in, I unwrapped the pie from within the muddy blanket. I stuffed the blanket in my back pocket, out of sight. I'd have to give it a good clean.

I walked up to the podium of the maître d', but she didn't see me. I coughed, trying to get her attention. Nothing. "Excuse me," I ventured, meekly. She looked to her left and right, a little puzzled. Eventually, she looked down and seemed relieved to see me.

"Thought I was hearing things!" she said. "How can I help you, Sir? Do you have a reservation?"

I held out the ad. "I'm here to try for the chef job."

"Right this way," she said with a smile, leading me into the back. She pointed towards a very muscular woman, "This is our head chef, Carla."

"You here for the job?" asked Carla sternly, looking up from the half dozen dishes she was juggling.

"Yes, ma'am," I replied, nervously. It all came down to this. I'd come all this way, worked so hard.

"Deon," she shouted, "keep an eye on all this." Deon dutifully obliged and took over the dishes with a lot less calm than Carla had had. "Have you brought me a dish, like the ad says?"

"Yes, ma'am," I said, nervously offering up the pie. "It was a long way here, so it's a day old I'm afraid."

Carla raised a sceptical eyebrow.

"It has acorns in it," I continued, "and mushrooms."

She placed a knife and a plate on the counter and brought over a step. I didn't take the hint straight away. "Well?" she asked impatiently.

"Yes! Sorry," I said. I climbed up and cut her a slice. I lifted it carefully onto the plate, before handing it to her.

She held it up in front of her face and inspected it very closely – the crimping, the pattern on top and, of course, the filling. She pulled a silver fork from within her jacket and took a bite. She tilted her head slightly as she did, as if to taste it better. Her face went through a series of emotions I couldn't exactly read. She finished chewing and swallowed.

There was an uncomfortably long pause, then she walked away. My heart collapsed. I knew it. I'd wasted her time. I'd wasted my time. I turned to leave.

"Hang on a minute," said Deon with a wink. "Don't go yet."

I looked up at him, puzzled, but listened and stood there in agonising silence.

Carla came back and threw an apron at me. "This is the smallest size we have. I hope it fits."

My eyes widened and a smile spread across my face. "You mean—"

"She has such a penchant for drama," said Deon, rolling his eyes.

"That's a damn good pie," said Carla. She smiled too. "You ready to work hard?"

"Yes, ma'am."

"When can you start?"

"Well," I said, "right away, really."

"Good. Tomorrow, six o'clock sharp."

I stepped back out onto the streets of the capital and breathed a breath of new beginnings. I was grinning from ear to ear. It was time to find somewhere to stay! And write a letter to Millie! And get the blanket thoroughly washed. I was ready for my new life in the capital to begin.

People of the Capital

The Capital, 3241

The Dragon King has the power to change his form. He does so often and wanders the streets of the capital. He loves to people-watch. Despite being both a king and a god, he is humble and in touch with the people he rules. This people-watching may be part of why, a consequence of that, or both. He writes notes sometimes. No one reads them but him, usually. Here are some.

The Pigeon Queen
There's a woman who, during the half-hour lunch break she gets from her job at the apothecary, feeds the pigeons. She'll throw a crumb of bread to a solitary pigeon. It'll take an immediate break from its strutting, dash straight towards the crumb, and swallow it whole. The woman will then throw down another crumb.

This time, a second pigeon, sat on the roof of a nearby building, takes notice. It swoops down to join its companion for the feast. Crumb after crumb, the group grows. Three, then five, then a dozen, then three dozen. They seem to appear out of thin air. She always makes sure to pack an extra bread roll.

Others see the birds as pests, but this woman loves them, and they bring her joy. She doesn't know it, but in their own language, the pigeons call her kind-hearted, and they love her too. The kind-hearted woman treats them well when others just shoo them away.

Some people, who have forgotten the happiness that can be found in simple things, call her the 'pigeon queen', in an attempt to mock her.

"Here she is again, the Pigeon Queen."

They really don't see how dumb they sound.

The Gardener and His Roses

There was an old man, who loved to tend his garden. It was beautiful. He had all sorts of plants, but his pride and joy was his roses. And for good reason!

He was one of the few people I interacted with regularly. No matter what form I took, he'd always give me a wave as I walked past. I'd always wave back. Sometimes we'd talk, briefly.

"Wonderful weather, isn't it?" I'd say.

"Delightful," he'd say back, with a large grin.

"I love your roses."

"Thank you very much. They're my pride and joy."

Short conversations of that nature, completely meaningless in the grand scheme of things, but ever so meaningful in the not-so-grand scheme of things.

I always found him there, rain or shine, until one day I didn't. His roses looked sad, as if they missed him. I heard that he was sick.

The next day, I walked past again. The roses had wilted a little. After that, I had business to attend to so didn't go past for several days. When I did return, the roses were dead.

I couldn't bring myself to go back to that part of town for a long time.

The Young Lovers
Otieno is a boy of sixteen. He's training to be a woodworker, just like his father. He has a real gift. He works diligently and takes pride in what he does. He makes the most beautiful pieces.

Today he finished a bowl he'd been working on for a while. Around the outside was carved a field of tulips. Every single flower was a work of art and could have made the piece exceptional alone. There were hundreds of them, each with their own character. It was the kind of bowl you could look at for hours without getting bored, and those really don't come along very often.

The bells rung five times just as he was finishing. He was done for the day. After work he likes to go and meet his sweetheart. Ha-Neul works at a blacksmith at the edge of town. They meet there and walk beyond the city limits. They climb the hill that sits a mile or so away and sit together under a large rowan tree. They look at the view. Sometimes they talk, fervently and passionately. Other times they sit in silence, just enjoying each other's company. They're deeply in love.

The Crow King
There's a man who lives on the third floor of a house, who's befriended some crows. Crows are very intelligent birds. Every morning and every evening, they fly up to his open window. He feeds them treats. In return, they bring him gold.

It started with them bringing him twigs, scraps and rubbish, a token of their appreciation for his kindness. But one day a crow brought him a gold piece. That crow got extra treats, and the flock took note. Now, they scour the streets for any dropped money.

He's become fairly wealthy. His friends and family are always impressed by his generosity. One or two have become a bit suspicious. He works a junior job in a mill, so how has he always got so much money? No one knows the truth, besides him. And me, I suppose. But he's never miserly, so people usually don't push the topic too hard. He gives to his friends and family. He gives to those less fortunate. And of course, he keeps a bit for himself.

He and the pigeon queen should meet. I think they'd get along. Or perhaps they'd be enemies, in a there-can-only-be-one sort of way?

The Portrait Artist

Varnika lives above a tea shop. She's studying magic. Her tutors always reprimand her for not practising. She does practise, every day. Just not the magic they want her to learn.

She likes to paint, people especially. She hears the orders come through from the shop downstairs.

"One green tea, with two sugars, please."

"Could I have a breakfast tea, with just a smidge of milk, no sugar?"

"Black tea. Quickly, please, I've not got all day."

Everyone orders something slightly different in a slightly different way. Everyone has their own preferences and idiosyncrasies. She likes to imagine from those few spoken words that person's life. Then she paints them.

She puts brush to canvas, without any need for pigment. The dry brush produces any colour she wills. She's gotten very good at erasing, too.

There's a wall in her flat full of these portraits. Sometimes, as she's walking around the city, she'll spot someone who matches one of them exactly. That always makes her smile.

The Sweeper

Every spring, trees all across the capital bloom. Flowers of pink and white and purple grow by the thousands. The streets are lined with colour, and in the shining sun, nature throws us a parade.

After a while, the flowers start to fall. The streets become swamped with huge piles of petals. I think this is even more beautiful. Couples lie in the piles together. Children throw them in the air. It gives the city a beautiful ambience.

There's one man who really doesn't like them. He uses his broom to sweep them up, with no small amount of zeal. He goes around with huge empty bags, fills them with the petals, and burns them. He's employed to do it, and it needs to be done at some point, but it's always a shame to see it happen.

He doesn't have to do it with such enthusiasm or so soon. It could be left for a day or two. Every year I consider passing some rule to that effect but never do.

Beauty is in the eye of the beholder, after all, and it's impossible to please everyone. His joy is worth no less than mine. I imagine he waits all year for the pleasure. Nor is he the only one that finds them annoying; I do hear other people complain.

I do my best to be fair, and to run things for everyone – not just for me – but despite that, it'd be really nice to have the petals around for a little bit longer. The city is beautiful at this time of year, and so what if a little bit less work gets done? Some things are more important than work. Once the man retires, I might change things.

When you've lived for a thousand lifetimes, people who are truly unfamiliar to you seldom come around. One of them came along today, as the Dragon King was walking the streets. He wore unfamiliar clothes and spoke with an unfamiliar accent.

On Dragons

The Capital, 3241

"Gather round! Gather round!" The preacher's voice wasn't loud, but everyone heard it. His tone held a subtle but unmistakable confidence, and he oozed charisma. He was very good at convincing people to believe what he wanted them to believe, and so he was a very good preacher. He understood the nature of people very well.

In the form of a middle-aged man, the king looked on attentively and smiled to himself. The smile faded as he heard a shrill screaming from behind him. "I wanna see! I wanna see!" The din came from a girl of around six. He graciously lifted her up onto his shoulders, and in return, she pulled his hair. The king rolled his eyes. *Kids!*

Seeing the crowd had become sufficiently large, the preacher began in earnest. "People of the capital!" he cried, pausing a moment for the murmur of the crowd to die down. "You all know of the dragons," he continued, "the Sun, the Moon, the Earth, and the Stars. The four great powers in this world that provide us, the evanescent masses, with everything we need in order to live and to thrive. The gods are powerful, and the gods are good. And yet, they're often forgotten by people in the city." He looked around accusingly, and his face became stern. "People like you."

The sternness gave way again to the easy smile.

"It's easy to do. You live a life separate from the bare elements and have lost your connection with the divine. But the gods should never be forgotten. Ask the farmer where he'd be without the Sun and the Earth. Ask the sailor where he'd be without the Moon and the Stars. Day and night, dawn and dusk, summer and winter, everything in this world is their creation. Everything you have here in this spectacular city, everything small or large, is given to you by the grace of the divine dragons.

"Gorgeous lady, in the front... yes, you. That dress is beautiful! May I ask from what it's made?"

She looked nervous and didn't answer.

The priest flashed a smile. "It's not a trick question."

"Cotton," she replied, hesitantly.

The priest repeated her answer more loudly, for the crowd. "Cotton! Grown in the Earth, fed by the Sun, and no doubt weaved with magic, that gift given to us from the Stars! Have you thanked the dragons for your fine dress, my lady?"

She blushed. "No," she admitted.

"Heed my words carefully, all who are listening here today." He closed his eyes and took a deep breath. His voice became loud. "The fury of the Dragons is great! Trembling earth, climbing waves, barren soil, and virulent disease – the power to change the very world, all with the wave of a hand!

"But their power is limited not just to grand disasters, no. Your brother whose leg never quite healed after that accident, your friend who for years has never gotten that promotion she feels like she deserves, your uncle, struck with melancholy, who has become blind to the joys of the world – these are problems you're all familiar with. You know people who suffer from them, or you even suffer from them yourselves. These things may seem arbitrary, but they're anything but. Wouldn't you like to see yourself and the people you love free, happy, and safe?"

A murmur of yeses came from the crowd. One man shouted, "Of course I do!"

"Of course you do," repeated the priest. "And that is achievable, my dear people, because the gods' love is even greater than their wrath. If you show love to the gods, the gods will show you love in return! The gods are good! Let me tell you a story, one not many people know."

The king raised an eyebrow.

"The God of the Sun and the God of the Earth are in love! Yes, in love! They, like us, know the tragicomic joy of that most domineering emotion. And yet, the two are always apart. They could spend eternity together in bliss, but they don't. Why is that? They choose not to because if they get too close it upsets the balance of this world. If the Sun were too close to the Earth, it'd get hot. The rivers would dry up, the crops would wilt, and all of us would die.

"For us, they stay apart. For us, they forsake their hearts' desire. Their love for us is even greater than the love they have for one another. The distance between them is what makes life possible. They work together to create all the beauties of nature. Every tree, flower, and fruit is a testament to the sacrifice they've made for us and is a celebration of their benevolence."

He turned back towards the woman in the cotton dress. "Is a thank you too much to ask for all they've done for us, and all they've given up for us?"

The woman shook her head fervently.

"Now is the time for you to correct your mistakes!" The preacher pulled a dandelion from his pocket and placed it behind her ear. "The dandelion, a humble flower, a flower many of you may consider a weed – this is the symbol of the gods!"

"It grows from Earth," he began. He held his hands together, palm to palm. "This is the shape of the stem. Follow my lead."

Keeping the bottom of his hands together, he curled his hands into round fists. "It flowers in a golden sphere. This is the Sun."

He opened his fists, forming an open circle with his fingertips touching. "It seeds into a white sphere. This is the Moon."

He parted his hands, spreading his fingers wide. "The seeds float in the wind, uncountable lights in the sky. This is the Stars."

He brought his hands back in front of him. "This motion is a way of showing your thanks to the gods. Commit it to your memory."

The little girl on the king's shoulders held her hands out, poorly attempting to mimic the motion. The preacher spotted her struggling and made his way through the crowd. He smiled at the girl, covering her hands with his own and helping her make the motions. "Well done," he said. "You're a fast learner." He looked down at the unassuming man holding her up. "Your daughter has a bright life ahead of her," he said. "I sense she'll live a life close to the dragons themselves."

The king couldn't help but laugh.

"I don't joke, Sir," said the preacher. "She will. I can feel it with every bone in my body."

"I know," replied the king. "In fact, you have no idea how right you are."

The preacher looked a little confused by the reply but never lost an ounce of composure. He made his way back to the front of the crowd. "Commit it to memory, all of you! And thank the gods every chance you get! The temple is not far from here…"

He continued to preach, but the little girl had lost interest in the words. She yawned. The king took her down. "Come on," he said, "let's go find your parents."

As they made their way back, she held her hands together like she'd been shown, two fists forming the sphere that was the sun.

Rise to the Sun

Ormath Mountains, 3262

She never looked down. She'd learnt that a long time ago. It doesn't matter how high up you are, all that matters is the next move. Whether you're a foot off the ground or a thousand feet in the air, the next move is always the same.

She'd almost made it to the top. She just needed to get over the ledge, and onto flat ground. Her arms were tired, her whole body was tired, and her heart was beating in her ears. With a great exertion, and what was almost a scream, she pulled herself up.

Afterwards she lay exactly where she was, with her cheek against the cool rock. All her focus was on regaining control of her breathing. Her limbs were being pulled down by a heavy fatigue, crushed under its weights. But her mental discipline was strong. Her mind was the master of her body, and she flung off the weights. Her tent had to be up before the sun was down.

The top of this cliff was exposed – even in the sun, it was cold. When night fell, if she was still outside, she'd freeze. She didn't like the look of the storm clouds gathering in the distance, either. The fair weather wouldn't last. The view was impressive, though.

> Beneath her peak flowed a sea of grey crests,
> Of mountains a-towering in kingly stance,
> Whose ridges and gorges aplenty were tests,

She had passed with a stubborn defiance.
Beyond to the north stood forests of green,
And to the west the serpentine river,
Which in golden hour's warm light did sheen
As across land the sliver did slither.
At a boundless ocean, it came to end,
In muddy a delta mighty and wide.
Behind her, the mountains she was to ascend,
Higher than the summits of any beside.
In desperate pursuit of her life's one quest,
The top she'd reach for, at her heart's behest.

But she didn't have time to ponder her dreams now. The ridge was fairly wide. Plenty of room to pitch a tent, so she got to it. A familiar routine, and it was done just as it got too dark to see.

She huddled inside and lit her small lamp. She pulled some food from her bag. It could generously be called 'sailors' biscuit'. The 'bakers' mixed together flour and water, put it in the oven, then forgot about it for a week. It was harder than the mountain. It was calorie dense, though, and that was what she needed. She'd picked some berries earlier in the day, and that was her lunch – rocks, and berries she was only ninety-five percent sure weren't poisonous. At this point she was willing to risk it. Good food was just a memory.

She took out her water bottle and said a little prayer before eating – not thanking the gods for the meal, rather asking to come out of it unscathed. She made the familiar motions with her hands – palms together, open into a circle, close into a fist,

"Mighty gods, hear my prayer!" she began. "May these berries not kill me, and may my teeth survive this biscuit. Oh, mighty gods, hear my prayer." She said this quietly to herself with half a smile. The words weren't particularly serious, but they gave her both comfort and the confidence she needed to dig in.

Once she was done chewing, she pulled out her journal and made a log of the day's events. Progress had been good. She was another day closer to finding the God of the Sun. She placed her journal away lovingly after finishing and went to bed contented, hoping to get some much-needed rest. She woke up with a start.

> The wind it blew in strong and harsh gales,
> Showing the mountains an unbridled wrath,
> Shrieking its song to the valleys and dales,
> To strip bare whatever did come in its path.
> Recalcitrant raindrops ride currents to fly
> In a mimic of the starlings' mad dance.
> Twisting and turning 'til nowhere is dry,
> And the storm clouds can make their advance.
> With crackling of lightning foll'wing in tow
> Splitting the heavens and searing the sky,
> The old man of thunder who drifts so slow,
> Caught up eventu'lly and let loose his cry.
> His deep rumbling bellow demands you hark,
> As the flashing fades and leaves you in dark.

You could barely see your hand in front of your face. She boldly stuck her head out from the tent. She stuck it back in very quickly. She wasn't going to make much progress today, and that frustrated her.

The wind was coming from the south. She figured it'd be a good idea to go down the northern side of the mountain where it was sheltered – leave her tent pitched because she couldn't take it down in the wind – and just do some scouting around the area. She wasn't one for sitting around, even if she knew it was the best decision.

So, she put on her pack and got ready to leave. She thought for a moment and then took her pack off. She left the tent and, staying low to the ground, went to collect some rocks. She made a few trips, waiting for lightning to illuminate the ridge, spotting a good one, and then scrambling to collect her prize. She got a few good, heavy rocks to weigh down the tent while she was gone, just in case. These few short trips had left her soaked to the bone and completely windswept. However, she wasn't one to change her mind once she'd made it up. The thought occurred to her, but she dismissed it without hearing it out.

She reshouldered her pack, before taking it off again. She wasn't going far or going for long. She took out most of her food, most of her water, and anything else she deemed non-essential for a short trip.

She put her pack on, for good this time, and stepped out of her tent. She shut it tight behind her and began walking very slowly and very cautiously across the ridge and towards the north. The relief was immediate as she got down onto the slope beneath the ridge, shielded from the wind and the rain.

She sat for a moment on the slope, feeling like she was in the eye of the storm – no longer a victim of it, merely an observer. Nature never failed to impress her. When it really flexed its muscles, nothing could compare, nothing but the dragons, of course. It really put their power into perspective. It made her feel small, but she'd be all the more proud when she overcame it. She wasn't scared of this storm – it was a challenge she was prepared to meet.

She got up and started walking along the slope, one foot in front of the other, testing the strength of each foothold before taking a step. She screamed as she slipped. She didn't test them well enough, it seemed. A patch of shale was her undoing. She lost balance, and a small avalanche carried her down and down and down. It hurt.

When she came to a natural stop a hundred metres or so lower, she shouted, loudly, some words the thunder was kind enough to censor. She was grazed and cut all over, and her leg had twisted at a weird angle. Her knee hurt – a lot. She cursed again, and this time there was no thunder to cover her. Luckily, there were no children around. So far as she knew, no one was around, not for a very long way.

She didn't move, waiting for the worst of the pain to pass. She assessed herself and breathed a sigh of relief. Her wounds weren't that bad – painful, and annoying, but not particularly serious. Her knee was tender, but it was nothing time wouldn't fix.

She looked up and waited for the next flash of lightning. It illuminated the slope. It was a long way, and she wouldn't be able to climb the route she'd fallen down. She'd have to go far to the side, away from the slate. She was confident she knew her way back though, which was reassuring. The only problem was getting there. She got up, and instantly realised she'd underestimated the damage to her knee. She shouted some really creative words into the storm.

Up was out of the equation, for now. She waited for the flash of light and looked at her sideways options. Her heart rose. There was a cave opening no more than a hundred feet away. The ground was fairly level, but it still took her a few minutes to hobble the distance. She collapsed down against the wall of the cave. *Well, this is an adventure,* she thought, not willing to admit she was wrong. The wind shifted, and rain came pelting in. She groaned and half-walked-half-crawled her way deeper in.

She was absolutely dumbstruck. Around the corner, a brilliant light shone. It was like a doorway to another world.

> Pitter pattering of rain came to halt,
> And instead played a sonorous tune.
> Flowers, they sang in cadence without fault,
> And the sunshine was bright as high noon.
> A meadow beholden to dragon divine
> Of lush beyond ken and beauty sublime,
> A place of pure worship, a living shrine
> To a God so-powerful, strong in her prime.
> This valley paradise, hidden from sight
> Was the home of the deity of sun.
> There, in the centre, she stood, bright in might,
> Expression was kind, her speech thus begun,
> "Welcome, weary trav'ler come from afar,
> Years of toil, and now here you are."

I'm glad you made it," she said. Her lips formed a smile that was full of sharp teeth, but still welcoming – a heartwarming, genuine smile.

"You were expecting me?"

"Of course I was." She stepped forward and lifted her front leg. She placed the tip of her claw against the woman's forehead.

Her pain melted away, her cuts healed, and her bruises faded. Even her knee was good as new. The woman looked down at herself, amazed. She felt better than she ever had. All she could think to say was, "Thank you."

"You're very welcome," said the dragon, smiling. "Think nothing of it." She sat down and curled up slightly.

The woman couldn't help but be reminded of a cat.

"Sit," purred the dragon, and the woman did.

She sat cross-legged in the most beautiful meadow she'd ever seen, in the middle of a stormy mountain range.

The dragon looked at her intently. "I have a favour to ask of you," she said with that lovely smile.

Sunburn

The Capital, 3262

The king read the letter again, and then again for a third time. It worried him. The woman saw the worry on his face, and it worried her. She was knelt in front of him, having just handed him said letter.

The king sighed. "Thank you for bringing this to me," he said. "I understand that the God of the Sun wants you to return to her?"

"Yes, Sir."

This made him even more uneasy, and that, in turn, worried her further. It wasn't the reaction she'd been expecting. But she was too scared to ask what worried him, too scared to ask any questions. Had she gotten herself caught up in something, an argument between two gods?

"You can go," said the king. He wrote a short note on some paper and handed it to her. "Give this to the steward. He'll outfit you with anything you need for your journey. Any provisions you want, you can have."

The woman bowed her head graciously. "Thank you."

"Good luck," muttered the king distractedly.

It was a long walk out of the hall, and her steps rung out on the hard floor. The door creaked as it opened. It creaked even louder when she closed it. The king made a mental note to have it fixed. It was a very old door. He'd been meaning to have it fixed for a hundred years or so. Something else always demanded his attention though, and it never got done. The letter demanded his attention now.

What is Sun up to? Why has she issued this quest? Why does she want it kept secret? Why did she send that woman with a letter, instead of speaking to me herself?

He's been quiet for so long, and it's better that way. Why poke a sleeping bear? The reward isn't worth the risk. She must see that.

And I don't like the language she used. Nothing but thinly veiled threats. It's written in a way which leaves me no real choice. I'll make the preparations immediately, just like she wants. He sighed. *What is she up to?*

Aoki and Maria sat in the waiting room. They were in a remote wing of the palace, one not many people ever got to visit. Maria had gotten there on time. Cai had aimed to be early but got lost, and so he was on time too. They nodded at each other and sat in silence. The chairs were very nice, beautiful and comfortable, without being overly opulent. Maria sat perfectly straight. A distant ringing of bells telegraphed noon. A minute later, Aoki walked in.

"Hello," he said.

"Hi," replied Cai.

"Hello," replied Maria.

Aoki smiled warmly. "Sorry, I'm late," he apologised.

Cai smiled and replied "It's all right."

Maria nodded. Aoki sat down, slouched. They looked towards the floor and sat in silence.

"I'm Aoki," announced Aoki after a while, in an attempt to initiate conversation.

"Maria," said Maria.

"Cai," said Cai.

"Pleasure to meet you both."

"Likewise," said Maria.

Their gazes turned awkwardly back to the carpet. It was a beautiful carpet. It matched the chairs.

Cai noticed a large sword at Maria's side and a knife at Aoki's. He had no weapons himself. "Do either of you know why we're here?" he asked.

Maria and Aoki both shook their heads.

"I got a summons from the king this morning," Cai continued. They all had. "I reckon we're going on some sort of mission. Maybe—"

The look on the face of the woman who walked in silenced him. It was the look a stern headmistress might give to a misbehaving child, one she really hated. She strode with unashamed confidence, said nothing, and sat down.

"Aoibheann," said Cai, with a curt nod.

Aoibheann nodded her head slightly to acknowledge his greeting. The group returned to silence. Aoibheann got progressively more irate. She'd arrived late on purpose so she wouldn't have to wait, but here she was, waiting anyway. It annoyed her to no end.

The bells rang for one o'clock, and the next person came in, finally. Aoibheann gave him a burning look.

"Arjun," he said, introducing himself with a small salute. "And don't you forget it."

The others were annoyed at him too. He pretended not to notice and took the last seat. The sun shone right in his eyes, so he got up and sat on the floor instead.

As he did, a voice came from the ascending stairwell. "Come on up."

Aoibheann was the first to rise. She strode purposefully towards the stairs. Maria was right behind her. Aoki and Cai followed. Arjun waited until they were all out of sight, then he got up too, slowly. He muttered something to himself about just getting comfy.

The door at the top of the stairs opened into an office. There was a large desk overfull with stacks of papers, and behind it sat the king. A slight breeze blew from the balcony, ruffling the papers. One really caught the wind and began to fly, doing all sorts of gymnastics as it fell to the ground. Maria caught it and handed it to the king.

"Thank you, Maria," he said kindly. She bowed. He looked at all five people in turn. "Thank you all for coming. I'm sure you're wondering why I've asked you here."

"Yes," snapped Aoibheann, "I am."

Maria gave her a horrified look. The king ignored the answer to his rhetorical question. "I have a big favour to ask of you all," he continued. "Although I'm afraid you really don't have much choice."

Cai and Maria shared an apprehensive glance. Aoibheann stared at the king. Arjun stared out of the window.

"I'd like you all to go on a quest," explained the king, "to the frozen north beyond the borders of this kingdom. You'll leave tomorrow."

"If we don't have a choice, you're not asking a favour, you're giving an order," said Aoibheann sternly. "You're ordering me to forget everything and leave the city tomorrow? For how long?"

"I'm afraid I am giving an order, Aoibheann," said the king sternly. "I don't know for how long you'll be gone for. Months, maybe. But I don't ask this frivolously. It's for the good of the kingdom, and you'll all be suitably rewarded."

For the first time, Arjun looked directly at the king. He raised an eyebrow.

"What's the aim of this quest, your highness?" asked Maria.

He hesitated for a moment. "I can't tell you."

"You can't tell us?" exclaimed Aoibheann. "You're sending us to the end of the world and won't tell us why?"

"You'll have to trust me."

"And if I say no?"

The king raised an eyebrow at her. "You can't say no."

"I don't appreciate being threatened," said Aoibheann coldly.

"I'm not the one threatening you, Aoibheann," said the king. "You know that."

Her eyes narrowed, and the retort died on her lips. She was suddenly silent.

"Your highness," asked Aoki, "how are we supposed to complete this quest if we don't know what our goal is?"

The king picked up a sphere from his desk, a few inches in diameter. It was black and covered in runes. "This will point you in the right direction," he explained. "It's like a compass." He tapped an image of a dragon with his claw. "This rune will always point in the direction you need to go."

"I have a young daughter, your highness," blurted out Cai. "I can't just disappear for months, not knowing when I'll be back."

The king looked pained. "I'm sorry, Cai. I really am. But there's no one else with your skills here in the capital. You're essential to the mission."

"I have to go?"

"I'll make sure your daughter is well looked after, Cai. I'm sorry. To all of you. I wouldn't ask unless it was necessary."

"For the good of the kingdom," Cai muttered. He furrowed his brow, paused, and then sighed. "Fine, I'll do it. But can I ask one condition?"

"You can always ask."

"I want one more day to spend with my family."

The king thought for a moment, and his compassion won over. "That's a fair thing to ask; I can't deny you it. You can leave the day after tomorrow at the crack of dawn and no later."

"Thank you, your highness," said Cai, with a slight bow.

"Maria?" asked the king.

"Your will is my command, your highness," she replied dutifully.

"Thank you. Aoki?"

"I've always wanted an excuse to go up north. It sounds like fun."

"Thank you." The king nodded. "And you, Arjun? You've been quiet."

Arjun smiled a lopsided smile and bowed an overly exaggerated bow. His voice was dripping with mockery. "Of course, my overlord. Anything for you."

"Show some respect!" exclaimed Maria.

"It's okay, Maria," said the king. "Thank you, Arjun. You may only tell your close families what you're doing, and you must swear them to secrecy. Word can't be allowed to get out about where you're going. While you're in the palace, speak to the steward. She'll equip you with food and supplies; weapons from the treasury, too, if you so desire."

Aoki whistled. "I could do with a new dagger."

"And a new set of armour would be nice," agreed Maria. "Thank you, your highness."

"Take anything you want," he said, "as a token of good faith. Which one of you would like the sphere?"

"I would," said Aoibheann, quickly and assertively.

The Dragon King stood up. Rising to his full height, he dwarfed the people in front of him. He appeared suddenly very powerful. Aoibheann was unfazed. The king dropped the sphere into her open hand.

"Take good care of it," warned the king.

Aoibheann nodded.

"Good luck. I dare say you may need it. Go now and say your goodbyes. Meet at the crack of dawn, the day after tomorrow. Aoibheann, Arjun, don't be late."

Everyone but Arjun bowed, and they left the study. Aoibheann stormed off and slammed the door to the waiting room loudly. The other four lingered.

"Well," said Cai.

"Well," said Aoki.

"It's a great honour to be chosen for such an important mission," declared Maria.

"I suppose so," acknowledged Cai. There was a lot of scepticism in his voice.

"I've never been to the proper north before," mused Aoki. "I wonder what it's like. It'll make a great story."

"A story you won't be allowed to tell," retorted Cai.

"Ah, yeah," said Aoki, visibly disappointed. "I forgot about that."

"We'll do our duty," said Maria. "That's what's important, not bragging rights."

"Why's it so secretive, though?" asked Cai.

Aoki's face lit up. "There must be one hell of a prize afterwards."

Maria rolled her eyes.

"We've got to follow a mysterious orb to the end of the earth, in a secret mission on order of the king! There's definitely one hell of a prize afterwards," said Aoki excitedly. His tone soured. "I'm not sure about some of the company, though."

"You know her, Cai?" asked Maria.

"A little. We were in a few classes together at the University."

"You're a mage!" exclaimed Maria.

"I am."

"So that's why the king said you were so essential! What can you do?"

"I'm a summoner."

"And Aoibheann?" asked Aoki. "What's her power?"

"Fire," said Cai. "She is, as I'm sure you've seen, quite arrogant. But to be honest, I'm glad she's coming with us. What I want from this journey is to come back alive and unharmed. Aoibheann makes that a lot more likely. She might be the most powerful mage I've ever met."

"She seems to have taken charge already," pointed out Maria.

"She has," agreed Cai.

They all looked a bit crestfallen at that.

"So, why do you think you were chosen?"

"I'm not sure," admitted Maria. "I'm in the army. I'm not exceptional, but I'm a good fighter, and I've trained to be a doctor."

"Very useful skills. And you Aoki?" asked Cai.

"I'm an archer, a hunter, and a ranger," he said. "I can make sure you don't all die in the wild."

"Very glad to have you on board then," said Cai, "both of you. How about you, Arjun?"

Arjun had sat back down, in a chair this time, a little way apart from where the others stood.

"I do this and that."

"That's not really an answer," said Maria.

"I know," he replied.

Maria was taken aback. "If we're going to be travelling together, it's important we know. We could be in life-or-death situations!"

Arjun just shrugged.

"What skills do you have?" she asked. "What experience?"

He shrugged again and stood up. He walked out without another word.

"I can't believe him!" exclaimed Maria. "What's his deal?"

"It looks like there might be two difficult members of this party." Cai sighed. "This trip is going to be fun."

"It is!" said Aoki, completely ignoring the sarcasm.

"We'll have plenty of time to talk when we're on the road," said Cai. "Right now, I'm going to spend time with my family."

"Yes," agreed Maria. "I need to say some goodbyes too. I imagine it's easier for me and you, Aoki. We're used to it. I'm sorry, Cai."

He nodded. "Thank you."

"I'll see you by the gates!" she said.

"I'll see you by the gates," he said.

The weather was mild. The air was still and crisp without being too cold, perfect for a journey. A pigeon sat on the battlements and cooed smugly. The cockerel wasn't up yet.

Maria sat by the gate. She'd been early again. She'd spent the past hour and a half rather bored. She took stock of her equipment for the tenth time. Her visit to the treasury the day before had been quite fruitful. She wore a brand-new set of lightweight leather armour, with two new daggers strapped to her belt. Her sword gleamed, although that wasn't new. She sat on a pack full of supplies and a medicine kit. Her load was heavy, but she was strong enough to carry it if it got too cold for the horses.

Aoki and Aoibheann arrived together. They had obviously taken a similar route at a similar time, but they were walking some distance apart and not talking. They'd both visited the treasury, too. Aoibheann wore a fine silk robe, coloured crimson. Aoki had a dagger strapped to his waist that could only be described as outlandish. Its hilt was completely encrusted in enormous jewels. As soon as he got close enough, he unsheathed it and waved it in front of Maria.

"Look at this!" he said, face full of joy. "They just gave it to me! For free!"

"It's beautiful," agreed Maria.

"And sharp too," he said, sheathing it. "It's the best dagger I've ever seen." Aoki looked the soldier up and down. He smiled. "It seems I'm not the only one who's got some new kit! That armour is so shiny. It must be new."

"It is," confirmed Maria, twisting around to show the back. "I wanted something strong but easy to carry, and they delivered perfectly. That robe is beautiful, Aoibheann!"

"It is," she said, as if the praise wasn't high enough. "Are we waiting again?"

"It's not dawn yet," said Maria with an edge to her voice. "Nobody's late. Look, here comes Cai."

He waved to them from across the courtyard. "Hello," he said to Maria and Aoki. They nodded their acknowledgement. "Aoibheann?" he asked.

"What?"

"Are you really going to wear bright red silk on a freezing cold secret mission?"

"I don't get cold. And I don't need to hide either."

"What if someone shoots an arrow at you?"

"I'm too powerful to need armour, Cai." She sighed. "I see you're wearing a full set."

"I am. I value my life."

Aoibheann snorted with contempt.

"We match!" said Maria, pointing to her own armour.

Cai looked down. "We do!" he said.

"Check this out," said Aoki, showing him the dagger.

"Are you going to show that stupid thing to everyone we meet between here and the north?" asked Aoibheann, already fed up.

"Anyone who'll look," replied Aoki, "at least until the novelty wears off."

"It is a very impressive dagger," admitted Cai. "But maybe don't go showing it off, or you'll attract unwanted attention."

"No one would be stupid enough to try and rob us," Aoki pointed out. "Not when we have Fireball here with us."

"Fireball?" Aoibheann repeated. "Fireball? Do you want to be burnt to a crisp?" The message came across loud and clear. Aobheann looked around. "Where is that last eejit?"

"That's rude," said Arjun, stepping out from the gatehouse.

Maria looked shocked. "How long have you been there?"

He looked smug. "If you were more alert, you'd know," he replied.

Maria sneered at him.

"Now we have two wise crackers. Wonderful," Cai muttered to himself.

"I spoke to the stable master," said Arjun. "He's prepared some horses for us."

"Let's go," commanded Aoibheann, refusing to let him take the lead.

The sun was just rising as they left the city and walked the short distance to the stables. The glare from Aoki's dagger was almost blinding when the light caught it. The man waiting for them squinted.

"You're not the stable master," said Aoibheann. "I've never seen you before."

"I've given him the day off," said the man with a wink. "The king sends his regards. He wanted to wish you a safe trip."

"Where is he then?" asked Aoibheann.

"A dragon would draw attention, but he's closer than you might think," he said. "He wants to thank you and give you this." He held up a small bag and wiggled it. He threw it to Aoibheann.

The party crowded around, as she opened it, and saw the gold inside.

"There might not always be inns, but when there are, take full advantage of what they have to offer."

"Thank you," said Aoibheann.

"I will," promised Aoki.

"Thank the king for us," asked Maria.

"He appreciates your gratitude," said the not-stable-master with another wink.

He led them inside and showed them five of the finest horses. They stowed what they could in the saddle bags and mounted up.

"I won't delay you," said the man. "Remember, time is of the essence. Good luck."

"Thank you," said Maria and Aoki in unison. Cai and Aoibheann nodded.

"The sphere is pointing us along the road," announced Aoibheann. "Let's go." Without waiting for a reply, she urged her horse on.

"She really has made herself the leader, hasn't she?" complained Aoki. He did follow, though.

Cai held back a little and looked over his shoulder at the city behind him. Maria noticed and recognised the look on his face. "What's your daughter called?"

"Morgana."

"How old is she?"

"She's four." He sighed. "She's probably still asleep."

"We'll make it back alive, and we'll make it back quickly. I promise."

He put on a smile. "Thank you, Maria."

"Come on," she said kindly. "We're falling behind."

He lingered a little longer, then, eyes front, set his horse to a canter.

On the first day the going was easy. The sphere led them along well-established roads, and they'd covered a lot of distance by the time the sun set. When Arjun suggested they call it a day in a prosperous market town, there'd been no complaints. They'd found the most expensive inn they could. Everyone was feeling more upbeat, despite the rough start to relations. If this was how the journey was going to go, it wouldn't be so bad after all.

Aoki smiled as he sank into the most comfortable bed he'd ever had the pleasure of lying in. Even Aoibheann smiled, when she was in the privacy of her room. Maybe it'd be closer to a holiday than a chore. They met downstairs for dinner.

Before long Aoki's plate was stacked high with half dozen kinds of poultry, smothered in gravy. Arjun's was stacked slightly higher. Aoki noticed that fact and ordered some more. Arjun laughed at him.

"I could get used to this," remarked Maria, between mouthfuls.

"Don't overeat," said Aoibheann, looking at her with contempt. "You need to be alert tomorrow."

"No, we don't," replied Arjun. "We're not anywhere dangerous."

"Anywhere is dangerous for people like you."

"You're not going to protect little weak me?" he asked, sounding hurt.

"Not if it's a danger caused by your own ineptitude."

"Rats!" Arjun exclaimed in false distress, before resuming his eating.

Aoki sourly put his extra portion to the side.

"Can we try not to argue?" asked Maria. "If we're going to be spending all this time together, we should try to get along."

"If you listen to what I say, I won't argue with any of you," said Aoibheann.

"Unbelievable!" muttered Cai.

Aoibheann looked him in the eye. "I'm the leader of this party."

"Are you?" asked Maria. "Says who?"

"It doesn't need to be said."

"Aoki is the most experienced traveller. Maybe he should be in charge."

Aoki looked around with a hint of panic in his eyes. When Aoibheann didn't even glance in his direction, he gratefully dug back into his meal with his eyes down.

"I'll take his advice when I feel it appropriate," stated Aoibheann. "If you want to challenge my leadership, Maria, you're welcome to. But it wouldn't end well for you."

"You might be surprised," countered Maria.

"I doubt it."

"You think you're better than us, don't you?"

"Yes, I do. Because I am. Only a God could kill me, Maria."

The two glared at each other, and Maria's hand rested on the hilt of her sword. Cai decided to intervene before it could escalate further. "Any large decisions will be made as a group, agreed?"

Everyone chimed in with an 'aye', except for Aoibheann. "I won't take orders from any of you." She sighed. "But if it'll stop you all whining then, yes, fine."

"Thank you!" said Maria. *Was that so hard?*

"This food is really good," said Aoki, breaking the awkward silence that followed.

"He's right," agreed Arjun through a mouthful.

"How's your salmon, Aoibheann?" asked Cai.

"It's very good," she admitted. "How's the mushroom pie?"

"Impeccable."

"Who wants a drink?" asked Aoki.

There was a loud noise of agreement from Arjun, which was seconded by Cai and Maria.

"Just one," warned Aoibheann.

"Two," countered Aoki.

"Fine," she said. "Two. But anyone who isn't up on time tomorrow—"

"Yeah, yeah," said Arjun. "You'll burn us to a crisp."

Aoki set off towards the bar. His heart sank as Aoibheann called after him.

"Wait!" she said. She threw him a gold piece. "Get me one too."

They retired to their rooms a little later than they should have that night, but in much better spirits.

"Do you know the game 'I spy'?" asked Aoki.

"Aoki, you've been suggesting games non-stop for the past four days," said Aoibheann "When are you going to run out and be quiet?"

"Never," he replied. "Most people don't realise how boring adventuring can be. It's mostly travelling. You've got to have ways to keep yourself entertained."

"How do you play?" asked Cai.

"I pick something I can see and say, 'I spy with my little eye something beginning with…' whatever letter it starts with. Then you have to guess what it is," he explained.

"Why am I not surprised it's a children's game?" asked Aoibheann.

"You wanna play?" asked Aoki.

"No."

"I will," said Cai.

"Me too," said Maria.

"You in, Arjun?" asked Aoki.

He scoffed. "No."

"Okay I'll go first," said Aoki. "I spy with my little eye, something beginning with T."

"Tree?" guessed Cai.

Aoki paused, hesitant to answer. "Yes."

"Unbelievable!" cried Aoibheann. "Out of anything you could have chosen, anything at all, you chose tree?"

"I'm starting off easy!" said Aoki. "You have to ease into it. Go on Cai, it's your go."

"I spy with my little eye something beginning with…" He looked around. "H."

"Horse?" asked Aoki.

"No."

"Hay?"

"No."

"Harness?" asked Maria.

"No."

"Hill?" she asked.

"No."

A pause.

"Helmet!" shouted Aoki triumphantly.

"Wrong again," said Cai.

Aoki twisted his head around, in his best impersonation of an owl. He looked everywhere, somewhat frantically. He came up with nothing. "You're good at this, Cai," he admitted.

"Thank you."

"No, he isn't," said Aoibheann.

"What's the answer then?" asked Aoki.

"Easy," she said, pointing to the verge. "The answer is hyacinth."

"It's not, actually." said a smug Cai, smiling.

Aoki laughed.

"Hauberk?" she asked.

"Nope."

"How do we know you aren't changing your answer?" she accused.

"I promise," he said.

"Swear it," said Aoibheann, "on your daughter's life."

Maria raised an eyebrow at Aoki. They both laughed.

Aoibheann turned round to face them. "What are you two laughing at?" she snapped.

"You don't like losing, do you?" asked Aoki.

"Shut up," she said. "Swear it, Cai."

"I swear," he said.

Aoibheann was visibly upset. "We're moving. I bet it's no longer in sight."

"It's still within sight."

She thought for a moment. "Horseshoe!" she exclaimed.

"Good guess," he said, "but no."

"Handsome man?" asked Aoki, pointing to himself.

Cai laughed. "I'm afraid not."

"Hunter?" asked Maria.

"No"

"Hilt!" shouted Arjun, from the back.

"First try," said Cai, giving him a short round of applause.

Aoki looked down at his belt in dismay.

"I could see it if I was blind," said Arjun.

"Well done," said Maria.

"Well played," said Aoki. "See, it is fun, Aoibheann."

"It's a game for children."

"You're only saying that because—"

"Be quiet!" she barked.

"Hey! You—"

"No. Be quiet," she said. "Look!"

The sphere in her hand had begun to flash. It glowed bright red for a half second, before fading, and lighting up again.

"What does it mean?" asked Maria.

"The rune is pointing to the forest," she said. "We should go. Now."

"You want us to leave the road?" asked Arjun.

"Now," she said urgently. "And stay quiet."

She turned her horse sharply to the left and galloped into the forest. Arjun tarried, looking down the road. He didn't see anything. After waiting a few moments, he followed along with the others. They rode through the brush until they were out of sight of the road, and the sphere stopped flashing. They were still and silent. Arjun began to say something but was silenced by a look full of fire.

They heard a distant clamour. It got louder and louder as it came along the road – the clank of heavy armour, the barking of orders, and the shouting of replies. Aoki dismounted quietly, motioned with two fingers to show the others what he was doing, and snuck back to the road. He saw the army patrol. They passed by without a glance in his direction, and he rejoined the group.

"An army patrol?" asked Aoibheann.

"An army patrol," Aoki confirmed.

"That voice giving orders sounded familiar," said Maria. "I think that was Lieutenant Port. I used to serve under him. He's a good man."

"So, we're hiding from the army now?" asked Cai.

Aoibheann looked down at the sphere with a new curiosity. "This is a secret mission, remember," she said. "It's a secret from the army too. We should avoid them wherever possible, especially if they might recognise Maria. But how did the sphere know?"

I thought you didn't need to hide, thought Maria.

"What do you know about it?" asked Cai.

She looked puzzled. "Nothing," she said distantly. "I thought it was just a glorified compass."

"Can you read the runes?"

"No," she admitted. "Can you?"

"Not at all," he replied.

"This is powerful magic," she said, still inspecting it.

"So, whenever we're in danger, that thing will light up and show us how to escape?" asked Aoki. "That's pretty damn useful."

"We don't know that," said Aoibheann. "It'd be foolish to rely on it to warn us."

"Where's it pointing now?" asked Cai.

"It wants us to go further into the woods."

"It does seem to know what it's doing," admitted Maria.

"So, instead of a road and nice inns, we go the whole way camping in a forest?" asked Arjun incredulously. "You've got to be joking. We know where we're going – north. Why can't we keep going like we have been?"

"We follow the sphere," said Aoibheann.

"And if it gets too overgrown for the horses?" asked Cai.

"Then we walk."

"Let's vote," said Cai. "All in favour of following the sphere, raise your hands."

Everyone but Arjun raised their hand. "Didn't the king say that time was of the essence?" he asked. "We can't walk the whole way."

"He raises a valid point," agreed Maria.

"The king told us to follow the sphere," said Aoibheann.

"There's no way I'm not following the psychic orb," said Aoki. "Not a chance."

"We follow the sphere," repeated Aoibheann firmly.

Arjun muttered something under his breath.

Before long they had to dismount and lead their horses deeper and deeper into the forest.

"Is that a lake?" asked Maria, as she caught a glimpse through the trees.

"Looks like it," said Aoki.

"It's getting late," said Aoibheann. "We'll camp there."

"It'll be full of bugs," warned Aoki.

"We should find somewhere else," suggested Maria. "I hate bugs."

"That's not my problem," Aoibheann replied. "Come on."

While Aoki and Maria went out to hunt, Aoibheann and Cai worked on setting up the tents. Arjun sat on a log.

"Are you going to help?" asked Aoibheann.

Arjun picked at the dirt underneath his fingernails. "No."

"Then we won't put up your tent," said Cai.

"That's fine," he said. "It's warm out."

Aoibheann was furious but held her tongue. Cai watched her cautiously. He recalled some of the rumours he'd heard. The 'Flame of the Dawn', people called her – to her face, at least. Behind her back, she was 'Von the volcano'. But no matter what they called her, the stories were the same. He was wondering how many of them were true when he noticed something. There were mosquitoes everywhere, but whenever one got close to Aoibheann, it would burn up.

"No wonder you weren't worried about the bugs!" he cried. "Can you extend that to me?"

Aoibheann began chanting in a language unfamiliar to the others. It was guttural, and her voice was loud. She clasped her hands together. Arjun raised an eyebrow from where he was sat. The lake, the entire lake, began to boil. It bubbled vigorously, hissing and spitting. Enormous pockets of steam rose to the top and popped violently.

"What are you doing?" Maria screamed.

Aoibhean didn't reply.

"Are you insane? Aoki's in there. Stop!"

Aoibhean kept chanting, and Maria stepped towards the mage.

Cai stepped in her way. "She knows what she's doing," he said. Maria went to move past him. He stepped in front of her again. "Trust me," he pleaded.

Their faces were red, and their eyes met. Cai's gaze was intense and calm. Maria's was wild. The heat was unbearable. She drew her sword from its sheath. She strode forward, shoving Cai aside with her left hand and brandishing her weapon with her right. Sweat poured from her face as she stood beside Aoibheann.

"Maria!" shouted Cai from the ground behind her. "Please. Don't interfere."

The chanting got louder, and Maria stood still, a silhouette in the steam with her sword above her head. The chanting got louder again and faster. And then it stopped. It had taken less than a minute. Aoibheann took a deep breath and staggered, almost falling over. Cai rushed to support her and helped her sit down.

"I'm fine," she mumbled.

Cai nodded and turned to Maria. "Let's go."

"Go where?" she shouted.

"Come on." He grabbed her hand and led her through the steam.

"Seeing as you're contributing to my team," she said loudly, to emphasise the point, "I will protect you from the bugs." She held both hands out wide and spun around. Every mosquito in the radius around the camp burnt up – every mosquito that is, except for the ones around Arjun. He seemed unfazed, though.

As they finished setting up, Aoki and Maria came back. Aoki carried two rabbits, and Maria had her hands full of berries.

Aoibheann's stomach growled. "Maybe you're not so useless after all," she remarked.

"You're welcome," said Aoki cheerily. "I'll get a stew going. Did you collect any firewood?"

Aoibheann laughed. "I don't need firewood." She clicked her fingers, and a roaring fire started in the middle of the camp.

Aoki's eyes widened, and he rushed over. "Sweet!"

"Maybe you're not so useless after all," said Maria.

Aoibheann gestured with her hand, excluding Maria from the mosquito protection. Maria waved her hands frantically, trying to swat at the onslaught of bugs. "Okay, I'm sorry, I'm sorry," she said. "I didn't mean it."

"Thank you," said Aoibheann with her fakest smile. She didn't re-extend the protection.

"It's a big lake," said Cai. "I feel like I should have heard of it. Do you know it, Aoki?"

"Nope," he said. He walked up to the water and wet his hand. "It's nice and cool," he declared. "If I had a spear, I'd go fishing." He turned to face the man sat on the log. "Hey, Arjun, didn't you bring a—"

Aoki screamed as a tentacle burst from the lake. It grabbed his ankle and pulled. Maria and Cai jumped up ready to act. They weren't fast enough. Aoki had been pulled under the water.

They stepped into the lake, or rather where the lake had been. There wasn't a drop of water left. Cai paused and looked around. He couldn't see any further than a few feet, and the ground was obscured. He pointed his free hand outwards, and a ghostly bird emerged from it, a great bird, larger than any Maria had ever seen. It flapped its wings, and the rush of air began to clear the vapour around them. As the lakebed was revealed, Maria recoiled. It was covered in what must have been fish, charred beyond recognition.

"She protected us," said Cai. "She still is protecting us, actually. Aoki will be safe" – he swallowed heavily and looked down nervously at the baked earth – "from her at least. Come on."

They ventured forward, down the banks. It was steep to begin with, before levelling out. They soon noticed one charred mass that stood out from the rest. They began to run. Maria took the lead, ready for action. But there was no need. It was just as charred as the fish. Its enormous, contorted body was still. Maria nudged a tentacle with her sword, and it crumbled into dust.

There came a weak shout. "Hey! Over here!"

"Aoki!" replied Cai. The relief in his voice was unmistakable. He powered through a tentacle, towards the voice. Aoki lay on the lakebed, his clothes still wet. He coughed and spluttered. "Are you okay?" asked Cai.

Aoki coughed again. "What just happened?" he asked weakly.

"Aoki, are you hurt?" cried Maria, rushing in. She bent down and brushed away the remains of the tentacle that was over him. "Look at me."

He did.

"How many fingers am I holding up?"

He answered correctly.

"What day is it?"

He answered correctly again.

"Let me look at your ankle." She rolled up his trouser. The entire leg was covered in welts.

Aoki lifted his head. "Again," he asked, "what on earth just happened?"

"You were pulled into the lake," said Cai. "And then Aoibheann evaporated it."

"She evaporated the lake?"

"Yes."

"The whole lake?"

"All of it except for you."

"Okay," he said. He put his head down again and muttered a prayer under his breath.

Maria slung him over her shoulder and carried him back to camp.

Aoibheann was sat by the fire eating rabbit stew. "We need to leave," she said between mouthfuls, "right away. Pack up."

"What?" asked Maria. "Aoki's hurt. I don't think he can walk. He needs to rest."

"He can ride," said Aoibheann. She looked Aoki up and down. "You're welcome, by the way."

"Thank you," he croaked.

"What was that thing?" asked Cai.

"I don't know nor do I care," said Aoibheann. "Get packing. Oh, and Maria?" She turned towards the soldier. "Don't ever threaten me again."

Maria looked at her angrily but didn't reply.

"Understood?" asked Aoibheann with force.

"Understood," muttered Maria.

"So we left the road to hide, and now you've filled the entire sky with steam," said Arjun. "Well done. Now everyone within a hundred miles knows we're here."

"And what were you doing, eejit? Sitting on a log?"

"You're not familiar with subtlety, are you? You should meet her sometime, she's lovely."

Arjun shot up as his log burst into flames.

"Come on," said Cai. "She's right. We need to leave. Where's the sphere pointing us, Aoibheann?"

Maria stopped packing for a moment. "It didn't warn us," she realised.

"We were never in any danger," dismissed Aoibheann.

Cai handed Aoibheann her pack. He gave her an inquisitive glance. "And we were in danger from the soldiers?"

She paused. "Perhaps it warns of danger to the quest, not danger to us," she suggested. "The army finding out about the quest could have put it in jeopardy. Aoki being eaten would be of no consequence."

"Thank you," he croaked.

"We need to be wary of it, like I said," warned Aoibheann. "Now let's go. We need to be far away by morning." She led the way, and as usual, the others followed. Aoki fell asleep slumped over his horse.

Cai caught Maria's concerned look. "Will he be okay?" he asked.

"Somehow, yes," she replied. "Once he's rested, he'll be fine. There's no serious damage; I fixed up his leg. He'll be scarred, though."

"I doubt he'll complain about that," said Cai. "He can tell everyone the story of Aoki the Kraken Slayer."

They both laughed, but Maria got serious again quickly. She slowed her pace to put distance between them and the others. She spoke in a hushed tone. "So, that's what she can do?"

"Yes."

"I didn't know anyone could do that," she said. "It's terrifying. When you said she was powerful, I didn't think—"

"Neither did I," said Cai. "I had no idea the level she'd reached."

"I'm scared," admitted Maria. "She hates me."

"You looked like you were about to chop her in half!"

"Well, I…" She stopped herself. "I never could have hurt her, could I?"

"No."

"How can we refuse her anything?"

"She's not a monster," said Cai. "And she's on our side, remember. She's not a bad person."

"How well do you know her?"

Cai hesitated. "Not that well."

"How powerful are you? What was that bird you summoned?"

"I can summon animal spirits," he answered.

"Any animal?"

"No. I have to have helped that animal pass on to the next world."

Maria looked suspicious. "So, you're a necromancer?"

"Of sorts."

"If it came down to it, could you beat Aoibheann?" she asked.

Cai held up his hand. "I'm not having this conversation," he said firmly. "She just saved Aoki's life, remember." He looked forward, at how far ahead the others were. "Let's not fall behind," he said, picking up the pace.

The whole party was on the edge of exhaustion. Arjun yawned so deeply and loudly, it would have been dismissed as performative in any other context. He was so engrossed in his yawn he didn't notice a somewhat ghostly-looking ant crawl up his boot. It bit him on the ankle, and he yelped. Aoibheann laughed, then she yelped too. Then Maria.

"Keep an eye out," said Cai, wearing a smile no one else saw. "There must be a nest nearby."

Slightly more awake, they kept walking.

The king had to fly above the clouds to avoid being seen. He hated flying in the moonlight. It made him feel exposed. The cold light gave him chills. It only took him a few hours to cover the distance that had taken the messenger weeks. He glided on currents only he knew, weaving between the mountaintops. He came to land in the secret paradise of the Sun.

"I thought you'd have come sooner," she said playfully. "I've been waiting."

"I have a kingdom to run," he replied. "I was busy."

"Diligent as ever, I see."

"What do you want?" he asked.

"What do I want?" she replied. "Why, you're the one who's come to visit unannounced."

"I don't have time to play games."

She smiled. "You really don't."

After a full night's journey, the party made camp again. Aoki woke and half-dismounted, half-fell from his horse. Maria rushed to support him and helped him to bed. He was asleep again very quickly. Aoibheann left a small fire burning beside him to keep him warm. They all slept very broken sleep and stayed in bed until noon.

"Thank you, Aoibheann," said Aoki, with real feeling. "You saved my life." He grabbed a sausage from over the fire and turned his head. "And you two as well, Cai and Maria. Thank you." He paused. "From what I hear, I have nothing to thank you for, Arjun."

"You're welcome," the accused replied through a mouthful of breakfast.

Aoki looked straight at Aoibheann and smiled. "You care about me."

She avoided his eyes. "It'd be a stain on my reputation if a member of my party died."

"I really thought I was a goner!" he said cheerfully. "You're a hero."

"If you were more competent, I would never have had to save you." The disdain in her voice was frank.

Aoki looked upset.

Aoibheann rolled her eyes. "Your rabbit stew was good," she admitted. "So you're good for something."

The hunter beamed.

"How are you feeling?" asked Maria quickly. "I tended to all of your wounds."

"I'll be good as new soon," he said, stretching out all four limbs. "Thanks to you. I'm going to have so many stories when I get back. I knew this quest was going to be good! Aoki and the Thing from the Deep. It has a certain ring to it, doesn't it?" He got no reply save for a feign-encouraging smile from Maria, but that was all he needed. "Where to next, skipper?"

"We'll do a light half-day's march," said Aoibheann. "Last night we bore due north, and the sphere is pointing us north today again."

"It's going to start getting cold soon," warned Aoki. "We might have to start huddling together at night for warmth." He smiled and raised an eyebrow at Cai. "Your wife doesn't need to know."

"I'd rather freeze."

"Aww, come on!"

"Agreed," said Aoibheann. "Not that I ever would freeze."

"Is your magic weak in the cold, Aoibheann?" asked Cai.

She scoffed.

"A water mage in a desert isn't usually very strong," he continued. "It's only natural that in the cold you'd—"

"I'm beyond mages like that, Cai," she said.

"I suppose you are," he admitted. "What—"

A deep shout came from the trees. "Hail!"

Maria grabbed her sword, and Aoki, his bow.

"Let me do the talking," said Cai to the others quietly. He shouted back cautiously. "Hail!"

A lone man walked into their clearing. He was tall, and so obviously strong. He had scruffy black hair down over his eyes, and a long, well-maintained beard. He was very handsome. When he spoke, his voice was deep and smooth.

"My name is Corryn," he said affably. "Pleasure to meet you."

"Likewise," said Cai. "It's a lovely day."

Corryn looked to the sky at the shining sun. "It is," he agreed. His gaze turned to the fire. "That smells lovely! What are you cooking?"

"We've got sausages and bacon."

"Lovely," he said.

There was a long silence. The party looked at each other and at him.

"Well," he said eventually, "I'll be on my way. Safe journey to you."

"And to you!" said Cai.

The man turned to leave, but Aoki stopped him. "Would you like to join us?" he called after him. "We have plenty to go around."

"What are you doing?" hissed Cai.

Aoibheann bit her tongue and clenched her fist. The food over the fire began to cook a lot faster.

"Thank you," said the man, turning back. "It's always a pleasure to share a meal with fellow travellers."

Aoki motioned towards the campfire, and the man made a point of sitting down next to Aoibheann, right in Aoki's spot. He stood behind the two awkwardly.

"Where are you headed?" asked Cai.

"Did you see the smoke last night, above the lake?"

Aoibheann and Cai looked at each other through the side of their eyes.

"We saw it, yes," said Aoibheann.

"I've been sent to investigate it," said the man. "Do you have any idea what might have happened?"

"No," said Cai.

"Are you sure?" asked the man. His voice was relaxed and silky. He reached for a piece of bacon. "No idea at all?"

"I'm afraid not," said Cai firmly.

The man began to chew. "It's good," he said, motioning to his mouth. His eyes lingered for a moment on the fuelless fire.

"Very good." He addressed Aoki directly. "So, where are you all headed?"

Aoki made to reply, but Cai answered before he could. "That'd be spoiling the surprise."

"Apologies," said the man. Holding up his hands. "I don't mean to pry."

They ate in silence. It was a hearty breakfast and a delicious one.

When he was done, the man slapped his thighs with his hands. "Well, I won't outstay my welcome. Thank you for your kindness; may it be repaid to you in turn."

Aoibheann breathed a sigh of relief as he looked about to stand up. She let her guard down, just for a moment, but that was all he needed. The form of a man crumpled and fell like it was made of paper, and an eight-legged monster emerged. The hairs on its legs bristled and its mandibles opened. It leaped towards Aoibheann.

Aoibheann was fast to react, and it began to burn, but momentum carried it forwards. Her eyes grew wide. Her pupils ignited, and her body erupted in flames, but momentum carried it forwards. Three feet left. Two feet. One.

Aoki's boot caught it firmly in the abdomen. It grazed Aoibheann's ear as it flew past. Its momentum had shifted just enough. Maria stood paralysed in fear as the spider landed beside her. She held her sword in front of her with white knuckles but couldn't muster the impetus to swing it.

Aoki drew his bow and shot it straight through the head. It wriggled, and he shot it again. He knocked a third arrow and shot it through the thorax. It burst open into a thousand swarming children.

The spawn were immediately engulfed in an inferno. A firestorm so hot they became nothing in an instant. Aoibheann's eyes glowed. Maria's sword was caught in the blast, and she dropped it with a cry as the heat flowed into her hand. The fire went from red to yellow to white as Aoibheann's incantations became screams. Everyone fell back as the heat became unbearable. Aoibheann's voice cracked, and the words of power caught in her throat. She stopped. All that was left behind was soot. Breathing heavily, she stormed up to Aoki.

"YOU CRETIN!" she screamed. She stuck her finger in his chest and his shirt smoked. "YOU INVITED THAT—"

"The sphere flashed!" he shouted. "The sphere flashed!"

"I don't—" she began. She was still shouting, but her anger had lost its edge.

"When he turned to leave," interrupted Aoki, speaking quickly, "the sphere flashed. You didn't see it, but when he arrived, I grabbed it just in case. It flashed when he was going to leave."

Aoibheann closed her eyes and took deliberate, heavy breaths. Maria held a dagger in hand, poised like a cat ready to pounce. Aoibheann opened her eyes and the fire in them was gone. "Thank you, Aoki." Everyone relaxed a little. "You saved my life." She sounded uncomfortable and was shaking. She turned to Maria. "I'm sorry."

Maria looked at her with a deep, bitter anger that didn't manage to hide her fear. She clutched her right hand close to her chest.

"Let me see your hand," Aoibheann asked.

"No," replied Maria.

"Let me see it," Aoibheann insisted.

"No."

Aoibheann took a step forward, and Maria took a step back. Aoibheann stopped and softened her tone. "I can fix it."

Maria hesitated, then held out her hand as far away from herself as she could manage. Aoibheann approached and gently touched the blistered and burnt skin. Maria winced. A stream of light flowed out from Maria's hand and into Aoibheann. The blisters faded and the burn receded. Only a small patch remained. Aoibheann let go, and Maria snatched her hand back violently.

"You're welcome," said Aoibheann, angrily.

"I'm welcome?" shouted Maria incredulously "I'm welcome? You're the one that did it!"

Aoibheann cut off her own snide retort and quieted her voice. "I'm sorry, Maria. I really am."

Aoki broke the uncomfortable silence. "What was that thing?"

Cai and Aoibheann looked at each other. Cai was pale. "That was a shapechanger," he said, "and maybe an assassin."

"You think it was looking for us?"

"I don't think this was a chance encounter," said Cai. "It seems we were told to keep this quest secret for a very good reason."

The realisation they were being hunted was sobering.

"And I invited it into camp," said Aoki distantly.

"We've killed it now," said Cai. "It obviously already knew who we were. If it had left, it could have come back and killed us in our sleep or brought reinforcements."

"You did the right thing," said Aoibheann quietly.

"But who is after us, and why?" asked Cai.

No one had an answer.

"There might be more of them."

"Why is it never something with a normal amount of legs?" complained Aoki. "Two, I'm okay with. Four? Fantastic. Any more than that, no thank you. First that lake monster, now this. I'm okay with bugs when they're the size of bugs, but that thing..." He shuddered.

Maria went to pick up what remained of her sword. It was unusable, melted into a pile of deformed metal. "I loved this sword," she said.

"I'll buy you a new one," said Aoibheann.

"From where?"

"I don't know," she replied. "At the next available opportunity."

"Are there many masterfully forged swords with irreplaceable sentimental value for sale in the forest?"

"Maria, she's trying to help," said Cai.

"She could have killed me!" said Maria, exasperated.

"Yes, but she didn't," he countered. "And she did kill that swarm. What were your plans for dealing with it?"

Maria had no reply.

He turned to Aoki. "Good reactions. You're obviously a capable fighter."

"Thank you."

"Right now," said Cai, "We need to get moving again. Once we've put some distance behind us, we'll take a day to train together. We should have done it a long time ago. We're in danger now. We need to know what each other are capable of. Sound like a plan?"

Maria and Aoki nodded.

"I'm not training with you," said Arjun. "But we should definitely get going. Dummy's right about those things with all the legs."

Aoibheann stayed quiet as they once again broke camp in a rush. She put a dark cloak over her crimson robe. A new paranoia fell over them as they travelled. The sound of a deer in the undergrowth had their hearts racing and weapons drawn. Even the birdsong caused them stress. Was that a bird or some hunter's signal? There was no talking. They moved with a sense of urgency.

The moon wasn't bright, but Aoibheann lit their way as they kept going late into the night. They followed the sphere north and crested a small hill. The trees were thin, and the sightlines were good. They unanimously agreed on it as a campsite and decided to take turns on watch. The people off watch didn't sleep much more than the people on watch.

They woke at dawn and wordlessly broke camp before another day's hard march. At around midday, Aoki, who was leading the way, gestured to those behind to stop. He held a finger to his lips and pointed at a bird in the branches. He mouthed, "Turkey." He silently drew his bow, aimed for a breath, and let loose. The arrow hit the turkey through the neck.

"Yes!" he cried, throwing his fist in the air. "We're eating good tonight!"

"That was a good shot," remarked Maria.

"What can I say," he said with a cheeky smile. "I'm the greatest archer the land has ever seen."

"Get over yourself," said Arjun, but he was impressed too.

After that, conversation gradually returned. Aoki baited Arjun into an argument over who was a better fighter, discussed with Maria how they should cook the turkey, and told an obviously embellished story about one of his adventures. He was good for morale. While he was busy arguing with Arjun and Aoibheann about the merits of and issues with various methods of 'borrowing without permission', Maria once again got Cai alone at the back of the party.

"I told you so," she hissed. "She's dangerous."

"We don't know what we're up against now," he replied. "We need her help."

"We're up against her! She hurt me, Cai. And don't tell me you didn't feel the heat as well."

"She's a powerful person. She's been untouchable for a very long time, and she almost died. Her own mortality looked her straight in the face, and it shook her. You saw how she was afterwards. She never meant to hurt you. Her apology seemed genuine."

"She protected us before when she used her magic. This time she didn't because she was scared and angry. What happens if we get into another life-or-death situation and she loses her cool? I was worried about her deliberately causing us harm. Now I'm worried she'll do it accidentally, too."

"And what do you suggest we do?" asked Cai, frustrated. "You want us to abandon her, is it? After she saved our lives?"

"I don't know," Maria replied, equally frustrated. "But she scares me. And I hate her."

Cai looked sad. He'd thought that was the case, but hearing it said so plainly really drove the point home. "We all need to get along. You said it yourself a while back, do you remember?"

"A lot has changed since then."

"When we train tomorrow, I'll talk to her about making sure she protects us from her magic."

"Thank you." Maria managed a smile. "I can't wait to see what you can really do."

Cai smiled back. "Do you fancy your chances?"

She scoffed. "You wouldn't stand a chance, little boy. Even without my sword, I'll beat you."

"As if, I—"

"Hey, what are you two scheming about back there?" shouted Aoki.

"She thinks she can beat me in a spar," Cai shouted back. "She's misguided."

"Ha!" shouted Aoki. "I could beat you both at the same time."

The two gave each other a knowing look, silently agreeing to prove him wrong. The mood was lifted, but a niggling paranoia still hung above them.

The rest of the party watched on as Maria and Aoki circled each other warily. They each held the sheath of a dagger. Maria lunged forward and Aoki dodged back.

"Stop running away and fight me!" she shouted.

He lunged at her from the right. She stepped left and moved to grab his arm. She caught it and held it tight against her side. Aoki tried to move in close and felt a sheath against his throat.

"You're dead," Maria said with a big smile.

Aoki smiled back. "Best of three," he said.

They went again. Maria was taller and had a longer reach. She used that to her advantage, stopping Aoki from coming in close. She swung wide whenever he approached. Aoki put some distance between them, before quickly bending down to pick up some dirt. He threw it in her face and attempted to get in close, but a wild slash held him back.

Maria had one hand up to her face, rubbing her eyes. She spat. Through her blurry vision she saw Aoki approach again and swung wildly. But he was expecting it, and dodged, before grabbing her arm and pulling, bringing her off balance and stumbling towards him. He stuck his sheath into her chest.

"Ha!" he shouted. "Now you're dead!" He turned to Cai. "I can't believe that worked, oldest trick in the book."

"So, we're playing dirty, are we?" Maria asked. "Okay then. Let's go again."

Aoki nodded sombrely. "Winner takes all."

Maria instantly drew the second sheath from her belt and threw it at Aoki's head, who managed to dodge just in time.

"Hey—" he started, before having the wind knocked out of him as he was tackled to the ground. Maria repeatedly mimicked stabbing him.

Cai laughed. "She makes it look easy."

"I'm not a close-range fighter," he complained. "I'm an archer."

"You did well," said Maria, standing up. She offered him a hand. "You have good reflexes and a good fighting brain."

He took her hand. "You're not half bad yourself," he admitted.

"I don't usually fight with daggers, remember?" she said. "And I still crushed you."

"You'd never get that close," he said. "I'd sit up in a tree and shoot you from a hundred yards."

"Do you often watch women from up in trees?" asked Arjun.

"No!"

"You're both obviously capable fighters," said Cai. "I'm impressed. Will you be taking part, Arjun?"

"No."

"Aww, come on!" goaded Aoki. "Fight me!"

"Based on your performance, that'd be a huge waste of my time."

"Then fight me," said Maria.

"You're not much better."

"If you're so good, then prove it!" said Maria. "You've done absolutely nothing so far. Why are you even here?"

"For the pay cheque."

"Your life's on the line now, Arjun," said Cai. "It's more than a pay cheque; it's about staying alive. We need to know we have each other's backs. And we need to know what you can do."

"I can look after myself."

"Can you?" asked Aoki. He tried to slip behind Arjun and grab him in a chokehold. Arjun seized his arm and flipped him over his shoulder. Aoki landed on the ground, hard. He had the wind knocked out of him again. He wheezed.

"That's proof enough for me," said Maria.

"Me too," agreed Cai.

Aoibheann smiled a little. She went to help him up.

Cai strode into the middle of the clearing. "Should we show them how it's really done, Aoibheann?"

"You go ahead," she said. Her smile faded. "You've all seen what I can do."

Cai nodded. He took a deep breath. He held his arms out, palms facing the sky. A slight shadow seemed to pass in front of the sun. It wasn't dark per se, but it wasn't bright anymore. Shining, rippling ghostly shapes emerged from the ground all around him. Dozens of them, big and small. They formed into familiar shapes as they grew: a bear, a snake, a bull, hornets, ants, rats, eagles, wolves.

Cai lowered his hands, and the animals started moving. The bear lay down and rested its head on its paws. The bull started grazing. They all minded their own business, showing no interest in each other or the people around them.

"Amazing!" said Maria.

"You're a walking zoo," snorted Arjun.

Cai gestured his hand, and the bear walked up to Arjun. It grew in size with every step and stood much taller than the man it was approaching. It growled from deep in its chest. Arjun took a step back and held his spear in front of him. A growl from behind made him spin around. Two wolves bared their teeth. Two hornets crawled along the back of his neck. He stood very still.

Point made, the bear turned and meandered back to lay in its spot. The wolves walked back to Cai, and the hornets flew away. Cai scratched a wolf behind the ear.

"That. Is. Awesome!" said Aoki. "That's incredible! You're a one-man army!"

Cai gestured, and everything except for the bear and the hornets faded away. The sun shone a little bit brighter. "The more things I summon, the harder it is," he explained. "I can't maintain that many for long."

"You change their properties?" asked Aoibheann.

"I can change them to an extent. Their spirit has to stay true to what they were in life. I couldn't give Shar there wings, for example. She'll always be a bear. But what I can do is make her a bigger bear."

Aoibheann nodded. "You've become powerful," she said. "You've come a long way since our time at the University."

"Thank you," he said. "How much precision do you have with your magic, Aoibheann?" he asked.

"A lot," she answered.

"Could you put an aura of fire around something, without burning it?"

She replied without hesitation. "Easily."

Cai motioned at Shar. Aoibheann chanted a few words, and the bear was cloaked in flame. Her claws and teeth were especially augmented and burned impossibly hot. As Cai gestured with his hands, she grew again, even bigger than before. She stood up on her hind legs, and her head almost poked above the trees.

"Well, that's absolutely terrifying," said Aoki. Arjun's eyes widened.

The flames faded, and Shar came back to all fours with a crash. Cai went over and scratched under her chin. "Good girl." She nuzzled her head against him. He turned to Aoibheann. "We work surprisingly well together, it seems."

"I don't think anyone would want to mess with us while that thing's around," said Maria.

"It's not particularly stealthy though," said Cai. "Best leave it as a last resort."

"Agreed," said Aoibheann.

"Can I ask one more thing, Aoibheann?" said Cai.

"Sure."

"How much energy does it take to protect all of us from your spells?"

"It's not trivial, but not arduous, either."

"Can you make sure you always do it?"

She replied through bared teeth. "I didn't do it on purpose."

"I know, I know. But it's important, always."

"You think I don't know that?"

"Yes, but—" interrupted Maria.

"You stay out of this!" said Aoibheann, embers flying. "You have no idea what you're talking about." She took a deep breath and turned to Cai. "I'm doing my best."

He nodded. "Thank you," he said. "We should take the rest of the morning to train together. We'll get going again this afternoon."

While Cai and Aoibheann worked on combining their magics, Aoki and Maria paired up to spar again.

"Go easy on me," he said. "I'm covered in bruises already."

She went to swing, and he flinched. She dropped out of her fighting stance. "Why don't you show me your archery?"

"Ah, so you want to see the archer supreme?" he said. "That's more like it. I suppose I can bless you with a sneak peak."

"Shut up."

"Okay, okay." He picked up his bow. "What should I shoot?"

Maria looked across the clearing. "The oak," she said, pointing.

"Okay." Aoki took his stance. He drew his bow, aimed for a moment, and shot.

"Nice shot!" shouted Maria. The arrow hit its mark. "And again?"

The second arrow hit just above the first. As did the third, and the fourth.

"You really are a good archer," conceded Maria. "I'm impressed."

He beamed. "Impressed enough to help me collect my arrows?"

She rolled her eyes. "Just about."

"Thank you, Maria!" he shouted, running off towards the trees.

Maria followed. "Aoki," she said, seeing the arrows up close. "They've almost gone straight through."

"They're always a pain to get out," he said, grabbing a shaft and pulling. The arrow didn't budge.

"How strong are you?"

"Very."

"Not that strong!" she shouted.

Cai heard her shout and came to look. "Not that strong," he agreed.

"Hey!"

"And your bow isn't strong enough to do that, either," said Maria.

Aoki looked down at it, a little perplexed.

"That's a lightweight bow. It'd snap in half before being able to shoot a foot deep into an oak!"

"No, it wouldn't."

"Yes, it would."

"Has it snapped?"

"No," said Cai, jumping in. "Because you're a mage."

"I don't think so," said Aoki with half a smile.

"I've never seen you miss."

"Yes, that's because I'm good."

"Do you ever miss?"

"I—"

"Ever?"

Aoki paused to think. "No."

"Even the best archers miss sometimes. You have magic – weak, untrained magic, but magic nonetheless."

Aoki looked down at his hands. He held them out, and flipped them over, examining them closely.

"You can't see it," said Aoibheann.

"But how can I have magic?" asked Aoki.

"Some people are born with it," said Cai.

"Maybe you're more interesting than I thought," said Aoibheann. "Can you do anything else?"

"I don't know! I only just found out!"

"Shoot at the tree again. Point your bow to the side but think about hitting the tree."

Aoki walked across the clearing and took his stance. He aimed straight at the tree and then turned his bow a couple of degrees to the right. He closed his eyes, concentrated, and let loose. When he opened his eyes again, he saw the arrow planted just an inch above the others.

"I knew it!" said Cai.

Aoki didn't know what to say. It was an unfamiliar feeling.

"It curved mid-flight," observed Maria. "That wasn't a natural flight path."

"Did you never get suspicious?" asked Cai. "I've never seen anyone shoot so powerfully before or so accurately."

"It's always come easily to me," he explained. "But I just thought I was really good."

"You never stopped to think?" asked Aoibheann. "Why am I not surprised?"

"When we get back, you should visit the University," said Cai.

"Can either of you teach me?" he asked excitedly. "Will I be able to do things like you can? Do firestorms? Summon giant bears?"

Cai looked sympathetic. "Probably not."

"No one can do what I can do" Aoibheann huffed.

"Most magic is quite narrow in scope," said Cai. "Yours probably focuses entirely on archery."

"Can you explain it to me?"

"We don't have the time or the specific expertise."

"Oh," said Aoki, looking disappointed.

"I'm sorry," said Cai. "But you should experiment. Test the practical limits of what you can do right now."

"Do I need to speak that language like you do, Aoibheann? Or do a specific pose?"

She laughed at him. "My magic is celestial," she said, looking to the sky, "divine; yours is primitive. You should be able to control it using just your intuition."

"Primitive?" asked Aoki bashfully.

"I don't agree with her choice of words," said Cai. "But she's right. Your magic seems to be subconscious. You shouldn't need to try too hard to use it."

"So, I can just hit whatever I want by willing it?"

"Try it."

Aoki turned around and aimed his bow towards another tree. He shot and hit it squarely in the middle.

"What if you turned back around and tried to hit that same tree?" asked Maria.

He did so, and his arrow took its natural course.

"So, you at least have to be pointing in the general direction," remarked Cai. He picked up a stone from the ground. "Try and hit this."

He lobbed it across the clearing, and mid air an arrow collided with it.

"Incredible," said Maria, smiling.

But Aoki didn't look happy. He just looked down at his hands, quietly. "How do I know what's my skill, my strength, and what's magic?"

"In your case, it might be hard to tell," said Cai.

"Why aren't you happy?" asked Aoibheann. "You're a mage!"

"I feel like a fraud. I always knew I was good…" he said. "But turns out I'm just a cheat! I'm not a good archer at all; I never was."

"You're better than an archer now!" said Aoibheann.

"Of course you'd say that."

"What?" she said. "But you are!"

"It doesn't matter," said Aoki. "I'll explore what I can do. You two do your practice."

Cai put his hand on Aoibheann's shoulder and guided her away.

Maria turned to leave, too, before noticing. "Where's Arjun?" she asked with a hint of urgency in her voice. They all surveyed the clearing. He was nowhere to be seen. "Arjun?" she called cautiously, and not too loudly.

The four instinctively stood back-to-back. Cai raised his hands and summoned a spectral swarm of fruit flies. They began to fly out in every direction. He didn't need to scout. Arjun walked out from the trees, holding a handful of berries and chewing loudly.

"What the hell were you doing?" asked Maria.

He looked down at his hand and back to Maria. He stuck his hand out, clearly showing the berries.

"Yes, you were collecting berries," said Maria. "But the question still stands. What the hell were you doing?"

"Do you not possess one single iota of intelligence?" hissed Aoibheann.

"I possess enough to know these would have gone really well with that turkey we had the other day."

"Funny," said Cai.

"You do know we're being hunted?" asked Aoibheann.

"I know that."

"You do understand how, in that context, wandering into the forest alone without telling us might be a bad decision?"

Arjun just shrugged. "I'm fine."

"How do we know you're not another shapechanger?" accused Maria. It was an unsettling question.

"I pinkie promise," Arjun replied, taking a step towards them.

A wall of fire burst up in front of him for a second.

"Don't come any closer," warned Aoibheann.

"Have you gone insane?" he shouted. He gave Cai a pleading look. "I'm me!"

"Aoki," whispered Cai, "Could you lightly graze his arm?"

Aoki lifted his bow and pointed it at Arjun.

"Hey! What are you doing?" shouted Arjun, holding his hands out and shrinking as much as he could. "I'm me!"

The arrow just caught his arm.

"Red blood," sighed a relieved Cai. "He's human."

"What a surprise!" screamed Arjun, walking towards the campfire. He added grumpily, "I'm keeping all these berries to myself."

Maria rolled her eyes. "You would have done that anyway." She grabbed a bandage from her kit and wrapped it around his arm.

"You can't wander off like that," said Cai sternly.

"I thought Aoibheann was in charge?" replied Arjun.

"Don't wander off like that," growled Aoibheann.

"Yes, ma'am," said Arjun, with a mocking salute.

"You realise your life is in danger?" asked Cai. "How are you still not taking this seriously?"

"I won't wander off," he said. "Promise. Now come on, it's time for lunch."

Arjun ate his food under four sets of dirty looks. They broke camp, and after they had a few hours of marching behind them, they emerged from the forest.

"Finally!" exclaimed Maria.

"Does this mean we can ride again?" asked Arjun.

"Yes," said Cai. "But we'll still have to be vigilant. In the open, we're exposed." He turned to Aoibheann. "Where's the sphere pointing us?"

"Take a guess," she replied.

"Due north, got it." He surveyed the lands out in front of him. "Do you know this area at all, Aoki?"

"I've not been here before," he replied. "But I've heard some things."

"Like what?"

Aoki thought. "I think there's a town somewhere in the very far north," was all he came up with.

"Insightful," remarked Aoibheann.

"I hope we pass through it," said Arjun. "It'd be nice to sleep in a bed."

"Agreed," said Aoki. "Those inns! Ah! It was heaven!"

"It's hard to believe that was only a few days ago," said Maria. "A lot has changed since then."

"Things have definitely taken a turn for the worse," agreed Aoibheann.

Cai turned to look behind him. "Yes." He sighed. "My family is back there somewhere."

"We'll make it back," promised Maria.

"You know, I sort of enjoyed the relative peace and quiet in the beginning. But now I just miss them."

Aoibheann rolled her eyes. "You always were overly sentimental."

"There's no one you miss?"

"No."

Cai shook his head disapprovingly. "We're in more danger than I'm comfortable with."

"Then let's not wait," said Maria. "Let's go. Riding through pasture should be a breeze."

"And no one will be able to sneak up on us," said Aoki.

"Can you summon an eagle to scout for us?" Maria asked Cai.

"Now that I don't have to walk, yes. Doing it all day will leave me drained, though."

"It's a worthy trade off," said Aoibheann. "Come on, let's not waste any more time."

They'd only been riding for a few minutes before Cai motioned at them to stop. His eagle flew back to him and gently touched its beak to his outstretched finger.

"There's a shepherd up ahead," he said. "Maybe we should take a detour."

"For a shepherd?" asked Aoibheann. "Really?"

"If he really is a shepherd," said Maria.

"Do you see where we are?" said Aoibheann. "There's obviously going to be a shepherd. The sphere hasn't warned us. We keep going where it leads us."

"This is probably his land," said Aoki. "In my experience, they're not always too receptive to trespassers."

"You've all become timid," said Aoibheann. "We follow the sphere. We won't detour to avoid a shepherd."

I seem to remember you being quite timid these past few days, thought Maria.

Aoibheann started riding. After a moment, the others followed – her orders were often disapproved of, but seldom disobeyed. They passed the shepherd and exchanged greetings. Aoki talked to him about the weather.

"It's going to rain soon," said the shepherd. "I'd find shelter if I were you. I'd invite you into my home, but I'm afraid I don't have the room. You could have the barn, if you'd like, but it's awful draughty."

They politely declined, thanked him, and went on their way. Aoibheann was smug. They were able to cover ground quickly on horseback. Before long, surely enough, the sky was full of dark clouds.

"Shepherds are always right about that kind of thing," said Aoki. "We're going to get wet."

"We can deal with it," said Aoibheann. "That forest detour has already delayed us too long. We can't stop."

"Can you keep us dry?" asked Cai.

She rolled her eyes. "You lot are pathetic."

"Please?" asked Aoki, earnestly.

"Fine," she said. "But remember you already owe me your life, hunter. I don't know what else you have to offer."

"I'll make you some more stew."

"Make it for me twice," she said.

"Nice to know the value you place on my life."

Pretty soon it began to not just rain but pour. The clouds thickened, and the wind picked up.

"I can't scout for us in this weather," shouted Cai, raising his voice just to be heard. The rain came to within an inch of him before turning to steam.

Aoibheann nodded. "We keep going," she shouted back.

The wind whistled a high note, and they all knew that if Aoibheann wasn't there they'd be very cold. Each member of the party and their horse were completely surrounded by an aura of steam.

Cai rode alongside Aoibheann. She put on a facade of nonchalance, but he could see the concentration beneath. She pretended not to see him looking. Eventually, she sighed. "It's good practice," she admitted.

An hour passed, then two. They could barely see, but the directions provided by the sphere had conveniently become much more accurate, guiding them around every obstacle.

"My parents always told me," said Aoki, "that when it hails like this, the gods are sad. The cold tears they cry from up on high fall down to earth – and if they're not comforted, their tears will come to bury us all."

"Maybe we should pray," suggested Maria.

"The gods have better things to be doing," said Aoibheann, "than flying around crying on people."

"How would you know?" asked Maria.

Cai took the opportunity to ask a question that'd been on his mind for a very long time. "I've heard rumours about you, Aoibheann," he began tentatively, "rumours that you know the God of the Sun,"

"We've met," she said curtly.

"You've met a god?" gasped Aoki.

"More than one."

"What were they like?"

Aoibheann didn't answer initially. When she did, she did so slowly. "I don't worship them anymore."

"Oh," said Aoki uncertainly.

"Do you think that the Sun is involved in this?" asked Cai.

She didn't turn to face him. "I've thought it since the moment I got that summons from the king."

"I was worried that might be the case."

"Isn't that a good thing?" asked Maria. "We have a god on our side!"

Still staring straight ahead, Aoibheann answered. "It isn't that simple, Maria."

"Why not?" she asked.

Aoibheann didn't reply, and neither did Cai.

"Why not?" Maria repeated.

"We should find somewhere to rest before it gets too late," suggested Aoibheann.

"Agreed," said Cai.

"You're just going to ignore me?" asked Maria.

"Maybe you should try that prayer," Aoibheann said, sneering.

"I will!" she said. She held her hands palm to palm, in the familiar gesture. She bent her fingers to form a circle, then closed her fists. Then, she opened her hands and spread her fingers. She spoke some words only she could hear, then blew over her hands, sending the words to the gods like dandelion seeds in the wind.

The hail stopped; the sun beat its way through the dark clouds and reclaimed the sky. Aoibheann looked wide eyed at Cai, before spinning furiously around. Maria looked very self satisfied.

"So there's no doubt," muttered Cai.

"Problem solved!" she said, wearing her sweetest smile.

"You have no idea the situation we're in, do you?" shouted Aoibheann. "Oaf!"

Maria kept smiling. "Thank you! We're blessed."

"Maria," said Cai, his voice full of disappointment, "you really don't understand, do you?"

Her smile faded.

"We're not blessed," hissed Aoibheann. "We're pawns. Tools! Being used in the schemes of a god who cares a lot about the success of those schemes and not at all for our lives. If she thought it'd give her even a tiny chance of achieving her goal, she'd kill us all without hesitation." Aoibheann lit a fire in her palm and stared at it curiously, as if she was seeing fire for the very first time. Maria stared at it, and her, wearily. "You think I'm powerful, Maria?" continued Aoibheann. "You're scared of me; don't think I don't see that. You're terrified. Well, I'm scared of her, the same way you're scared of me. We're nothing to her."

"You're scared?" mocked Arjun.

Aoibheann stayed silent.

"She'd be a fool not to be," said Cai.

"I didn't know," said Maria. She hung her head. "I'm sorry."

"You should be," snapped Aoibheann. She dropped Maria's rain protection for a moment, leaving her soaking wet. "She's probably laughing at us right now."

"So, if we're going to the far north," said Aoki, "on a quest for the God of the Sun, does that mean…"

"Yes," said Cai. "We're about to do something that's going to upset the God of the Moon – maybe quite a lot. We're up against a God."

"I didn't sign up for this," said Aoki with panic in his voice. "Why don't we just turn back?"

Aoibheann snorted. "The Sun isn't forgiving."

"Turning around isn't really an option," said Cai. "But not every divine quest is big, you know. Sometimes it's something quiet and simple."

"We won't be directly fighting the God of the Moon," said Aoibheann. "Sun knows as well as we do how that'd go. Moon hasn't been seen in a long time. He's asleep, so far as we know."

"So maybe we just go up there," said Aoki. "Do what we need to do while the dragon is gone, and then we go home?"

"Exactly," said Cai.

"Okay," said Aoki, mainly to himself. "I can do that. I can do that."

"What if the dragon does show up?" asked Maria.

"Do you really need me to answer that?" asked Aoibheann. "You," she paused for dramatic effect, "would die in a second."

Maria turned to face Arjun. "Why don't you seem to care about this?" she probed.

"I'm not an oaf like you," he said. "I already knew, just like those two."

"How?" she countered. "How did you know?"

"That's a good question," reaffirmed Cai. "Not many people know what the gods are really like."

Arjun shrugged.

"Don't just shrug," commanded Aoibheann. "What are you hiding? You've done absolutely nothing so far, but you must have been chosen for a reason."

"Okay, you got me." He held his arms out. "I didn't actually know. I was trying to be stoic." For the first time on the trip, his voice came across as genuine. "I'm scared too, okay?"

The ground got increasingly bleak as they went. The lush grasses and forests they'd become accustomed to were long gone. There were no flowers and no trees – only desolate fields covered in patchy grass. Except for practical considerations, they mainly travelled in silence. Cai's eagle soared above them, ever vigilant.

They stopped for dinner by a small river, where Aoki shot some fish. They had provisions of dried food, but it tasted awful. Aoki proved his value to the team's morale day after day. He was a good cook, as well as a good hunter.

He didn't enjoy hunting anymore. It made him feel empty, knowing now that he was using magic to do it. It felt more like slaughter to him than hunting. He still did it, though. The party needed the fresh food – and he really didn't want to see Aoibheann try to hunt. She'd probably set half the world on fire. He thought about asking Cai to do it, but maintaining his magic every waking moment was taking its toll; he was visibly fatigued.

As if on cue, Cai's eagle came flying towards them. Cai visibly tensed, which led Aoki to do the same. It had seen something.

"It looks like you were right, Aoki," said Cai, after communing with it for a moment. Relief came over his face. "There's a town up ahead."

"Yes!" said Arjun. "We can sleep in beds tonight."

"How far?" asked Aoibheann.

"A few miles. We could be there today," replied Cai. "But do we trust them enough to visit?"

"They're probably just fur traders," said Aoki. "We could stock up on supplies, get some rest, and maybe even find a sword for Maria."

"And if they ask what we're doing?" replied Cai.

Aoki shrugged. "Trying our luck hunting for fur."

"Going to that town is exactly what someone looking for us would expect us to do," said Aoibheann. "But the sphere hasn't warned us, so we go. We should stay vigilant and keep to ourselves as much as possible."

It took them two hours to reach the town. There was a weather-beaten sign near the limits reading 'Fox's Perdition'.

"They don't mince their words, do they?" said Cai.

"I'd have dry humour too." said Maria. "If I had to live in a place like this."

Fox's Perdition had seen better days. Or maybe it hadn't. It was the kind of place that might have been built decrepit. It was closer to a village than a town, really. Most of the buildings fell along a single muddy street, and they could generously be described as ramshackle. A sign hung out from one of them, showing a roaring red lion.

"That'll be the inn." Arjun smiled, taking the lead.

It was small on the inside. There was a man behind the bar, three men sat around a fire and, once the party had entered, not much room for anything else.

Cai nodded in greeting to the barman, who nodded slightly in return. His expression was impassive.

"Newbies," he said without enthusiasm. "What brings you to our little slice of paradise?"

One of the men around the fire burped loudly, as if to emphasise the point. Water dripped from the ceiling.

"We're just passing through," said Aoibheann. "We're going to try our luck hunting for furs."

The barman laughed derisively, and the other men joined in.

"You don't strike me as the type, little miss," he said, looking her up and down. He licked his lips. "You're much too pretty. Why don't you stay behind here? We'll take good care of you, won't we, boys?"

They roared with laughter. He pointed at Maria. "You take that one with you though; she's more of a man than any of my sons are! Ah, ha, ha! Look at the size of her!"

Maria turned red and raised a fist. The barman's reaction was not what she intended.

He held his hands out in front of himself in mock fear. "Ooo, don't hurt me, miss!" He laughed. "See that, lads, I'm trembling."

Aoibheann lowered Maria's hand. "She's stronger than any of you and no less of a woman because of it," she said. "We didn't come in here to be ogled or insulted; we came here to find lodgings. Do you have any?"

The barman turned to Cai and Aoki. "Gods, she's an ache! How'd you put up with her?"

Cai looked at him coldly. "Do you have any rooms?" he asked.

The barman looked taken aback by the lack of agreement. "Rooms are all full," he said aggressively. "You can sleep in the barn out back." He winked at Aoibheann. "But you're welcome to share my room."

"Don't let his wife know!" shouted one of the men from the back.

The barman laughed at that. A large bead of sweat rolled down his forehead. He dabbed at it with an oily cloth and looked a bit confused.

Cai touched Aoibheann's arm gently. "Hot flush?" he asked the barman.

"Hell's come to get him early!" shouted one of the men.

"Shut up, Merv," snapped the barman.

"We'll take the barn," said Cai.

"Three gold pieces," he grunted.

"Three?" asked Cai in shock.

"You're really testing my patience. Sleep outside if you want."

"We will!"

"Fine, fine. Two. And I'll let you sleep on the hay."

"You weren't going to let us before?" asked Aoki.

"We'll take it," said Cai quickly.

Aoibheann rummaged around in her bag, as if she was struggling to get the money together. There were hundreds of coins there. She found the equivalent of two gold in change, and put it on the counter, avoiding the barman's open hand.

"Through there," he said, pointing. "If you want dinner, find somewhere else. Don't come back in here."

"We have horses, too," said Cai.

"I don't care," said the barman, turning his back to them. "Tie them up outside."

Cai nodded.

As they turned to leave, Aoki's cloak opened a little, and his dagger caught the light. The party left through the back door and were presented with the barn, a hundred or so metres away.

"It doesn't actually look that bad," said Aoki. "It has a roof."

"It beats camping," agreed Cai.

The men went to see the inside. Maria motioned for Aoibheann to hang back.

Maria coughed. "Thank you," she said awkwardly, "for sticking up for me back there."

"Don't take it personally," said Aoibheann. "I was defending women, not defending you."

"Ah," replied Maria sheepishly. "Well, thank you anyway."

Almost reluctantly, Aoibheann muttered, "You're welcome." She faked a smile and walked away.

Aoki was right; the barn really wasn't that bad. It was well built and kept the cold out. There was plenty of hay to be used as bedding. Arjun had already fashioned a makeshift bed in a big pile of it.

"I'm sorry," said Cai as she came in, "about them. That can't have been pleasant."

"I chose to put up with it this time," sighed Aoibheann. "If only they knew who I was, they'd be on their knees."

"Get up, Arjun," said Maria. "We're going to see if there's any merchants."

"I'll stay behind," he said.

"No, you won't," said Aoibheann decisively. "We're not splitting up. Anyone in this town could be an enemy. And if you leave my sight, Aoki will have to shoot you again."

"Because you think I might be a bug?"

"You do look like one. We can't take any chances."

Arjun fake laughed. "Very funny," he said.

They left together. Aoibheann kept the sphere under her cloak and surreptitiously checked it every chance she got. Along the main street, they met a travelling trader. He was a lot more friendly than the locals and sold Maria a sword. It wasn't particularly sharp or well balanced, but it was a sword. Maria knew what she was doing and could turn it into something pretty useful, even with the limited equipment she had in hand.

Cai bought a charm, a small wooden carving of a swallow – it was supposed to be good luck. The trader said it'd make sure he "got back south again safe, just like the swallows do every year." Aoibheann rolled her eyes at it. Cai hung it around his neck. Arjun stole and ate some dried fish while the others were occupied.

There wasn't much available in the way of fresh food, so they ate their rations in the barn. Aoibheann handed Maria the sphere. She took first watch while the others slept. She pulled a small whetstone from her bag and was about to begin sharpening her new sword when she hesitated. She'd begun to feel like a burden. She didn't have magic like Aoibheann or Cai, or even Aoki. At least she was better than Arjun, she thought, but that wasn't saying much. She really didn't want to wake the others, so she decided to sharpen her sword outside.

As she opened the barn door, a breeze rushed in. She quickly shut it behind her. The air had a real chill to it. The area was softly lit by a lantern hanging above the door. She sat on the ground at the edge of the light and began her meditation.

She ran her blade up and down the stone in even and rhythmic strokes, shaping its crude edge into something at least indicative of a real weapon. She missed her old sword. It had been a gift from her father, after she'd joined the army. He'd saved up his pay and bought the finest sword he could afford. He wasn't strapped for cash, so the finest sword he could afford was very fine indeed. Maria smiled sadly. The craftsmanship had been of the highest quality, and she'd lovingly maintained it for years. More than that though, it reminded her of her father. Now it was a puddle. Her anger at Aoibheann flared up, and she left her meditative state.

She didn't let the anger consume her. She calmed her breathing and continued her process. She forced herself away from the subject and thought again about her father. She'd been a good fighter ever since she was small, and so it was no surprise to anyone when she announced her intent to become a soldier, but that didn't stop her mother's face dropping when she heard the news, as if her worst fear had come true. Her father had supported her, though. He'd never stopped supporting her, until the day he died. He was a good man. He'd never really understood her but was behind her one hundred percent, nonetheless – no matter what.

It might not be the same sword, she thought, *but your love is still in it, Dad.* She smiled a bittersweet, nostalgic smile. *Every time I sharpen it, a little part of us will be put in it.*

She held it out in front of her and looked closely. She flipped it over and looked closely again. She was proud of the job she'd done. It was no masterpiece, but it'd serve its function. She took a fighting stance and tried a few practice swings. The balance was good.

She snapped back to reality as a twig snapped behind her. She recognised the figure of one of the men from the inn earlier.

"'Ello," he crooned with a toothy smile. "Sorry to disturb you so late at night m'am, but I—"

Two pairs of hands roughly grabbed Maria from behind. A knife was held to her throat.

"But I'll 'ave to ask you to keep quiet and drop that sword," continued the man, his smile widening.

Maria did as she was told. The daggers were taken from her belt.

"There's a good girl! She's smarter than she looks, lads, which isn't saying much!" He laughed loudly at his own joke.

More men came out of the dark, about a dozen in all. The leader nodded his head, and two went to fling open the barn doors. "Wakey, wakey!" he shouted as loud as he could.

The party didn't hesitate in following that order. Aoki reached for his knife as soon as he woke, Arjun for his spear. Aoibheann and Cai raised their hands ready to unleash their magic.

"Don't get any funny ideas!" commanded the man. "Any of you make a move, and Mrs Mountain gets her throat cut."

Aoibheann's eyes caught alight as she stared at the leader. She lowered her hands.

"Nothing personal, lovely," he explained to her. "It's just the way things work around these parts. This is what's gonna 'appen. You're going to put your hands in the air, slowly get up, and go stand over there with your faces against the wall. Then we're gonna take all these expensive things of yours. We won't kill you if ya be'ave."

Aoki dropped his dagger on the floor, and Arjun followed suit with his spear. They slowly got up, and all went to the far wall. They stood there, each with a knife in their back.

The gang leader went straight for Aoki's dagger and whistled quietly. "Well, I never." He put it down when he saw another man eyeing it up greedily. "We share the spoils evenly, remember, lads. If any of you try and hide something, I'll kill you meself."

They began rummaging through the bags, pulling out everything. Every member of the party was very roughly patted down. They found the unlit sphere in Maria's pocket and threw it onto the pile with everything else.

"You there," demanded the ringleader, pointing at Aoki. "Where did you get this?"

"I got it from the capital," he replied. "From the royal armoury."

"You 'ear that, lads? These lot must be nobles. Maybe we can ransom 'em." His smile faded as he came up close to Aoki and whispered in his ear. "If you 'ave money for a dagger like this, you 'ave no reasons to be in this dump and no reasons to be a trapper. What are you really doin 'ere?" He stuck the point of Aoki's dagger into Aoki's back, a little harder than was comfortable.

Aoki said nothing.

The man got really close and breathed heavily in his ear. He enunciated every word. "What are you doin 'ere?"

Aoki swallowed heavily. "We were sent on a mission by the king."

"And what sort of mission would that—" he began. He stopped mid sentence because he got cold, very cold. It had never been warm in the barn, but the cold felt different to before. It was deep in his bones. He turned around sharply, and saw he wasn't the only one affected. "To me!" he roared, and all of the men converged. They stood, shivering, in a semi circle facing the door, weapons outstretched.

The prisoners were left unattended, and Aoibheann, radiating heat, spun around, hands outstretched. She didn't hesitate for a moment, letting loose a wave of fire. The robbers stood no chance – only char was left.

"You and that dagger!" she screamed at Aoki.

Cai looked down, horrified. "I know they were robbing us, but—"

A fresh rush of cold came in, and the embers extinguished. The sphere lit up, in the same colours of warning as it had before. Aoki rushed to pick up his bow, and Maria picked up her dagger as she joined them by the wall. Arjun pulled his spear from the pile, as Cai summoned Shar and a pack of wolves. They stood ahead of the party, wordlessly alert, watching the door.

The cold got more and more intense. Crystals of frost began to form on the frame of the door, slowly at first, but they began to multiply and grow exponentially. It began an inexorable creep towards them. Aoibheann shot out a probing wave of fire to melt the frost, but it reformed almost immediately. The barn was only intermittently lit, by the eerie red flashes of the sphere. They heard heavy footsteps approaching, quickly.

Aoibheann tensed, ready for action. As soon as movement appeared in front of the doors, she launched an explosion of fire. The barn was lit with overwhelming brightness, blinding the others. The explosion didn't reach its target – it hit a wall of frost which contained it in its entirety. Steam filled the room. Aoibheann concentrated her power into a dozen small pellets, shotgunned straight ahead. They pierced straight through the wall, which shattered.

The flashing light cast a shadow on the contorted face of the intruder. Its eyes were filled with unmistakable hate. They were the eyes of something that knew nothing else.

It strode closer with a hobbled gait, and Shar leaped to action. She launched herself at its side and dug in her teeth. Cai's wolves surrounded it, biting at its heels as it struggled to be free from the weight of the bear. Aoki shot an arrow, perfectly aimed at its eye.

It howled, and the cold intensified to such an extent that everything around it began to freeze solid. The wolves, the bear, and Aoki's next arrow mid-flight. Aoki's fingers were encased in ice. They quickly melted as Aoibheann refocused. She launched fire at the beast again, chanting loudly. The beast shot ice in return, and red met white, as the two forces struck.

Aoibheann upped the intensity. A drop of sweat formed on her forehead and rolled down into her eye. The temptation to wipe it off was enormous, but she didn't. She squinted in irritation, and the frost gained ground. She took a breath and, masterfully, centred herself. She pushed, chanting deliberately. The frost began to falter. She took a step forward. She knew she was stronger. She poured more and more of herself into the words she spoke.

All at once, the beast's power gave way. The fire that had been kept in check suddenly met no resistance. A tempest of fire, every ounce of Aoibheann's power, was unleashed. It swirled and raged around the party, consuming everything. It expanded exponentially, covering the barn, the inn, and the entire town.

Aoibheann's calm broke as she scrambled madly to contain her power. She chanted an opposite incantation, closing her hands, bringing the fire within herself, but it was under control much too late.

The enemy had been defeated, and the town had been turned to ash. Aoibheann fell down, and Cai rushed to catch her.

"Aoibheann…" he muttered, "what have you done?"

"Why now?" asked the king. "We've had peace for so long."

"That's exactly why," the God of the Sun replied. She snorted. "He's out of practice."

"You couldn't have waited a month? A week?" he cried. "You knew full well there weren't many mages in the capital. You knew who I'd have to send."

She opened her mouth in a broad smile, revealing her sharp teeth. "I wanted them there."

"You're playing with fire," cautioned the king.

"And you're playing with words. How droll," she countered. The God of the Sun snapped. "Of course I play with fire."

"Sending them was a mistake. You don't know what they're capable of."

"I know it better than you do."

The king looked at her warily. He decided she was telling the truth. "You could have at least told them what they're doing."

"Now where's the fun in that?" she said smirking.

Aoki had suggested they travel west, towards the sea. It was a deviation from the sphere's guidance, but with the land becoming increasingly inhospitable, the coast would be the best place to keep themselves fed. One seal, he'd explained, could sustain them for days. They might come across seabirds, too, for a nice treat.

It was sound advice, and they'd followed it. It had taken them about a day of travelling due west from Fox's Perdition to reach the water. After following the coast north for another day, they'd truly left the rest of the world behind. There was nothing around them but white – snow and ice covered everything.

Aoki hunched over a pile of blubber and dried dung. He was expertly striking two flints together but having a hard time getting the makeshift fire lit. Aoibheann watched on silently. The rhythmic clacking was muffled by the snow. Even under their thick clothes, the party were shivering. Finally, the right spark came, and it caught.

"Here's our fire," announced Aoki, proudly standing up and stretching. "What's for dinner?"

"Seal," Maria grunted.

"And something more," remarked Cai. He pointed to the sky. "Look."

His eagle was coming back and had a gull in its claws.

"I stand corrected, seal and scrawny bird." Maria sat as close to the fire as she could bear. She rubbed her hands together vigorously.

Cai held the sphere in his hands. He examined the runes that covered its surface.

"Any chance it's decided to send us south?" asked Arjun.

"No," replied Cai. He clutched the sparrow charm that hung from his neck. "I'm afraid not."

"How much further north do you think we'll have to go?" asked Maria.

"I don't know." Cai exhaled. He sat next to Maria. "The going will only get tougher from here."

Aoki joined them, and the three sat shoulder to shoulder. "The days are getting longer," he remarked. "It should be dark by now."

Cai squinted up at the evening sun. "We're lucky it's summer, I suppose."

"Lucky?" grumbled Arjun under his breath. "Lucky."

"Does anyone want to hear a song?" offered Aoki.

Arjun physically recoiled, his eyes wide. "Lucky," he muttered. "So lucky."

"I didn't know you could sing!" exclaimed Maria.

"A little." Aoki chuckled amicably. "One song in particular comes to mind."

"Let's hear it," requested Cai. "Do you want to join us, Aoibheann?"

She stood a little distance away, behind the others. She shook her head and turned her back.

"Time," Aoki whispered in response to Cai's worried look. He nodded in return. Aoki made a show of clearing his throat. "Ladies and gentlemen, boys and girls," he belted out in his best announcer's impression. "Today you're very lucky, oh yes, you are! Today you get to hear the vocal delights of the great Aoki!" He managed to fit way more syllables into his name than had any business being there. He whooped and cheered for himself, mimicking different voices. Maria joined in.

"Just get it over with," said Arjun, sighing. "Or I'll walk off into the snow."

Aoki began singing, slowly and emotively. His voice was smooth.

"Win-ter snowwws,
No bo-dy knowwws,

The sec-rets that you froze.
Oh, winter snows,
A hush falls o'er land,
As you grip it in your hand.
And life all dies,
as you open your eyes."

There was a pause, and the tempo suddenly picked up. Aoki's voice became more crass.

"You can do one, Mr Winter,
you son of hoar-frost.
Take your snow
And get lost.
You can do one Mr Winter!
You can do one Mr Winter!
You can do one Mr Winter,
you son of hoar-frost.
Take your snow
And get lost.
You can do one Mr Winter!
You can do one Mr Winter!"

Maria clapped.
"Thank you, thank you," Aoki mimed a bow.
"What in the world was that?" asked Arjun, almost offended.
"I thought we'd just established it's summer?" said Cai.
"Well, yes, but—"
"I wish we had some ale," interrupted Cai. "I would have enjoyed that song a lot more with some ale."
"Are you saying you didn't—"

"I agree," interrupted Arjun. "A lot of ale."

"And some wine, too," added Cai.

"Don't listen to them Aoki," reassured Maria. "I enjoyed it. You have a wonderful voice."

"Thank you," cried Aoki. "At least someone here can appreciate true art!"

"I didn't say it was—" started Maria, but she cut herself off. "Never mind."

"You do have a good voice," admitted Cai. "I'll give you that."

"Do you know *The woman from Aor'ki*?" asked Arjun.

Aoki smiled. "I do."

"Absolutely not," warned Maria.

Arjun looked shocked. "*Voracious Veda*?"

"No."

"*The Confirmed Bachelors*?'"

"Do you not know any nice songs?" Maria asked. "Anything cultured?"

"This is my culture!"

She rolled her eyes. "Of course it is."

"I learnt those songs from soldiers," countered Arjun. "Get down from your high horse, army girl."

"We shouldn't stay up too late," announced Cai, always keen to diffuse conflict. "We should eat and then try to get some sleep."

"And we should all share a tent," added Aoki. "I know not everyone is keen on it. But you all felt how cold it was last night."

They all nodded, not particularly happy about it. As they pitched their tent after eating, Aoibheann quietly pitched her own.

The next day they came across a river. It was wide. Aoki knelt down and stuck his finger in it. It took all of his strength to push back against the current, and unsurprisingly, it was very cold. He drew his finger out quickly.

"Why?" he lamented, "Why is there always another obstacle?"

"I can ferry us across," offered Cai calmly, summoning Shar. He scratched behind her ear. "Bears are very good swimmers."

"Sweet!" said Aoki, quickly optimistic again. "But we're going to need to stay dry," he cautioned.

"You got that, girl?" Cai said to Shar. She grew bigger and bigger, until she stood at her full height. She dropped down unceremoniously into a crouch, and they all clambered onto her back. Cai grabbed a tuft of long fur and wrapped it around his hand in a makeshift hold. The others followed his lead. He looked over his shoulder with a grin. "Ready?" he asked. Before waiting for a reply, Shar got up. Her passengers were flung about. Arjun almost fell off, but Maria grabbed him by the arm. He nodded his thanks as she dragged him back into place.

"Why don't we travel like this more often?" asked Aoki, wrapping an arm around Maria's waist.

"I like it," she agreed. Aoki didn't see her blush.

Cai turned his head back towards them, and the look of exertion on his face answered the question. "Hear that, girl?" he muttered, stroking Shar's head. "They like you."

She snorted gently in response and began walking. She reached the bank, and stuck one paw in, tentatively.

"Maybe we should go towards the coast," said Arjun nervously. "There might be a delta, with a slower current."

"If the current is slower, the river will be wider," countered Aoki. He looked down at the sphere in his hand, which directed them straight across.

"Come on girl, you can do it," whispered Cai. "You can do it."

Shar took a step forward, her paws curled at the bank of the river. She snorted, then lithely let herself down into the water. There was a small splash, and she quickly felt the current. There was no helping being dragged along, but the opposing bank got closer and closer. A bead of cold sweat fell down Cai's forehead as Shar powerfully fought against the flow and swam towards the other side.

She swung paw upwards, with claws like knives piercing the ice. She swung her second paw up but failed to find the same purchase. The ice groaned. Unrelenting, the force of the water pushed on her. She swung the second paw up again, trying to find a grip, anything to let her pull herself out. She hung on as well as she could, but she began to slip. Like nails on a chalkboard, the sound of it was deafening.

All of a sudden it gave way, and they all plunged into the water. They held on as best as they could, hands wrapped around her long fur. Cai's concentration began to fail. The cold was overwhelming. Shock overcame his body and Shar began to look a little less real. What had been a very real, wild, animalistic struggle now looked more abstract, like drawings in a flip book. Jittery.

Aoki furiously shook Aoibheann, urging her to do something. She did nothing but hold on. Arjun's grip began to loosen. Maria grabbed his arm as the current took him, and with all her strength pulled him back. She wrapped her arms around him and the bear. Aoibheann shut her eyes as tightly as she could.

Aoki held on for dear life. Cai felt the sting of the cold and nothing else.

Shar wobbled out of the living world for half a second. She looked back at Cai, at the helpless people on her back. She became solid again and with a few strong strokes emerged from the water with a roar. She flung herself onto the bank, and dragged herself up onto the dry land, before fading, dropping the party from a few feet in the air. They landed heavily on the hard ice, what breath they'd managed to regain being forced out of them.

Aoki desperately pulled the flint and steel from his inside pocket. It had stayed dry, but his relief at that fact was short-lived. The kindling was soaked. Spark after spark fell from his quaking hands onto the tinder, but it just wouldn't light.

Aoki looked over at Aoibheann expectantly. She turned around.

"Aoibheann," he begged.

She paid no heed.

"Look at us, Aoibheann."

She didn't.

"Look at us!" he screamed.

She turned and met his eyes, then Cai's, then Arjun's, then Maria's. She saw their deathly pale faces and heard their chattering teeth. She dropped her eyes. "I can't," she said, almost to herself. "I can't."

Aoki stood in front of her and grabbed her shoulders. He felt her warmth, and she felt his cold. Her eyes avoided his again. "Look at me, Aoibheann," said Aoki, softly this time. "If we don't start a fire, we'll die."

She didn't reply.

"You aren't even going to save us?" cried Maria.

"Don't pity yourself," shouted Arjun. "Pity us instead."

"It's time, Aoibheann," said Aoki. "It's now or never."

A flicker of determination sparked in each of her pupils. "Stand behind me," she said. "Further than that," she added as they rushed to follow her order. "Further."

She focused her eyes on the kindling and took a deep breath. She held her hands out in front of her and took a second deep breath. She was shaking almost as much as the rest of the party, despite not being the slightest bit cold. She spoke a single word. She tried to make it purposeful, to channel a small spark, but she couldn't focus or articulate, and her uncertain emotions seeped into the word. Instead of a spark, she got an explosion. She stopped it immediately, contained it and drew it inside. But the damage to her confidence had been done.

The rest of the party flocked to the fire, soaking in the heat, but she didn't move. She had no control of her breathing. It was irregular and shaky, accelerating. Her mind was racing, and she couldn't concentrate. Images of the icy monster came back to her, images of her unrestrained power, and of the ashes of the town. *They were terrible people,* she reassured herself. *They were horrible people, all of them. Not all of them. The merchant was friendly.* She clenched her fists and drew her arms into herself. *You felt compassion for the barman's wife, didn't you? There were probably children there. I didn't mean to! But it was still your fault.*

"I didn't mean to!" she shouted out loud. The others turned and saw the tears falling down her cheeks. Her legs gave way. She lay on her side, fists still clenched, her nails drawing blood from her palms, her breathing shallow. She gave off more heat than the fire. Cai gently stirred.

Aoki rushed to her, put a hand on her arm. He felt her shake. "It wasn't your fault," he said.

She yelled through tears. "It was!"

"The God of the Moon is to blame, Aoibheann," Cai said softly. "The blood is on his hands, not on yours."

"No!"

"You were only defending yourself. Defending us."

"If I had more control, it never would have happened," she sobbed. "I killed them."

"Accidents happen, Aoibheann!"

Maria bit her tongue. *Accidents.*

"I should leave – alone. Go somewhere far away, far away from anyone else. I'm dangerous."

Maria no longer restrained herself. "You should."

"Maria!" shouted Cai.

"She's right," said Aoibheann. "I'm a monster." Her loud crying became silent, tears flowing down her cheeks. There was no sound at all, for a few moments.

"We can't force you to come with us," said Cai uncomfortably. "If that's what you—"

"We need you," interrupted Arjun, placing a cold hand on her shoulder. "If you want to atone for what you've done, and you can, then come with us. Do you hear me, Aoibheann? You can atone. You have to. You know what we're dealing with. If we complete this quest, we'll save the lives of everyone in the kingdom, and we need you to complete it."

"You can't know that," she said. "We have no idea what we're even doing! It could be completely inconsequential."

"It's not," he said with complete certainty.

"How do you know?"

He hesitated for a moment. "I was told."

All eyes moved from Aoibheann to him.

"You were told?" asked Cai. "By who?"

Arjun ignored the question and looked straight at Aoibheann. "The only way to get rid of the guilt you're feeling and regain control of your power is to see this through."

She met his gaze, intensely. Her tears stopped flowing, guilt momentarily replaced by suspicion. "Told by who?"

He didn't answer.

She asked again, firmly. "Told by who?"

He looked around and appeared conflicted. "The God of the Sun, a few days before we were summoned."

Cai looked shocked.

Aoibheann looked angry. "I don't believe you."

"It's true."

"Where did you speak to her?"

"In her valley, in the mountains."

"How did you get there?"

"She showed me the way."

"How?"

"In a dream."

"What did the valley look like?"

"Like a meadow of every beautiful thing in the world. The flowers sang."

"What does she look like?"

"Big. Orange. Small scar on her back left leg."

"What did she tell you exactly?"

"I can't tell you."

"I don't believe you."

"Why not? You were all wondering why I was chosen for this mission. This is why. I serve a role in this party. I just can't tell you what it is."

"I don't believe she told you."

"Why not?"

"You're lying."

"I'm not."

"Do his answers check out?" asked Cai.

"Yes," replied Aoibheann reluctantly.

"Then why don't you believe him?"

"Because she wouldn't have told him without telling me!" she shouted.

"You're jealous?" asked a stunned Maria. Aoki touched her arm to quieten her.

"I haven't just met the Sun," said Aoibheann, "I'm her champion."

Cai's eyes widened. So did Arjun's. The revelation was lost on Maria and Aoki.

"What does that mean?" asked the latter, tentatively.

"It means that she's given her soul to the God," said Cai, "sworn to always do her bidding in return for direct access to her power."

Aoki was stunned. "Is that true?"

Aoibheann breathed through her half-blocked nose. "Yes," she said, "it's true. I loved her once, I suppose, before I truly knew her. I lived to serve her, and I would have done it even without the pact. But as time went on… things changed. We're not close anymore. Despite everything that happened, I still thought she cared about me, though, in her own sort of way. I guess she doesn't if she'll tell him her plans but not me."

"She has her reasons, Aoibheann," said Arjun comfortingly. "It'll become clear."

"Do you speak to her often?" asked Cai.

"Not anymore. But the summons from the king... there was something about it – a little tickle in my mind."

"Which is how you knew she was behind it?" finished Cai.

"Yes."

A slight lull in conversation.

"So, your power isn't even your own?" snapped Maria. "You act like you're so much better than everyone, but you're just using borrowed power?"

"I wish it was borrowed," Aoibheann snapped back, "that I could return it. But there's no undoing what was done. The power is mine now, whether I want it or not."

"We're going to need that power," insisted Arjun, "if we're going to succeed."

"Cai is powerful—" she started.

"Not as powerful as you," he interrupted.

"You need to be there." The urgency in Arjun's voice was clear.

Aoibheann took a deep breath. "Okay, I'll come." She visibly hyped herself up. "I can redeem myself." She intended to say it as if it were fact, but it came out sounding more like a question, a question that Arjun answered.

"Yes," he said, "you can. But you have to take back control of your power."

She nodded. "Get behind me," she said again. She threw some snow on the fire, extinguishing it.

"Hey!" shouted Maria. Cai shot her a glare.

Aoibheann took the same pose she had before, and concentrated. She silently spoke the words in her mind, rehearsing them, as she had thousands of times before. She pictured for a moment the town but did her best to push the image down, to not think of it, to replace it with another image – that of her as a hero. The world ended, covered in ice, and her powers needed to save it. She needed her power to redeem herself. She needed to control it. Concentrate. Concentrate on the words.

She spoke them aloud, enunciated perfectly. The fire lit. The flame was bigger than she'd intended, but not massively so – a success. She laughed in relief.

"Well done," said Cai. Aoki clapped her on the back.

"Well done," said Arjun.

"Am I going crazy?" asked Maria.

They all looked at her.

"Am I going crazy, or have you all just forgiven her just like that?"

"Maria—" started Aoki.

"No, Aoki." she said. "Don't silence me. I know how much we need her. None of you will shut up about that fact, and yeah, you're probably right. But that doesn't mean we have to forgive her! She destroyed an entire town, remember? How many innocent people?"

"You're not helping," said Arjun.

"I don't forgive you," said Maria directly to Aoibheann. "And when we get back to the capital, I'm going to arrest you. You'll spend the rest of your life in jail for the crimes you've committed. I'll make sure of it, champion." The last word dripped with sarcasm. "I'll play my part in this party, for the duration of this quest. I'll watch your back, and even give my life if needs be. But afterwards, you" – she shoved her finger into Aoibheann's chest – "are going to jail. And the rest of you should be ashamed. I'm disappointed in you all. Aoki, Cai, I thought better of you both. Do you have no sense of justice?"

"I won't resist," said Aoibheann quietly. "When we're back, take me to jail. Take me to the gallows if you like. You're right about it all. Once this quest is done, I won't resist."

"You'll stand trial and be brought to justice," stated Maria.

"Once the quest is through."

"Yes," reluctantly conceded Maria, "once the quest is through."

The going was a lot easier over the next few days with the help of Aoibheann's abilities. They were kept warm and had no trouble lighting fires. It was almost comfortable, almost.

"I'm sick of eating blubber," said Aoki, in an attempt at jovial conversation. "If I have to eat any more blubber, I'll start blubbering." The light-hearted tone was obviously forced. Nobody replied.

He spotted a bird flying above and nocked an arrow. He hesitated. He reached back into his quiver and was reminded of how few he had left. He'd counted last night. Eight. He didn't want to risk losing one, so he let the moment pass. The bird flew over the horizon. He took some pride in knowing that he could have hit it. No matter how high up it was, how nimble it was, he could have hit it.

"I didn't recognise the species," said Cai.

"Neither did I," admitted Aoki.

Cai looked uneasy. "Maybe we should have stopped it. We don't know who's watching."

"You shouldn't tire yourself out. We might need to fight."

"And you don't have many arrows," said Cai. "We'd better reach our goal soon."

Aoibheann, who'd retaken control of the sphere, looked down at it. "All it says is north." She sighed.

Aoki held up his hand to shield his eyes from the sun. "Straight into those mountains?" he asked.

"Yes."

Mouth agape, Aoki looked up. "It's pretty high," he said. He gently kicked the cliff that stood in their path. "It's hard at least."

"Stop being dramatic," said Maria.

Aoki pulled a length of rope from his bag. "It's nowhere near long enough," he muttered to himself. "We won't be able to tie everyone together."

"I don't need a safety rope to climb this," said Maria.

"Neither do I," he replied. He glanced back at the rest of the party, who were resting further down the mountain. "But they do." He craned his neck to see the very top. "It's a long way to fall."

"This is where the sphere led us."

"The sphere only cares about the quest, not our lives."

"I thought the quest was more important than their lives?"

"Their lives?" asked Aoki accusingly. "Not ours?"

She stared at him with narrowed eyes and didn't reply.

"Even though the quest is more important than our lives," continued Aoki, "doesn't mean we should throw our lives away. We should find a way around."

Maria made a point of looking in every direction. "Do you see a way around, Aoki? Please, point me to the way around."

"If we go further—"

"We don't have the time to go further. We climb. Cai's summons can help."

"He can't summon and climb at the same time."

"Then he goes first. You lead him up, tied to you. We'll follow, with some creature to break our fall if we slip."

Aoki's eyes settled again on the top of the cliff. "It's high," he said, with worry in his voice.

"There you go," said Aoki. "That should do." He pulled the knot tight around Cai's waist. "Remember, if you lose your grip, do whatever you can to break your fall. If you start to freefall, I won't be able to hold you up, and you'll probably take me with you."

Cai nodded sombrely.

"Remember three points of contact at all times. There's lots of holds, so as long as you remember that, it should be an easy climb. Just watch what I do and copy every movement."

Cai nodded again.

"When we're done, we'll rest for a bit, let Cai get his strength back, and then we'll send down support."

Maria nodded.

"We'll see you soon and enjoy the view together at the top. Come on, Cai, let's get started."

"How are you doing back there?" he shouted, glancing down. The wind had picked up, and Cai struggled to hear. He did, however, see Aoki looking, and he nodded up at him.

That was good enough for Aoki. Despite the height, it had been a fairly elementary climb so far. In the harsh weather, they'd lost sight of both the bottom and the top. It would be easy to lose hope, to feel like you weren't making any progress. You just had to keep climbing. He didn't doubt they'd make it; he just hoped that he could get a fire started without Aoibheann's help. His fingers were getting cold. He reached for the next handhold.

A screech pierced through the wind, and Aoki only had time to look as a bird tore towards him. He buried his head in the cliff, heart beating in his throat, but needn't have. The bird changed its course. It slowed and perched on the cliff right next to the rope tying him and Cai together. With the long claw on its foot, it began to cut.

"Oi!" shouted Cai. "Shoo! Shoo!" He began to shake the rope, trying to dislodge it, but it did no good. He had a very limited range of movement – there wasn't much slack – and he was very aware that his friend was attached to the other end of it. 'Shoo' no longer cut it, and he began shouting obscenities. If Aoki wasn't so preoccupied, he would have been impressed.

The obscenities did no good, though, and the bird persisted. The claw tore through. The half of the rope that had been attached fell down and flailed in the wind. More obscenities came from Cai.

The bird did not relent. It swooped down towards him, talons outstretched. While desperately clinging on with one hand, he shielded his eyes with the other and began chanting. The talons cut deep through his thick gloves, but only superficially through his hands. His forehead caught some damage, and the bird moved sideways to claw at his ear.

Just then a spectral owl flew from the mist and caught the bird in its talons, its momentum carrying them both far away. Cai stopped his mumbling and sagged. His fingers held tight as the rest of his body relaxed as best as it could.

Aoki nimbly climbed back down, so that he was level with Cai. He reached over and helped clean the blood dripping down his brow. "No safety net," he shouted.

"No safety net," Cai shouted back.

"Are you going to make it?"

"Yes," shouted Cai with conviction. "I'm going to make it all the way back to Morgana, in the capital."

Aoki nodded. "Just follow my moves."

"Let me rest first," said Cai, "for a few moments."

They lay down at the top, exhausted. Blood flowed from Cai's face. His chest rose and fell heavily. "I knew we should have killed that damn bird," he wheezed. He laughed. So did Aoki. "For the gods' sakes!"

Aoki looked down at the broken rope. "What do we do now? Do you think you can send anything down?"

"Not yet," he said, spreadeagled. "I can barely lift my arms. Which means…"

"Which means we have to rely on the others to be patient, and not do anything impulsive?"

"Yes."

"This is ridiculous," said Aoibheann. "They've been gone for too long."

"Be patient," said Maria. "Aoki is a good climber. They'll send the rope down soon with support from Cai."

"I'm not waiting any longer."

"What are you going to do? Climb up by yourself?"

"Yes."

Maria sneered. "With those arms? Are you sure?"

"Ladies—" started Arjun.

"Shut up," snapped Aoibheann. "When I need to move some furniture, Maria, then I'll call you. But I don't need your help to save the world."

"Save the world? You only want to save the world to relieve your own guilty conscience!" screamed Maria. "By the gods, I—"

"By the gods?" interrupted Aoibheann bitterly.

"Yes! By the gods! By the gods, I hate you, Aoibheann."

Aoibheann turned towards the cliff without a word. She pressed her hand into the ice. Maria didn't see the relief wash over her face as she successfully applied just the right amount of heat to create the perfect handhold. She began her climb.

Arjun and Maria sat in silence for a while. "We don't need the rope," said Arjun. "Or any help. I can climb it, and so can you."

"We wait," said Maria firmly. "We do things properly."

They sat in silence a bit longer. Arjun followed Maria's gaze up to the shrouded clifftop. She caught him looking, and he raised an eyebrow at her.

"Fine!" she said. "It's been too long. Let's go."

Fog fell, and the weather worsened. It was just the two of them against nature itself. They were pelted with rain and buffed by the wind. They couldn't see the top.

Maria grabbed a knobble of ice and used it to pull herself up, putting all of her weight on it. It came loose. Her feet slipped, and only her left hand held onto the cliff. She grabbed the handhold with her right hand too and dangled there helpless.

Arjun looked down at her. He saw her grip was failing.

The handhold was too small. Her fingers weren't strong enough. Her right hand slipped back off the hold.

Arjun looked down at her. He slowly climbed down to where she was.

"Help me!" shouted Maria.

Arjun looked down at her and stopped.

"Arjun!"

She swayed as the wind caught her.

"Arjun!"

He smiled at her, then with his hard boots kicked her hand.

She cried out in pain as he kicked her again. She barely held on. "Arjun!" she shouted.

He turned to face upwards and resumed climbing with great skill.

The howling wind drowned out the last, helpless cry. "Help me!"

He was lost in the fog by the time she fell.

Before he reached the top, he made himself cry.

"Arjun?" asked Aoki. "Are you okay?"

"Maria—" he choked. "She…"

Aoki went pale. "What happened?" he asked frantically. "What happened?"

"I couldn't see – the fog – I heard a scream and—" he cut himself off with a sob.

Aoibheann sighed. She rubbed her temples.

"I'm going down," said Aoki, rushing to the cliff edge.

"You can't," said Cai, moving to block him. "It's too dangerous."

"I'm going down!"

"No, you're not."

Aoki went to push him out of the way.

"Stop it!" shouted Aoibheann.

"What if she's injured down there?"

"You know how high the cliff is, Aoki," said Aoibheann sombrely.

"We were so high up," added Arjun tearily. "But…"

A tear rolled down his cheek. A tear rolled down Cai's, too. The two men embraced. Arjun sat sobbing, and Aoibhean looked grim. They remained that way for several minutes.

"We need to move on," shouted Aoibheann above the whistling wind. "It's not safe here. The sun is setting."

"She'll have no grave," said Aoki. "Her body won't even decompose in the snow."

"When we get back, we'll honour her," said Cai. "She was a hero, and we'll make sure everyone knows that."

The climb was gruelling. Afterwards, Aoki said it had been the worst few hours of his life – overcome with grief but still forced to keep putting one foot in front of the other up the icy slopes. The wind howled and screamed. A part of him wanted to, too – to run, and howl, and scream until he was hoarse. Another part of him just wanted to stop – forget the danger, forget the quest, lie down and curl up in a ball. He didn't care about the consequences. The cold snow looked inviting. He stopped walking and stared at it wistfully. Cai put a firm hand on his shoulder. That was enough to bring him back to the present, and he started walking again.

Aoibheann, who was in the lead, was the first to crest the summit. She laughed, which angered Aoki, but when he crested, that anger faded. He laughed too, not a funny laugh, but a relieved one. In front of him was a valley, full of green, luscious green: meadows, vineyards, orchards. There were trees, actual trees. It felt warmer already; he could feel the bite of the cold receding. In the sheltered area around the river, he saw what looked like a small village.

"I've finally lost my mind," muttered Cai. "This can't be right."

"I've not seen a plant in weeks," said Aoki, stunned. It should have been a moment of celebration, but they all just felt numb. Arjun smiled a broad smile.

"How can this be?" asked Aoki. "It doesn't make any sense."

"You don't feel it?" asked Aoibheann quizzically.

"Feel what?" he asked, a little defensively.

"There's very powerful magic in this valley," said Aoibheann. She paused for dramatic effect. "The God of the Sun's magic." The realisation swept through the party. "I think we've reached our goal."

Cai laughed loudly. Aoki grabbed him in a tight hug, which lasted a few seconds longer than was comfortable for the hug-ee. He let Cai go and moved towards Aoibheann.

"Not yet," she warned, holding her hand out to stop him. "We're not done."

"Oh, come on," he said, hugging her anyway. Initially, she left her hands down by her sides, but eventually she hugged him back.

"Aoibheann's right," said Cai. "We're not finished yet. We still have a task to complete."

"And the return journey," said Aoibheann sombrely, the smile fading from her face. She drew the sphere from her bag. The glyphs on it were going haywire.

"She was so close to the finish," said Aoki. "After all we went through."

Arjun walked down the hill, with his hand held out. He felt a jolt and drew it back instinctively. It was hot. He stepped to the side and stuck his hand out again, tentatively. He felt another jolt.

"Aoibheann," he shouted. "Come here."

She walked down to meet him. It was a gentle slope, and the grass was vivid. It reminded her of the home of the God of the Sun. "What is it?"

"There's a barrier."

She held out her hand and sensed the magic around her. She didn't speak for a little. "Yes," she eventually confirmed. "there is a barrier." Another pause. She cocked her head. "You can't get through?"

"No, it's too hot."

"Oh, of course," she said quickly. "I forget sometimes." She waved her hand, and the fiery outline of a doorway appeared in the invisible barrier. "Go ahead."

Arjun quickly stepped through, and the others followed. While they went ahead down the hill, Aoibheann tarried. She put her hand against the barrier and examined it carefully. *Too hot to pass through?*

It wasn't long before the party got noticed. Before they'd made it even halfway down the valley, they were spotted by a man leaving the orchard. He froze.

"Hello, we—" started Aoki. The man dropped his apples and ran away, shouting at the top of his voice. Aoki turned sourly to Cai. "Not the welcome I was hoping for."

"He didn't seem hostile," remarked Cai.

"He didn't look like a soldier," remarked Aoki. "Maybe he's running to get one."

"This valley is under the protection of the God of the Sun," said Aoibheann. "These people aren't our enemies."

"Do they know that?" asked Aoki.

"We shouldn't be hostile," said Aoibheann.

"What's the plan, then?" asked Arjun.

"We speak to their leaders, I suppose," said Aoibheann.

"Let's hope they don't run off screaming too," quipped Aoki.

They walked slowly towards the village and saw no one else along their way. They didn't see anyone after they reached the village, either. Every door was shut, and it was completely silent.

"Looks like they've all run off," said Aoki. "Do I really look that scary?"

"They probably don't get many visitors," noted Arjun.

They reached what appeared to be the village hall.

"We were sent here by the God of the Sun," shouted Aoibheann, as loud as she could. "We're friends, not foes."

They looked around waiting for a reply, and all eyes snapped back towards the hall as the door creaked open. An old man emerged, and began chanting loudly in the same language Aoibheann did.

"What's he saying?" asked Aoki with a hint of panic in his voice, taking a step backwards.

"Stay still," snapped Aoibheann.

The old man kept chanting.

Cai braced for impact. Aoibheann stood completely relaxed.

The old man kept chanting.

"Is something going to—" whispered Aoki.

"Shush," snapped Aoibheann.

The old man kept chanting. His inflection shifted perceptibly as his chant grew to its crescendo. A huge ball of fire launched towards the party. Aoibheann calmly said a single word, and it was immediately extinguished in its entirety. The man's eyes widened.

"So, it's true!" he croaked.

"I'm Aoibheann, the Flame of the Dawn." She held out her arms, fires swirling around her. "I'm the Champion of the Sun, wielder of the God's ancient power. You have nothing to fear from me, father – I'm here to help. These are my companions."

The old man broke into a toothy smile. He turned back into the hall. "Come out, come out," he shouted.

The villagers poured out. The adults were mostly apprehensive, but the children didn't hide their curiosity.

One little girl poked Arjun, and he sneered at her. Another came up to Aoki and just stared at his face in wonder.

"Hello," he said awkwardly. The girl carried on staring.

"Maybe you were right about your face," said Cai, laughing.

"His face is funny," agreed the girl.

Cai burst out laughing.

"Go back inside," said the old man. "Sorry about them," he apologised. "They're heavy on cheek and light on manners. But I can't say I blame them. You're the first new people we've seen in a hundred years."

"A hundred years?" asked Aoki incredulously.

"Well," the man shrugged, "no one really knows for sure. A hundred is a nice number, though. Maybe I should have gone for 'in the time of my father's father's father…' That's a good one." He chuckled lightly to himself. "I'm one of the few that actually believed other people existed. Most people thought it was just a fairy tale."

"How is that possible?"

"I assume you've seen what surrounds this valley?"

"Yes," said Aoki.

"Ice, ice and more ice, going on forever."

"Not forever."

The old man gasped. "I knew it!" he said. "I knew it. You come from another valley?"

"We come from—" began Aoki.

"Another valley, yes," interrupted Aoibheann.

"How far away is it?" asked the man. "How many people live there? What's the climate like? How did you get here?"

"It's very far away," said Aoibheann vaguely.

"Why are you here?" shouted a woman from the crowd. "What do you want?"

"Carie, please," said the old man. "Show some manners."

"What do you want?" Carie repeated.

"We were sent here by the God of the Sun," answered Aoibheann.

"What for?"

Aoibheann hesitated. "We don't know."

"Well, I know!" said Carie, turning to face the crowd. "They've come here to eat our food and drink our wine!"

There were murmurings and worried faces in the crowd.

"Carie," said the man, "this woman is blessed with the power of the Sun, just like me, and just like this valley. I vouch for them."

Carie huffed and left. A few went with her.

"Come with me," said the man, leading them into the temple. "Let me tell you our story."

"Once, there was no ice at all. There were huge swathes of land, covered in green. There were forests and fields and even rolling hills made entirely of scorching dust. But winter overtook the land. The God of the Moon destroyed it all, and the great kingdoms of green fell. It was only thanks to the God of the Sun that we survived. She gave her blessing to this valley and protects us from the cold. The altar in this temple is the source of the barrier. You can see it, can't you?" he asked expectantly, looking at Aoibheann.

"Yes, I can," she replied.

A pillar of fire shot up from the altar and expanded into a dome covering the entire valley. The others saw a stone.

She rested her hand on it and instantly knew the purpose of their quest. "Its power is fading."

"I'm afraid it is," said the old man, dabbing his brow. "Our time is running out. I would guess we only have a few weeks left."

"And nobody knows?" asked Aoibheann.

"How could I tell them? I don't know how to fix it. I've failed in my duty."

"No, you haven't. You kept it going long enough for me to arrive," said Aoibheann.

"You can recharge it?" asked the man, the crow's feet around his eyes scrunching up in a hopeful smile.

"Maybe," muttered Aoibheann. "Do you know how it's done?"

His smile fell. "I don't," he replied. "It's magic is beyond mine."

"It's the magic of the Sun herself," agreed Aoibheann. "There's no doubting that."

"You have her magic too, right?" asked Cai. "Can't you pour some energy into it?"

"Maybe," she said. "What happens if the barrier falls?"

"The ice overcomes the valley," said the old man. "Our crops die, and we starve. If we live that long. You came from the south, didn't you?"

Aoibheann nodded her head.

"From the north... from the north something different comes. There are monsters – and they've become braver of late. They must sense the barrier is weak. Scouts have been seeing them more and more often and closer in. We don't have the means to fight them. My weak magic can only take us so far."

"What kind of monsters?" asked Aoki.

"Wolves that stand taller than a man and breathe a breath of pure ice. Giants taller than the tallest trees, who throw boulders the size of houses as if they were pebbles! Enormous sea snakes who fill the entire river with their writing bodies!

"Legend says of a demon, the great and terrible Nivarjinthor, whose power can rival that of the gods themselves! It has the power to draw every little bit of warmth from within a person, just from one single touch" – he tapped at the air in emphasis – "leaving them devoid of any life. It leads the armies of the cold, and only the grace of the Sun protects us from its wroth."

"Well, at least it's a good quest goal," said Aoki nervously. "Fix the magical barrier before the evil army destroys the town. Classic."

"Is it?" asked Arjun.

"It will be," said Aoki.

"We're late," interrupted Aoibheann, with her eyes closed and hands on the altar. "We should have gotten here sooner. You don't have weeks left," she said to the man. "You have… two days… maybe three."

"Can you fix it before then?"

"Yes," she said. "I think I can. But I'll need time to prepare. I've never done anything like this before."

"How long will you need?" he asked nervously.

"Give me until tomorrow morning."

The man looked relieved. "Praise the Sun! Thank you, Aoibheann. You've saved us. Thank you."

"I need somewhere to work privately," she instructed, "and writing materials."

"Of course," he said. "Follow me."

"How are you feeling?" asked Cai, shooting Aoki a sympathetic look.

"I'm trying not to think about it," said Aoki. "Let's finish this quest first. There's no time to grieve." He sighed. "How are you feeling?"

"There's no time to grieve."

Aoki nodded.

Cai nodded. "If Aoibheann can't fix this barrier, we might be in trouble."

"That's an understatement."

"If Aoibheann can't fix this barrier, we will be in trouble – a lot of it." Cai clutched the sparrow around his neck. It had become a habit of his, every time his mind drifted to his daughter.

Aoki noticed but didn't know what to say.

Cai continued, "We should speak to the local militia, if there is one. Hunters too, and blacksmiths – anyone strong and fit."

"I can stock up on arrows," said Aoki. "And we can see where we stand in terms of defence."

"I don't have high hopes," admitted Cai. "If it does come to a fight, we might have to do the heavy lifting."

Aoki nodded. "Make sure you rest up tonight. We'll need you." He looked over his shoulder. "Have you seen Arjun around, by the way?"

"Nope." He grunted. "It's just like him to disappear at a time like this."

The waxing moon rose in the sky. The village was quiet. Aoki lay in bed, snoring softly. Aoibheann lay slumped over a desk, snoring loudly. Cai sat in a chair, looking out of the window. He'd tried to get himself snoring but hadn't succeeded. He'd try again in a little while. For the moment he sat and watched the still world. He began to feel sleepy, despite all of his worries.

And then he was wide awake. There was movement. It was subtle. Maybe just his mind playing tricks, his paranoid, exhausted mind. But no… there was movement. He stepped back from the window and observed quietly, ready to raise the alarm.

It was Arjun. *That idiot. Where's he been?* Cai thought. *What a fool.* Cai watched him walk back through the village and into the room that had been assigned to him. *I'm going to give him such a talking to tomorrow. He can't be fooling about at times like these. He's so facetious.* Cai shook his head. Maybe that's just his way of dealing with things.

The surge of adrenalin left his body, and he felt the welcome hug of drowsiness. He climbed back into bed, and soon he managed to snore.

The next morning, surrounded by anyone who was anyone in the village, Aoibheann stood in front of the altar. The word had got out about what was going to happen.

A little girl looked up at Aoibheann in awe. "You're cool," she said, with a toothy smile.

Aoibheann ignored her. She took a deep breath and rehearsed the incantation in her head. She'd composed the spell last night and was confident it would work.

"There have been reports," whispered Aoki, "of monsters amassing around the barrier."

"I heard," she said.

He nodded. "Good luck."

She placed her hands on the altar, and her face soured. "This isn't right," she muttered. "The power is draining too fast." She turned to the old man accusingly. "Did you do something?"

"I've not touched it!" he said.

She closed her eyes. "It's getting faster." Her face contorted. She began chanting in her ancient, guttural language. Fire twisted around her. Sparks danced like butterflies. Children laughed and reached out to catch them. Their parents, very wisely, stopped them and then began to move backwards, as far as they could, until they were pressed tightly against the wall of the temple.

The sparks grew brighter and hotter as they spun around Aoibheann. She motioned her hands, and they converged in front of her, in a ball that shone like the sun. She lowered her hands and angled the ball towards the altar. The flames began to pour in.

A blast of cold came from the altar. Aoibheann lost concentration, and the fire died. She spun around. Arjun stood there, hands outstretched, covered in ice. Aoibheann saw the light of the barrier fade, and Arjun smiled his cocky smile.

Aoki drew his bow.

"Arjun," asked Cai nervously, "what are you doing?"

The ice grew around him, covering his entire body in a crystalline, spiky armour. Aoibheann launched a quick burst of flame. The ice shattered completely on the impact, leaving nothing behind. Aoibhean shouted a curse and kicked the altar.

"Is he dead?" asked the old man tentatively.

"He's gone," said Cai, "but not dead. I assume the barrier is down?"

"Yes," said Aoibheann. "It'll be battle after all."

Cai put a hand on her shoulder and a hand on Aoki's. The three looked at each other. Cai let go and turned to the villagers. "Take arms!" he shouted. The makeshift militia jumped to action.

Carie was calling down curses on Aoibheann, but she tuned them all out. "Cai," she said. "It's a good thing we practised."

He nodded. "Remember," he said, turning to the militia, "what I told you yesterday. The bear is on our side."

He stepped outside and took a deep breath. The shape of Shar's head began to rise from the earth. It grew and grew until it stood as high as him, and then taller again. It grew until it stood as tall as the temple itself. Aoibheann chanted as it did, imbuing it with fire. Its claws and teeth shone white hot, and its fur caught alight. The villagers stood in awe, and hope shone in their eyes. Shar let out a roar, and they joined in.

A dozen giants stood on the hill and let loose a roar of their own. They began a stampede down the hill, and Shar raced to meet them. She swiped a giant with her white-hot claws, melting through its chest. She grabbed another in her jaws and flung it about like a doll, throwing its limp body away.

The next giants were more cautious. Shar growled. Her flaming fur stood on end as the giants began to form a semicircle around her.

Aoki crouched on a roof, shooting arrow after arrow. His unerring aim was impressive. Every shot hit its mark, but they were mosquito bites to a creature 20-feet tall. A giant brushed away the arrows stuck in his arm without anything more than a look of annoyance.

Cai sat behind him, perfectly still, with pure concentration on his face. He held his swallow necklace in his hand, knuckles white. A few villagers joined Aoki on the roof with bows, and the rest stood ready on the ground with machetes, pitchforks, kitchen knives, clubs, or whatever else they could find. They were safe, so far.

Aoki noticed a figure halfway down the hill, walking leisurely through the frantic battle, a man encased in ice, with piercing eyes glowing blue. Even from a distance, Aoki could see where he was looking – right at him.

"Aoibheann!" he shouted, pointing. "Unless we stop him, we'll be overrun."

She nodded and steeled herself.

Aoki nodded back. "Good luck." He turned and drew his bow, before shooting an arrow straight into the eye of a giant.

"Aoki, I—"

"Tell me when you get back," he shouted, drawing his bow again.

The giants wasted no more time and began to close in on Shar. While she was busy, more creatures began to slip past. The wolves howled.

Aoibheann pursed her lips, and lingered for a second, before turning her back. She began chanting. The fire grew and squirmed around her, tightly held. She drew the power into herself and was overcome by a foreign but familiar presence, the God of the Sun. *This is what you wanted all along, isn't it?*

Aoibheann felt Her smug smile in her mind as new power flowed through her. She was even stronger now. The power swirled around her in a tempest, and she was encased in a sphere of flame. Her feet began to lift from the ground, and she was elevated well above the battlefield. The sphere around her grew, before collapsing in on itself, revealing the flaming wings of a dragon on her back.

Arjun's gaze left Aoki and moved to her. He smiled to himself, impressed. With a cry, he expelled all warmth from himself. He hunched over, and convulsed as he grew wings of his own, equal but opposite. He flew to meet Aoibheann, in the skies above the raging battle below.

"Aoibheann!" he shouted. He held his hands up in the air. "We don't have to fight."

"I can't believe I was so blind," she screamed. "The Champion of the Moon! I should have known. You never worked for the Sun."

"You're right. I hate her almost as much as you do, Aoibheann." His unblinking gaze never left her eyes. "I am the Champion of the Moon. But so what? The God of the Sun has wronged so many people, Aoibheann. She isn't 'good', and he isn't 'evil', you know that." He gestured at the battle below. "This is all a part of her plan. She knew who I was the whole time, and she sent you on this quest anyway. This is what she wants, for those people down there to die, and for you to kill me. She's using you. But it doesn't have to be that way. I can free you. I can break your bond with her."

"No, you can't."

"Yes, I can. I can free you."

"It's not possible."

"It is. I can cut your ties with the God of the Sun, forever. All you have to do is lay down your arms."

"And let you destroy this valley?"

"How many have you killed?" he asked. "More than this. And if you're left with your powers, you'll kill again, whether you want to or not. You'll lose control again. Could you live with yourself if that happened? You're already so close to not being able to. I saw it after Fox's Perdition. You're hanging by a thread."

"Shut up."

"I can stop that from happening. That's what you want, isn't it? To be free?"

"And what do you want, Arjun? You destroy this valley, and then what?"

"That's all I want. The God of the Sun stole this land, Aoibheann. This valley doesn't belong here. This is the territory of the God of the Moon, and he wants it back. That's all."

"I don't believe you'll stop here."

"You've listened to a lot of the Sun's propaganda, haven't you? When has the Moon ever taken any action but in self defence? All he wants is to be left alone in his own kingdom. He's tired. He wants to sleep in peace."

"The God of the Moon waged war with the other gods. He tried to destroy—"

"You've only heard one side of the story! You've only heard what the God of the Sun wants you to hear! Please, Aoibheann, you're smart enough to understand. I can free you from your curse. I can tell you the truth. We can be friends, and you won't ever have to hurt anyone again."

A glimmer of sad hope shone in her eyes.

"You hate the God of the Sun," continued Arjun. "Let her plan fail."

A realisation came to her. "If I'm the only thing standing in your way, why were you so keen to make sure I was here? When I wanted to leave, you convinced me to stay. Why?"

"I needed you to get me through the barrier," he admitted, "but—"

"You used me, of course."

"But I could have waited," he finished. "If you left, the barrier would have fallen by itself. I wanted you to stay so we could have this conversation. I'll admit, there were times I almost killed you. But when I found out you were the Champion of the

Sun, that you were just like me, I convinced you to stay so I can free you, Aoibheann. I don't want to kill you. I want to save you."

"Call off the attack, and I won't fight you. Call off the attack. Me, Aoki, and Cai, we'll lead the villagers safely down south. The valley will be yours, and nobody has to die."

"That's not possible."

"Why not?"

"They won't leave. We have no choice but to kill them."

"I can't let you kill them."

"Aoibheann—"

"I won't let you kill them."

"They have the Sun's power soaked into their very being! The food they eat and the wine they drink is so full of it! They can't—"

"I won't let you kill them."

The look of determination in her eye killed the retort on his lips. Without another word, he attacked.

Shar began to shrink. Slowly at first, but thereafter more and more noticeably. Aoki definitely noticed. She now stood shoulder to shoulder with the giants. It was getting harder and harder to hold them off. They charged her all at once, hit her, and held her down. Cai sent her back to the spirit world with a gasp. He flagged.

"We need to fall back," said Aoki.

"Where's Aoibheann?" spluttered Cai.

"She's gone after Arjun."

Cai looked down from the roof to see the villagers circling a wolf, jabbing at it with pitchforks. The old man chanted. It burnt to a crisp in a pillar of fire. The villagers cheered. The cheer died as a dozen more wolves followed. No longer occupied with Shar, the giants began in their direction too.

"Let's hope she succeeds," said Cai.

"Come on," said Aoki. He pulled Cai up and wrapped his arm around his shoulder. He shouted down to the villagers. "Retreat! Back to the temple! Retreat!"

They clambered down from the roof and began towards the temple, Aoki supporting Cai as much as he could. A howl from behind chilled their blood. Cai held his hand out, and the horns of a bull began to rise from the ground. The body just began to clear the ground as Cai wheezed heavily. It sank back down.

"I'm sorry," shouted Aoki, dropping Cai onto the ground and drawing his bow. He shot the wolf between its eyes, just as it began to charge towards them. Cai fell heavily, and the air was knocked out of his lungs. His swallow pendant fell from his neck, and he reached for it vainly as Aoki half-lifted, half-dragged him towards the temple. The old man stood at the threshold, fire in hand. He blasted another wolf, and Aoki and Cai got safely inside before the rest of the pack caught up.

Cai was breathing heavily and seemed to be fading in and out of consciousness. "Is anyone here a healer?" shouted Aoki. *If only Maria was here,* he thought to himself. *She could fix this.* He shook the thought from his mind. "Healer!" he shouted again. "He's the number one priority. He's the only one who might be able to save us."

Carie, who was stitching up a villager's wound, looked up from what she was doing long enough to spit in Aoki's direction, before carrying on. Aoki's lip curled as he felt rage beginning to overwhelm him. He took a step towards her. The old man put a hand on his shoulder.

"Your friend will be okay," he said coolly. "Don't do anything rash."

"None of us will be okay," snapped Aoki.

"I trust in the Champion of the Sun. These walls are thick; we just have to hold out."

A boom echoed throughout the temple as a giant fist crashed against the doors.

"And how thick are the doors?" asked Aoki.

The man's reply was cut short by another bang. The fist crashed against the door again and again, rhythmically pounding against the wood. Splinters began to show.

Aoki pulled all of the arrows from his sheath. There were six. His hand went to his belt, wrapping around the hilt of his jewelled dagger. He sighed deeply and nocked an arrow. A colossal hand burst through the door.

The elements swirled around them as they flew through the sky, spinning and twirling as they launched attacks at each other.

I can beat him if I don't hold back.

A shard of ice flew past her cheek.

He's not as strong as I am.

He darted back, and prepared to launch a boulder of ice, not at Aoibheann but at the church. She recognised his intentions just in time and moved to block.

He doesn't care about collateral damage.

He pulled back the boulder, and another shard of ice flew at her and grazed her side.

"You're sloppy!" goaded Arjun "Come on! Use all that power you have! Let it loose! Burn the world down, Aoibheann! Let loose your anger and your rage. Indulge it!"

Aoibheann held up a shield of flame to block a barrage of hailstones. *He knows me too well. This is what I get for trusting someone! He's getting under my skin.*

"You can't beat me like this! Come on! Give me a challenge!"

He's right.

His skin began to harden, and a sphere of ice grew around him.

Not this again. She launched a small ball of fire at the sphere, and it shattered easily. Nothing was inside. Aoibheann spun around. And again looking in all directions, moving back and forth as fast as she could. *Where is he?*

An icicle hit her squarely in the back. The thin layer of fire around her body dulled the blow, but it drove her forwards. More followed; one hit her arm, another her leg. A barrage came, and purely out of instinct, Aoibheann exploded. A huge wave of fire left her in all directions, turning all of the icicles to steam. She fought hard to withdraw it into herself, but it kept growing.

Not again. Please, not again.

She brought the expansion to a stop. Images flashed through her head of Fox's Perdition, a town in ashes.

Concentrate.

The images kept flashing through her mind. Her concentration broke, and the fire began to consume her. It grew and it grew, bigger and hotter. Arjun watched from a distance with a smile on his face.

Get out of my head.

The images kept coming back to her. She concentrated as hard as she could on the people in the village, on Cai, on Aoki. She held an image of his face in her mind, with his lopsided smile. She calmed herself. The fire began to withdraw. It drew back into her waiting palm, the giant sphere of flame compressing into a white-hot ball in her hand.

She launched it at Arjun, who barely managed to dodge. It singed his cheek. "That's more like it!" he shouted. "Use all that power; let it consume you, Aoibheann."

That's not going to happen.

"It would be so easy! Stop fighting it, and let the power consume you."

A hand of ice grabbed at Aoibheann's wing and dragged her down towards the earth. She shot fire at it, but the holes she made filled themselves instantly. While she was busy, Arjun launched an attack. She waved her hand, and a wall of fire blocked his barrage of ice. The barrage was weak. As she fell closer and closer to the ground, she realised that this was her opportunity. He was focusing too much on offence. As the wind rushed in her ears, and the ground grew closer, she closed her eyes.

Panic gnawed at her mind. She spent a valuable second telling herself she didn't have the time to panic. Pure energy grew in her palms. It wasn't enough, so she drew the wings into herself, adding it to the power.

Arjun tried to teleport away, but he was too slow. The ball hit him in the chest at inescapable speed. The ice in his veins thawed, his wings faded, and he fell the long fall down to the earth. Aoibheann frantically re-spread her own wings and broke out of the dive just feet above the ground.

She didn't hesitate in speeding to where he landed, ready to unleash her fury. She stopped, though, when she saw him. It was clear that it was over. She held her hand out and began to chant, before stopping abruptly. In a few mumbled words, she said a prayer, quietly, to herself. She held her hand back out and finished the invocation, turning his mangled body to ash.

With the power over them broken, the wolves and giants fled. Aoibheann flew straight to the village square, outside the temple. The doors were off their hinges, and cold bodies lined the floors.

She recognised the faces of villagers among the wolves and giants. She saw Aoki's unmistakeable dagger in the head of a wolf. Her heart dropped.

"Aoki!" she shouted. "Cai!"

Sickening silence.

A figure limped out of a side room, clutching his ribs. "About time!" Aoki coughed, smiling his lopsided smile.

Relief overcame her, and she rushed to hug him.

"Gently!" he squealed.

"Sorry," she said, blushing a little. She let him go. "Cai?"

"He'll be okay. He's hurt, but he'll be okay."

She was visibly relieved. "Good."

"Arjun?" Aoki asked.

"Dead."

Aoki grimaced and nodded. Others began to come out of the side room, realising it was safe. There were no cheers, no joy in the victory. They went to inspect the dead. There were eight, including the old man. Many more were injured.

Carie strode towards Aoibheann. The women stood face to face. "I want you gone," said Carie. It wasn't worded as if it were an order, but it was one.

Aoibheann nodded. "We'll leave as soon as we can. Aoki and Cai need time to heal. I need time to restore the barrier. We can help as much as we can with the repairs in the meantime, or we can leave you be."

"Leave us be," she said bluntly. "And leave as soon as you can."

Aoibheann nodded again. "Two days," she said.

Carie left to treat the wounded.

The God of the Moon felt a part of his power return to him – a small part, but nonetheless, it roused him. He remembered giving it away, years ago, to a man who swore to serve him. He looked around, and after a moment it dawned on him what must have happened. He snarled with rage. Someone had killed his champion.

He shook himself like a wet dog and stretched. His limbs hadn't forgotten their strength. He roared, anger beginning to overtake his mind.

"Do you feel it?" The God of the Sun smiled in her valley. "Do you feel it, brother?"

Gloom overcame the king's face. "I do."

The God of the Sun threw her head back and laughed.

"I really thought we were goners there," said Cai, sitting up in his bed.

Aoki sat in the chair nearby, and Aoibheann was looking out of the window.

"Me too," said Aoki. "I think I'll need a break from adventuring for a while."

"That doesn't sound like you," said Aoibheann.

"Well, I'm a changed man, Aoibheann," he replied. "I'm mature now, like a good cheese."

She laughed. "Obviously, not that mature." She rolled her eyes at him. "I guess you have the story you wanted."

"Yes," he said. His smile became a frown. "But it turned out a lot sadder than I expected. We haven't even had time to properly mourn. Arjun killed Maria, didn't he?"

"I think so," said Aoibheann. "I can't believe who he really was."

"It's really hard to rationalise," said Aoki distantly, "that someone you liked could really be like that. It's like the man we travelled with and the man you killed were two different people."

"We have a long journey home," said Cai, clutching his swallow necklace. "We'll have time to reflect. We'll make sure everyone knows she was a hero."

"I won't settle for anything less than a statue," Aoki replied with a half-smile. "A very big statue, covered in gold."

Aoibheann smiled. "That would be nice."

"And what happens to you when we get back?" asked Cai.

"That's up to the king to decide," she said curtly.

He nodded. "You got the barrier working again?"

"Yes. This valley should be safe for another hundred years."

"I don't envy the next group that has to come and fix it."

"Neither do I."

The conversation lulled.

"Are you ready?" asked Aoibheann briskly.

"I'm ready," said Cai. "Let's go home."

The God of The Moon

The Kingdom of Ice, 3262

The God of the Moon,
Here he had hewn
His kingdom from the ice and snow.
Pristine, and pure,
Yet it held no allure,
Only a long and cold river's flow,
With nothing to be heard,
Not one single bird,
Over the western wind's blow.
The kingdom mimics its master,
For life, it brings disaster.
Nothing can grow in this place of woe.

Except for his malice.
Sometimes it's hidden.
But gone?
No.

In this place, it feeds,
It multiplies,
It breeds,
And it begins to boil over.

Awakened, the dragon was subject once again to the rage that consumed him. Until, that is, the moon in the sky began to grow.

> The moon waxes,
> And the dragon subsides.
> The anger, it axes,
> And malice divides.
> The envy, it taxes,
> And hatred it chides.
> Love, it maxes,
> And good, it guides.
> The moon waxes,
> And the dragon subsides.

The dragon slept in his kingdom of ice. He dreamed, dreamed of the creation of the world, oh, so long ago, dreamed of himself, a dragon full of love and hope, pouring his very soul into his creation.

As he created his magnum opus – the moon itself – he poured too much of himself into it. His love, his happiness, his good intentions, all poured into his creation, tearing his very soul in two. As the moon began to wane, he awoke from his dream in a fury.

> The moon wanes,
> And the dragon thrives.
> The anger it gains,
> And the malice revives.
> The envy remains,
> And hatred arrives.

The love held in chains,
And good in archives.
The moon wanes,
And the dragon thrives.

The power of the God of the Moon ebbs and flows like the tides. As the moon grows, it takes the power from the dragon. As the moon shrinks, the dragon takes that power back. For one day only, does either hold full power – the moon on the day of the full moon, and the dragon on the day of a new moon. It was to a new moon, the dragon awoke.

This would be the last time
That his strength was taken.
He let loose the great roar of a creature in its prime.
The earth was shaken.

A walk, a canter, a run
Wings beating
With a power second to none,
But fleeting.

Higher and higher, he flew,
Above the eyrie of every eagle,
Perched on the mountains stood, so regal,
Above the winds he knew.

Higher and higher, he flew
To the domain of his foe,
Heaven's brim,
Where none could go
Besides his kin.

Too long he'd lived his life
In bondage to the tune
Of the incessant croon
Of the crescent moon
That caused him so much strife.

The hungry god had come to feed,
Luna he was to eat,
So this life he'd lead no longer.
He'd finally be complete.

Now was his moment,
Now was his chance,
To end this twisted dance.

Partition evil meets partition good,
In a clash of conflicting ideals.
To once and for all, restore full godhood
To the evil that'd hear no deals.

For the good wanted to reason,
As good often does,
Despite evil's treason
And sins because
There's no good in bloodshed,
When it can be averted,
But evil felt it must be fed,
And the moon dragon asserted,
"You will be mine!
No deal will be struck.
I'll destroy the benign,
You're all out of luck."

But as evil held triumph within its clutch,
Everything around it became hot to the touch.
A shining light, a solar eclipse,
And the balance of power flips.

Half a god against a god and a half,
And ringing in the ears of evil is a laugh,
That of the sun, who knows victory is near
And evil for the first time feels fear.

A deity deposed, defeated.
A battle begun at the world's birth is completed,
And the Moon Dragon falls to Earth with a crash.

Completely unheard, another dragon screams. It's a scream of grief. As the scream reaches its zenith, the firmament shakes, and a number of stars go out.

Michael

The Royal Capital, 3262

A tear rolled down the cheek of the Dragon King. His advisor gave him a funny look. He'd never seen the king cry before. "Is everything okay, my liege?"

The Dragon King didn't reply straight away. "Things are changing, Michael."

Michael cocked his head. "How cryptic."

"I'm sorry I can't be more forthcoming," replied the Dragon King. "But there's something that I need to do. And something I need you to do."

He got up and motioned for Michael to follow. The Dragon King was in the form of an elderly man, and he limped slightly as he walked. Michael was one of the few people who knew the king could change how he looked. He wondered now why the king didn't choose the form of a young man instead. He had to slow his gait considerably to keep pace.

He found himself in a part of the castle he wasn't familiar with. The corridors were old and dusty. They took a long winding staircase down.

Eventually, they reached a corridor which ended in a door. The king took a key from around his neck and opened it. The room beyond was immense, spotless, and brightly lit by torches. Rows and rows of shelves stood full to the brim with books, scrolls, and other curiosities.

Michael stood mouth agape. "What is this place?"

"This, Michael," said the Dragon King, "is my life's work." He looked upon it fondly, as he walked along the aisles. "A thousand years of knowledge, most of it known only to me. Magic, Science, Art, Medicine, Engineering, Governance, the Divine. There is information here about every possible subject. This information could change the world."

"Then why is it kept down here?"

"Because not all change is good."

The advisor looked shocked. "So, you've kept medical advancements to yourself?"

"Do you trust me, Michael?"

"Completely."

"I trust you, as well," the king replied, "completely, which is why I've brought you here." He pointed to a large fireplace at the end of the room. It lit. "You need to destroy everything here."

"What?" Michael stammered. "But this is your life's work! You said so yourself. The information here could help so many people!"

"It cannot fall into the wrong hands."

"What wrong hands? Who's going to find it down here?"

"I won't be able to protect it any longer."

"Why not?"

The Dragon King winced. Despite his calm demeanour, his head was spinning. "I need to leave."

Michael looked confused. "It'll be fine until you get back. You've left before."

The king gave him a kind, pitying look.

It took Michael a moment to realise what that meant. "You're not coming back."

The fire crackled. "I'm not." The king put his hand on Michael's shoulder. "You've been a good friend, Michael, and a great advisor – the very best, in fact. I have no doubt you'll be voted this country's first Premier, and that you'll lead the people to times of prosperity."

"You're just leaving? Where are you going?"

The king didn't reply.

"You've led the kingdom for centuries. The people love you!"

"I'm sorry, Michael," said the king. "I've spent far too long among humans. I've spent far too long neglecting my duty."

"What about your duty to us?"

"I'm sorry, Michael," repeated the king. The king turned, and walked away, a tear rolling down his cheek.

Michael watched him leave, tears on his own cheeks. He stood paralysed for a while, before coming back to his senses.

Alone in the grand library, he looked around. He picked up the nearest scroll and undid the clasp. The temptation to read it was strong, but something in the back of his mind stopped him from unfurling it. Instead, he walked to the fire and threw it in. Paper and metal burned alike in the divine flames. He took a deep breath, before going back to the shelf and picking up as much as he could. He walked back and forth, and back and forth, burning up the secrets of the world.

Bells began to ring outside. He recognised the tones – alarm bells. He double checked the door was locked and began to rush. The ringing continued for hours, and it had stopped for a few hours by the time Michael had finished. He surveyed the grand library and found nothing remaining.

He paused, with his hand on the doorknob. What was on the other side of the door? A world very different from the one he'd left. The golden age was over, and he felt things would never be as they were again. He opened the door and left without noticing the small box left in the corner full of scrolls.

"Hey, over here," shouted Gamel. "I've found something!"

The rest of his party rushed over. He unfurled one of the scrolls, and his eyes widened. It was covered in designs and schematics that were alien to them all.

Suggesting Treason

The Royal Capital, 4571

He's a caricature. He stood unnaturally straight, cigar in his left hand and schematics in his right. His large belly was hidden as well as it could be underneath his perfectly tailored suit.

He took a drag. He turned his head away from the man he was talking to and exhaled dark smoke right into my face.

He continued talking. "You can mass produce this design?"

He didn't even notice me.

"I can, and to the very highest quality," said the other man. He smiled shrewdly. "For the right price."

The smoker boomed with laughter. "Huh-huh-huh-huh!"

I hate that laugh. It was definitely the laugh of a smoker.

"I wouldn't expect any less from your firm, Mr McCorley. I hear your reputation is well earned."

"It is," said Mr McCorley. "We look forward to working with you, Mr Jones. Or should I be saying 'Sir Jones' now?"

I'm pretty sure he knows that's not the case.

Mr Jones took another drag. "Not yet, my boy. The new king doesn't quite get how things work yet. My application is," he made quotation marks with his fingers, "under review."

"It'll be pushed forward shortly, I'm sure," said Mr McCorley. "It's very well deserved." The last part was said with an interesting tone.

"Are you complimenting me, McCorley, or mocking me?"

"Just shooting the breeze."

Mr Jones hmphed.

He'll never let a subtle jab get in the way of business.

Mr Jones stuck out his hand. "Are we agreed?"

Mr McCorley brought his hand up from his side, then held it still, inches away from Mr Jones'. "There's something I need to ask you first."

"Naturally."

McCorley turned his head towards the prototype airship. Jones followed his gaze. "This contract will leave you with no small amount of military might."

"Yes."

"I've heard that this wasn't requested by the king."

"He's a very busy man. Only just taken the throne, and so young too! He needs experienced voices around him to make the decisions he has no time for."

"Of course," said McCorley. "I only ask one thing."

"Well?" said Jones, annoyed by the pause. "Ask. Don't mince your words."

"If you find yourself in a position of greater power, Mr Jones, remember who supplied you with these weapons."

Jones laughed again. "I won't forget, McCorley." He reached forward, closing the distance between their hands. He grabbed McCorley's firmly.

"Come, girl!"

I ran to open the door for him. How could he possibly open the door for himself?

He stepped out into the smoggy air. He took a deep breath and smiled. He threw what was left of his cigar into the street. It went exactly how he wanted it to go.

I ran over to his carriage and opened that door for him too. He climbed in rather ungracefully, and I shut the door behind him.

"Wait," he commanded. "Come in here, girl."

Fuck.

"Are you deaf?" he roared.

I opened the door hesitantly.

"You look like you've seen a ghost!" he cried. "Huh-huh-huh-huh!" His face softened. "I'm not going to hurt you, girl. You must have heard the stories about old Tamley."

I nodded.

"Well, I'm not him. Sit."

I did.

"You're new, aren't you? You've witnessed history today, my dear, on your very first day! You've heard things only a handful of people will ever hear."

I've worked here six months.

"I don't think I understood it, Sir."

He hmphed. "Of course you wouldn't," he said.

He was very mean, in a very non-personal way. Of course I wouldn't understand, that's obvious.

"You're from the country, aren't you?"

"Yes, Sir."

"Do you believe in gods? In magic, fairies, and dragons?"

"My parents do, Sir."

"And you?"

"No, Sir, they're just stories."

He pulled a second cigar from his jacket.

What was that, a minute?

"I suppose coming here has knocked some sense into you. It's easy to pick up sense when you're surrounded by this." He gestured vaguely around at the towering buildings and smoggy skies. "There's only one God here, girl. Do you know who it is?"

"Money, Sir."

"Huh-huh-huh! Spot on, girl. Money." He smiled as if he was the one who'd got the right answer. "You're sharper than you look."

I smiled as sweetly as I could.

"You saw that airship, didn't you, girl?"

"Yes, Sir."

"What do you think would happen if your people decided to rebel?"

"They'd lose."

"They'd lose. Spears and pitchforks against fifty flying cannons? Huh-huh-huh! It'd be a slaughter."

"Yes, Sir."

"I wonder what their dandelions would do for them then?"

"Nothing, Sir."

His eyes lit up. He's enjoying that image. He came back to reality. "They're stupid," he said, "but not that stupid. Once I show them what they're dealing with, they'll remember their place."

"The country folk will be yours to command, Sir."

"People look down on them. Individually, they may be worthless."

It's so casual.

"But who produces all of the food? Who digs all of the coal? Mines all of the iron?"

"The worthless country people, Sir."

He looked at me nastily.

"I'm sorry, Sir! I didn't mean—"

His anger turned quickly to mirth. "Huh-huh-huh!" He looked at me with genuine pity. "You might not see it yet, but you'll realise soon enough – the difference between us and you."

"Yes, Sir."

He continued. "When you own the people, the industry and the weapons, then who is left to oppose you?"

"Nobody, Sir."

"Nobody," he said, almost frothing at the mouth. "Nobody. Not many people know this, girl," he added, "but the king has no real power. He's only a figurehead."

Everybody knows that. There hadn't been a real king in living memory.

"But he's the king!" I cried. "Surely—"

"Huh-huh-huh! Count yourself one of the privileged few, my girl, you didn't hear it from me."

"Would you like to be king, Sir?" I ventured.

He kissed his teeth and then slapped me across the face. "Even suggesting that is treason, girl."

The answer was yes, but I'd overstepped. I felt my cheek go red. It stung, and I felt a bruise forming where that obnoxiously large ring had caught me.

We sat in silence for the rest of the journey. I stared out of the window, watching the smokestacks bellowing black clouds above the city. I was dropped off two miles away from home, and the carriage drove him to his front door.

I was reassigned the next day to the kitchens and never saw him up close again.

Good riddance.

Clang

Hamrow Woods, 4571

The rhythmic striking of metal echoed throughout the woods. Clang!
    Dark smoke billowed from fume hoods. Clang!
    Slag piled up in a heap ever bigger. Clang!
    Waste flowed into the river. Clang!
    The animals hated the clanging; their heads spun. Clang!
    They decided something must be done. Clang!
    Predator and prey put their differences aside. Clang!
    They were going to destroy the factory, allied. Clang!

They started by stuffing their ears.
    "That's so much better," said the squirrel.
    "What?" said the rabbit.
    "THAT'S SO MUCH BETTER!" shouted the squirrel.
    "WHAT?" shouted the rabbit.
    The owl, who was wishing now he'd just flown to the next forest over, wrote in the dirt: 'This is the plan.'
    The animals paid close attention.

As night fell, they put their plan into action. Soaring above, the owl directed operations.
    The mice snuck through pipes, narrow, but no challenge at all for the lithe rodents. They gnawed holes where they could.

The crows flew overhead, tactically dropping stones anywhere that seemed it might be disruptive. Exhausts, unset castings, and gauges were all victims.

The squirrels climbed up the walls and, nibbling at electrical wires, took out lights in a shower of sparks.

The rabbits ran, as was their strength, dodging between workers' legs. Powerful legs kicked over buckets of molten metal, spilling it all over the floor.

The bears walked around the perimeter, knocking over posts and frightening anyone who came near.

The hedgehogs snuck around, poking holes in whatever they could. No shoe or trouser was safe.

The owl was just thinking how well things were going, when a gust of wind blew her off course. A blast of hot air from a smokestack blew the stuffing from her ears.

Clang!

A hand reached inside the pipe and grabbed a mouse tight. Clang!

A thrown stone hit a crow's wing, prematurely ending their flight. Clang!

A broom knocked a squirrel to the ground. Clang!

A woman in iron boots kicked a rabbit around. Clang!

The bears were scared off by a clamour of pots and pans. Clang!

A hedgehog was grabbed by heavily gloved hands. Clang!

"What a nuisance," said the director. "These creatures are affecting productivity."

"We could get to work building a fence," suggested a worker.

"No," said the director. "That'd be too much effort and too much time. Fetch the flamethrowers. Burn the forest to the ground; we don't need it."

"But, ma'am," said one of the workers nervously, "that forest belongs to the king."

"These airships need to be delivered on time. If the king asks, it was an accident."

The workers saluted. "Yes, ma'am." They knew better than to speak out of turn for a second time.

The Hunt

Borders of the Hamrow Woods, 4571

I lie low in the undergrowth, trying to be as still as I can, but I'm shaking. I'm scared. I take deep breaths, trying to calm myself. I hear a rustle in the undergrowth.

What was that? Have they found me?

My stomach sinks. My body reacts before my conscious mind can process what happened. I scramble. I stand. I run, as fast as I can, away.

I hear a startled bird take flight and hate myself for being so stupid. It was just a bird. I hear shouting.

"There it is! I found it!"
"Due south!"

Tamay blew her horn, and the riders all set off in pursuit.

"Yah," shouted Guai Shou, urging his horse to go faster.

"Cut it off to the right!" shouted Toky.

Guai Shou split off from the group, while Toky and Tamay kept course. As they galloped, the wind blew harshly in their faces and branches cut them.

They gained quickly on the creature that was their prey.

They're right behind me. I can hear them.
But I can't stop. I can't look back. I can't.
I'm so stupid. Why did I run?

I can't outrun them. They're getting closer.

I hear someone out to my right. I angle left. I'm breathing so fast, and my legs are tired. I need to breathe deeper.

Concentrate. Concentrate you idiot.

Run. One foot in front of the other.

The crashing horses and the shouting is getting louder and louder.

Breathe.

Toky was a good rider, and the fastest in the group. The monster veered left, exactly as he'd intended. An animal is easy to predict. That part of the forest was more open and would make things easier for the riders. But it looked like that wasn't necessary. He'd closed most of the gap already. He threw a bola, and the monster tripped, its legs caught.

I hit my face hard on the ground, but the adrenaline dulls the pain. I don't have time for it.

I don't have time for anything.

I turn over and see the man and his horse over me, and I scream.

The creature let loose a piercing shriek, and it spooked Toky's horse. It reared and he fell to the ground on his back. His heavy armour made him slow to get up. The other hunters' horses panicked too and refused to get any closer.

What is this thing? How do I untie it?

I need to untie it now. It's so tangled.

He's getting up. He's getting up.

The more I struggle, the more it tightens. Be calm. Be calm.

I just need to grab the end and unwrap it…

He's up.

He got up and grabbed his spear from the ground – a perfect opportunity. He walked up to the monster and, without any hesitation, stabbed down.

I scream even louder than before. I can't help it.

Toky is blown back off his feet.

I pull the spear out of myself.

Toky hit his head.

I'm hurt. It hurts so deeply.
But I need to go. I need to get out of here.

Toky fell unconscious.

I scream again.
I can't untie the bola, but I can loosen it enough to slip out.
I get up. Every step hurts.
I'll heal. I always do, no matter what. But it takes time.
I just need to get away.

The other riders managed to take control of their horses and reached Toky.

"Quick, he's hurt!" shouted Guai Shou, dismounting.

"Let me see," said Tamay, dismounting too. She knelt down beside Toky and put the back of her hand by his nose. "He's breathing."

She gently lifted up Toky's head. Her hand was wet with blood. She searched frantically through her pack for a bandage.

"This is bad," said Guai Shou. "Is he going to be okay?"

"I don't know."

"For the gods sakes!" he shouted. He was overcome with anger. He shouted a wordless, wrathful shout. "It hurt Toky, and it's getting away!"

"He needs serious help. We have to take him back to the village."

"I'm going to kill it, Tamay."

Tamay hesitated for a moment, then said, "I could take him back alone."

Guai Shou nodded. "You take him back. I'll go on. There's a trail of blood. It can't be moving fast."

"Leave your horse. It won't be much use."

Guai Shou nodded. The two grabbed each other's forearms, in a well-practised handshake.

"Don't let it get you," said Tamay.

Guai Shou nodded again.

Without another word they parted ways.

I don't think they're following. I can't hear them.

If I can make it to the mountains, I'll be all right. No one can find me there.

I need a rest.

I can't have one. I need to go on.

I need to rest. There's no one behind me. I can rest for a little bit. I can't keep walking.

I sit down at the base of a tree. I must be far enough ahead.

I've left a trail.

There's a trail of blood behind me. Of course there is. I can't rest. I need to get up and keep going. They can follow me.

I'll stop bleeding soon. Then I can really get away. I need to keep going now.

The adrenalin is fading. It hurts. My legs are so heavy. But I need to keep going, one foot in front of the other.

Guai Shou knelt down and picked up some moss. He plugged his ears with it and then began his pursuit. He moved quickly and cautiously. He held his spear tightly, well-trained eyes and ears on the lookout for anything suspicious. It was an easy trail to follow. He only had one thought on his mind – to kill the freak.

I shouldn't have gone to that village.
Why do I go? Do I never learn my lesson?
It never goes well. I'm so stupid. I'm an idiot.
I was just so hungry. What can I do? They burnt down my home. I had nowhere to go.

"Why did it come here? I'll make sure it never goes anywhere again!" His foot got caught in the brush, and he jerked it violently free with a crash. He picked up the pace. There was a slight incline now. The creature was heading towards the mountains. That must be where it had its lair.

That must have been them. That was too loud to be a bird. They are following me. They're nearly here.
What can I do? I can't escape them. Not like this.
I'll have to fight. I'll have to stand my ground.
I can ambush them.
Yes! I can get them by surprise. I'll ambush them.

There had been a fairly clear trail of disturbance, but it stopped abruptly. That fact didn't escape the notice of the hunter. He slowed down, on high alert.

There's only one of them! Yes!
I can do this! I can do this.

He stepped slowly forward towards the end of the trail.

Wait... wait... wait...

There was blood on the trunk of the tree. Guai Shou looked up and instantly stepped back, his instincts taking over.

He's seen me! I waited too long! Idiot! Idiot!
I need to jump down. Now!

The creature jumped down from the tree. It landed heavily and staggered a bit. Guai Shou took the opportunity to lash out with his spear. It glanced off the monster's side, and he had to take a quick step back to avoid a frantic slash of claws. He stood, ready to strike, and the creature did the same.

He took the opportunity to take his first good look at the monster. It was pale, grey, and gaunt. Sharp claws and bared teeth were its weapons. It disturbed him. It was so animalistic – but so human too. Its eyes, its bright, wide eyes, flitting quickly back and forth from the spear to his own eyes. The piercing look it gave him made him feel dirty. His skin crawled, and he lashed out.

I dodge his spear. I can feel my side burn, but it's bearable.

The adrenaline is back.

I grab the shaft and pull. I'm stronger than him. I knew I was! He's stumbling forward. I can swipe at him.

Yes! Yes! A perfect opportunity.

Guai Shou let go of the spear and ducked. Predictable. He pulled a dagger from his belt and slashed at the creature's thigh. It screamed.

"KHAAAAAAAA!"

The sound was grating, primal but, for Guai Shou, muted by the moss in his ears. He was spared from the worst, but it still made him flinch.

I lunge forward, sink my teeth into his shoulder.

It's his turn to scream now!

I bite down even harder as he sticks his dagger into my wounded side. I can feel pain; I can taste blood.

Nothing else exists to me but those two sensations.

He twisted the dagger in the monster's side, but it kept biting. He dropped the dagger and grabbed at its face with both hands, trying frantically to prise apart its jaws.

He's not strong enough.

He wasn't strong enough.

I sink my claws into his face.

Guai Shou went limp. His legs gave way, and the two fell down. The creature still held him in its jaws. It didn't let go.

I need to be sure.
He's limp.
I need to be sure.
I don't think he's pretending. It's over. I can let go.
I let go.
I need to escape, properly this time. I need to go far away. I need to rest. I will heal. I always do.
I need to leave first. I need to walk away.
One foot in front of the other. One foot in front of the other. One foot in front…

The creature only made it a few steps before it, too, collapsed, exhausted.
Guai Shou lay completely still, deep in the woods.

Tamay came galloping into the village, Toky slung across her saddle. "Call the doctor!" Her voice was hoarse. "Call the doctor!"
There was an instant commotion, and a crowd formed. Toky's wife rushed forward, wailing. She put her head against his and muttered a prayer under her breath, again and again, through her tears.
The doctor came pushing through the crowd. Assertively, she called for him to be brought inside and to be given space.

I… What?
I get up and frantically look around. I'm alone. I'm alone. There's no one here. I must have passed out.

There's no one here except for him.

He's dead now; he must be.

I look at him again. His face is in shreds, but he must have been handsome.

I need to go.

I'm still looking. Why am I still looking?

I turn around and start walking. That rest was good for me. I can walk fine. It's getting dark. That's okay; I know the way back.

I can't go back. They'll come after me.

I need to go over the mountains.

What's over the mountains? I don't know. They're so tall.

I always knew I'd have to go, eventually.

The doctor worked as Toky's wife and Tamay stood helplessly watching. Time passed slowly.

After what felt like hours but was in fact only a few minutes, the doctor sighed with relief. "I think he's going to be okay."

Toky's wife let out a cry of relief and hugged the doctor tightly. The doctor hugged her back. Her shoulder was wet when she let go.

"Where's Guai Shou?" she asked.

Tamay hesitated, reluctant to speak.

"Where is he?" demanded the doctor.

"He went on alone."

"And you let him?" Suddenly the doctor was angry, outraged. "You let him chase that thing alone? After you saw what it did to Toky?"

"I—"

"You need to go after him!"

"I'll gather up some people."

"Take every horse we have and go! Go!"

Tamay nodded and left immediately.

"Where's Guai Shou's daughter?" asked the doctor.

It was Toky's wife's turn to hesitate. "I don't know. Earlier she was in the church, but she left. I don't know where she went."

It's steep here. But I can scramble up.

It was nighttime when they brought the body back. The doctor covered the young girl's eyes.

"But I prayed…" Her voice was quiet, broken, muffled by tears.

"I'm so sorry," said the doctor. "I'm so sorry."

There was nothing else she could say. They held each other tight.

Once I'm over this, I really am safe.
Over this ridge and…

"I'm alone," cried the girl.

I'm alone.

Zarachielith

Ashgrove, 4581

It was golden hour, and everything was bathed in warm light. The woman had her hood down. She knew it was supposed to be up, but there was nobody around. The hood limited her vision, and she wanted to take this opportunity to see, to really see. This might be her last chance to. She was about to do something that would make it difficult.

She stopped for a moment to appreciate the view: a small church on open grasslands which gave way to strong, healthy forest whose roots ran deep. The grasshopper band was playing their song, with a nightingale guest starring as the lead vocalist. It was an interesting mix of genres, but it worked. The starlings definitely approved – they danced along up and down and left and right, here and there and all around.

In a lot of ways, it was perfect. She breathed deeply, inhaling the fresh smell of the country. She squatted down to touch the grass, feeling it flow under her undulating hand. An old memory came to her mind, and it was dismissed with practiced skill. She stood and approached the church.

It was disused and had been for what looked like a very long time. There was an old, weathered sign on the gate, reading: 'DO NOT STEP ON THE CYCLAMENS!' She didn't need the sign to tell her. They were beautiful – nestled in the grass, a bright splash of pink on the green canvas. There's an ephemeral sort of beauty in all of nature, but these had more than anything else she'd ever seen.

The church had probably had a congregation of about a dozen. At one end was a stone altar. A single large candle stood upon it, plain wax, without any ornamentation or tray, about a foot and half tall, and six inches wide; an open book of prayers in front of it. It read:

'Oh, mighty gods, hear our words,
Oh, mighty gods, hear our words,
God of the Earth, provide us with bounty,
To assure that our plates never are empty.
God of the Sun, upon us shine bright,
So in your image, we may delight.
God of the Stars, let us be serendipitous,
And save the good from situations precipitous.
God of the Moon, spare us your wrath,
And we'll endeavour to always walk the right path.
Oh, mighty gods, hear our words,
Oh, mighty gods, hear our words.

She sneered. She hated that prayer, hated the gods, and everything they stood for. But what really bothered her about this one was how 'serendipitous' and 'precipitous' was such a forced rhyme. At least make your prayers well written.

The stained-glass window behind the altar had been smashed and badly boarded up. On the other end were three rows of wooden benches, and behind that a baptism well. In it was the feather of a crow and one small bone. Around it were dead butterflies. The floor was littered with them – at least a half dozen. She knew why. They came inside because it was warmer than the outside. Butterflies don't live long, so a lot of them died in there before making their way out. It didn't make it any less striking, though, or any less dramatically metaphorical. She smiled internally.

She took her place behind the altar. She cleared her throat and began to speak. Her words echoed through the church, and they felt powerful. Her voice was deeper than usual.

"I petition thee,
Thee that didst create the universe,
Thee that didst create the pretender gods,
Thou art Zarachielith: who no one hath seen.
The true god who doth not deceive.
Thou who hast power beyond our comprehension,
Thou dost decide who art mighty and who art feeble,
Those who art opulent or destitute, joyous or forlorn.
I am thy vessel, unto whom thou mayst bestow thy secrets.

Hear me Lo'Agathos, mighty daemon,
Fear thou me, for I am the blessed of Zarachielith.
Hear thy true name, Lo'Agathos, and fear me.
Hear me and make thine spirit subject unto me.
Be obedient unto me.
Thou, who art the scourge of the false gods,
The spells within your thoughts shall be mine.
The power within your soul shall be mine.
Hear me Lo'Agathos, mighty daemon, and fear me.

I petition thee, Zarachielith, the great and terrible god,
Who dwellest in the void beyond our ken,
To bind Lo'Agathos, base daemon, to my soul.

Hear me Zarachielith,
Hear me Lo'Agathos."

The last words bordered on a scream. She collapsed to the ground, drenched in sweat and lay there for some time. Eventually, she got up. It was dark by then.

As she was leaving, she stopped again to look at the cyclamens. She'd appreciated them before. Now they seemed to have a different quality to them. Without thinking, purely on an impulse, she crushed them under her boot. Regret washed over her for a brief moment, but she saw that they were still beautiful – a macabre beauty, a marred beauty, but all the more genuine because of it – as if she'd brought them into the real world from some distant Eden. Now that they were destroyed, they were perfect.

She put up her hood and left the churchyard. She felt power flowing through her.

Cakes and Rumours

The Capital, 4582

The room had large floor-to-ceiling windows looking out over the city. You couldn't see far through the smog, but despite that a woman stood looking out. She wore a long purple cape, with gold trim. It was, like the windows and the room they adorned, ostentatious. A second woman, dressed in the practical clothes of a soldier, approached.

"General," said the ostentatious woman without turning, "there's been rumours of a demon in the southeast."

"A demon?" asked the general.

"Yes."

A pause. "Are demons real?"

"No, they're not."

"What's this 'demon' been doing?"

"There's been conflicting reports. It seems like any misfortune that's happened over the past few months has been blamed on it: a missing child, a bad crop, dead livestock, that sort of thing."

"You think there's a group of bandits in the area?" asked the general. "Or is it just bad luck?"

The caped woman shrugged. "I'd guess bandits if I had to. But I don't have to. I'm sending you to find out."

"I'm going?" replied the general, with a lot less shock in her words than was in her feeling.

"Yes," confirmed the caped woman firmly. "I want to prove that I take them seriously, so I'm sending someone famous. Chances are it's nothing big, but it's not like you're busy anyway."

"That's true," admitted the general.

"And general?"

"Yes, ma'am?"

"Even though it's a load of nonsense, take their superstitions seriously. I want you to leave a good impression. The new king has caused a lot of damage to our relationship with the country people."

"I'll do my best, ma'am." Silence followed the statement, a silence that kept getting longer and longer. "Was that all ma'am?" the general ventured.

"Yes," replied the caped woman, "you're dismissed." Her gaze had never left the window.

"So, what did she want this time, general?" asked Ibra.

"We're going out to the country. There's been reports of a demon cutting about, and we're going to investigate," replied Fatima.

"A demon?"

"Yeah."

"Well, shiver me timbers! A demon!" said Ibra. He mimed a cartoonish panic. "I'd better brew myself a magic potion and pray to the sun for protection!"

"We have orders not to make fun of them as well, you dunce."

"It's all in good fun."

They looked at each other. Ibra was smiling. Fatima wasn't.

"Are you religious, Ibra?"

"No."

"Do you believe in demons?"

His expression changed. "I don't know. I… maybe? I don't think so."

"They don't exist here, in the capital. That's not in doubt. But you sometimes hear rumours, rumours from people you trust…"

He nodded. "Magic. Fairies. Monsters. Dragons. So why not demons?"

"So why not demons?" Fatima's gaze was intense.

Ibra averted his eyes.

"It is probably just bandits though."

"It's probably just bandits."

"I'm going to take three dozen soldiers, in addition to me and you."

"That should be plenty."

"Yes."

"When do we leave?"

"The day after tomorrow," she replied, "so you've got one more day."

He cocked his head and raised an eyebrow inquisitively.

She smiled and nodded. "Off you go."

As well as being second in command to the much-renowned General Fatima of the Royal Army, Ibra was a baker. He loved it. He owned a very popular bakery with his wife. They were always working on new recipes together, and their bakery was somewhat of a trendsetter in the capital. As he walked in the back door, his wife was putting the finishing touches on a truly remarkable cake.

"Don't move a muscle," she demanded, and he didn't. She was doing some very delicate piping work on a golden dragon. It had wrath in its countenance and rage in its eyes. It was breathing torrents of torrid white fire. It was mango flavoured. The torrents of torrid white fire were coconut. She had her tongue stuck out, as was her wont when she was really concentrating. "There we go," she said eventually. "All done."

"It looks incredible," said Ibra.

"You're a shameless flatterer," replied his wife.

"It's some of your finest work," he countered. "I'm impressed."

She smiled. "Thank you."

"I'm proud of you," he said. She smiled even wider as he continued, "This is the cake for the duke's son, isn't it?"

"It is."

"I think he'll love it. He's one lucky kid."

"Do you wanna get working on that honey cake prototype, and I'll get cracking on the frangipane tarts?"

"Sounds like a plan."

"What did the general have to say?"

"We're leaving the capital tomorrow."

"For how long?"

"I'm not sure. A few weeks maybe."

She stood in front of Ibra and held his face in her hands. "I'll miss you."

"I'll miss you too." He hugged her tight.

"Promise you won't get killed?" she asked.

"I promise," he replied.

"Promise you won't get maimed?"

"I promise."

"Promise you won't get stabbed?"

"I promise."

"Promise you won't—"

"I promise."

They did this little routine every time he went away. It was silly, but they enjoyed it, nonetheless. It put her mind at ease. They looked into each other's eyes. There was a twinkle in his and a twinkle in hers.

"Now get baking, my lovely; those recipes won't write themselves," she said good-naturedly, with a cheeky smile.

"Yes, ma'am!" he said, with a salute. They both laughed.

He'd been working on a new honey cake recipe for a while, and just couldn't get it right. He could make a good one. But good wasn't good enough. He wanted an incredible one. He wanted something new and exciting, and he felt like it was right on the tip of his wooden spoon. He worked on it for hours but went to bed frustrated.

He was frustrated in the morning, too. He hated riding and didn't really like his horse. He didn't like any horses, but this one especially got his goat, so to speak. His horse didn't seem to like him much either. Ibra's discomfort provided much entertainment to the others. Fatima raised an eyebrow as he jumped slightly. "It gave me a funny look, I swear," Ibra complained.

"A funny look?" asked Fatima.

"Yeah, like he was going to bite me."

"Most people who have to spend any time with you have that expression," said Rose from behind him, smirking.

Fatima laughed. "She has a point."

"No, she doesn't," said Ibra. "No human has ever looked at me like they were going to bite me."

"Not even your wife?"

"Well, maybe once or twice," he admitted. They all laughed at that. "But that's different. That doesn't change the fact that this horse is mean looking. You can't deny it."

Rose put her hands to her face dramatically, as if coming to a realisation. She gasped. "Maybe your horse is the demon!"

Ibra sneered at her.

"I'm being serious, Ibra! Where was he last week when that child went missing?"

"I wouldn't be surprised if he had eaten a child. Look at him!"

"The people out here probably can't tell the difference! Do they even have horses?"

Fatima brought her horse to a halt. The whole company stopped behind her, and the chattering that was happening suddenly came to a stop.

"What did I tell you two?"

Neither Ibra nor Rose replied. They looked like naughty school children being told off by the principal.

"I told you to show some respect. You think you're better than those people. You're not. This ends now. No more joking around. We're under orders to take these rumours seriously, but orders shouldn't be necessary – you should do it anyway."

"We were just joking, general. We—" Rose didn't get to finish.

"It stops now. And that applies to all of you," she said. She slowly and methodically looked every member of the company in the eye. There was silence the entire time. "You'll be compassionate to these people. Understood?"

A chorus of yeses came from the company. Fatima kicked her heels, and her horse started up again.

"She really expects us to take these backward bumpkins seriously?" muttered Rose to herself. "They're not worth saving, even if there was a demon." She didn't mutter very quietly.

Ibra turned around and looked at her with disappointment.

Fatima dismounted. "Come here," she said.

Rose dismounted too and walked up to her. Fatima was wearing leather gloves, with iron coverings over the knuckles. She took them off. With the back of her hand, she slapped Rose across the face, hard. It was loud, and Rose's face immediately reddened. Neither woman said a word, and they kept intense eye contact. Rose's eye was welling up, but she didn't look away.

Fatima broke the silence. "Don't speak like that again." She turned around, got on her horse, and resumed the journey.

Rose's eyes didn't leave her until the entire company had passed. Then she mounted up, too, and followed.

They spent that night at an inn.

"I really was joking earlier, you know," said Ibra. "I have no ill will towards these people."

"I know," said Fatima. "But Rose wasn't joking."

"She hates you."

"I think she does," said Fatima. "It might be a problem."

"If I'd known her attitude, I never would have invited her along."

"It's not your fault, Ibra. You can't have known."

"Why not send her home?"

"I'm hoping she'll learn a lesson."

"Maybe. Or maybe she'll just double down, become even more entrenched in her beliefs."

Fatima sighed. "What's her problem?"

"I don't know," replied Ibra.

A knock came at the door.

"Come in," said Fatima.

It was the innkeeper, and he'd brought two hearty-looking bowls of stew along with a large flagon of beer.

"Thank you very much," said Ibra, his stomach growling in concordance.

"Thank you," said Fatima, taking one of the offered bowls.

"I'm sure it's not up to the standards in the capital, ma'am, but it's quite popular around here. It's my grandfather's recipe. He ran this inn a long time ago. Then when he died, my father took over. And when he died, I took over. And I've been running things ever since. The secret is to let the rabbit sit in spices for three days before you throw it in the stew, that way—" He stopped himself. "Ah, but I shouldn't disturb you. My father always said I talked too much." He laughed a gentle laugh. "He used to say, 'Marvin, you do talk too much. You could talk the ears off a basset hound.' They have very big ears, you see, and so—" He caught himself. "And there I go again! I really do talk. But there is one thing I wanted to ask you. You see…"

"Ask away, Marvin," said Fatima. "Please, sit down."

He took an empty chair. "Well, you see, it's just nearby… recently, there's been rumours, you see. People have been talking, and people have been scared, you see. And seeing as you're soldiers, I thought I might ask you, you know?"

Ibra put down his spoon and began paying attention. "What sort of rumours?"

"Well, it started about two weeks ago. No, let me see, it was… twelve days ago. No, thirteen! Thirteen. So Walar Goll who lives on the edge of the village, you see, he woke up one morning, and his wall was gone."

Ibra and Fatima looked at each other. Fatima opened her mouth as if to say something, then closed it again, a little befuddled.

"I'm sorry?" asked Ibra.

"Just a great big hole in his house, you see. And now I think that's rather peculiar if you ask me. He came into the inn that night, and he ordered a bowl of stew. That same stew you're eating there yourselves. It's quite popular, you see. And he said to me, 'Marvin, I woke up this morning, and my wall had disappeared.' Of course I didn't believe him at first. No one did. But then a group of us went to see, and sure enough his wall was missing! It was mighty peculiar. A whole wall gone missing! Ain't that queer?"

"What do you mean by missing? Like knocked down?"

"Absolutely no trace of it! I'll tell you this free of charge: my jaw was on the floor. I kid you not! I turn to him, and I say 'Walar Goll, what happened to your wall?' I did. And he told me he didn't know! And then, now here's the peculiar part. That wasn't the only incident! A few days later, someone lost a chimney! And the day after that, someone lost a fence! This village won't have one thing left in it by the end of the month! Mark my words. Only the God of the Stars knows what's going on, and she's not telling!"

"And you'd like us to investigate?" asked Fatima.

"Well, a couple of members of the village saw you coming, you see, and they asked me to ask you to see if you could see about maybe looking into it. Of course, I'm sure you're too busy, your ladyship ma'am and your lordship Sir." He got up from his chair and bowed deeply.

Ibra looked over at Fatima.

She thought for a couple of moments. "We'll send most of our force ahead in the morning, but a half dozen will stay here for a few days to investigate. Ibra, you can lead them."

Marvin bowed even more deeply. "Thank you, ma'am; thank you so much. Just wait till I tell the folks downstairs. They'll be on the ale like it's Moringston eve! But to be perfectly honest, between me and you, you see, they're on it like it's Moringston eve most nights! Ha! Any excuse. It's very good for business, I must say. They're a very jolly group for the most part and— ah, but there I go again, talking your ears off. I'm sorry, I always talk too much! I'll leave you two in peace and go tell the folks downstairs! I'm so sorry for disturbing you, and thank you so much."

"You're welcome," said Ibra.

"Marvin?" asked Fatima.

"Yes, ma'am?"

"Once you've told the folk downstairs, would you like to join us while we eat? We've got business out of the way, and it'd be nice to have your company."

"Of course, ma'am." He blushed a little. "Although I'm not sure I'm the best company. I'll leave my daughter running the bar for the rest of the night."

"Bring up another flagon of beer," she said, passing him a gold coin. "And an extra glass."

The three of them had a great time, talking long into the night about nothing of much importance, probably much too long into the night.

Ibra woke the next morning to a loud banging on his door and an equally loud banging in his head. Fatima swung the door open. "I'm leaving you with five soldiers, including Rose. I want you to investigate what's been going on and then follow us up in no more than three days." Straight to business.

"How are you up so early?" he groaned.

"How are you not?" she asked. "Get up and get going! You've got a job to do!" She picked up a boot from by the door and threw it at him.

He wheezed as it landed on his chest. "Okay, okay, I'm getting up."

"I'm just about to leave. Good luck, Ibra."

"You too, general."

"Please do find out what's happening here. I'm curious."

"I'll do my best."

She nodded at him, and he nodded back.

After she'd left the room, he stretched, letting out a loud 'mmmhhhh' sound. He got dressed at a somewhat leisurely pace and went downstairs. Fatima was already gone, and his group of soldiers sat downstairs waiting for him.

"Ey! He's finally up."

"We've been waiting all morning!"

"What time do you call this, Ibra?"

"The sun's starting to set!"

"Okay, okay, I get it!" he said. He looked outside. It did seem to be past noon. "We're going to speak to a man called Walar Goll. He lives on the outskirts of town. I assume Fatima has briefed you?"

A chorus of agreement.

"Good. Then let's not waste any more time. Let's get going."

It wasn't a long way – the village was small. Mr Goll's house was nice, cosy, like the cottage you'd expect a wealthy grandparent to retire to. The garden was immaculately maintained and quite beautiful. The architecture was familiar, with a simple rectangular floor plan, and an arched roof. There was one thing about it that wasn't familiar, though, and that would be the lack of wall. On the side facing them as they approached, the entire wall was missing. Mr Goll had hung some sheets from the roof – for privacy, presumably.

What was just as strange was the fact that nothing else seemed affected. *Shouldn't the roof have collapsed? Shouldn't the flowers be disturbed? Shouldn't there be some signs of people?* All these thoughts ran through Ibra's mind as he knocked on the door.

The man answered, and he looked relieved to see the group of soldiers. "Have you come to help?" he asked, hopefully.

"Yes," replied Ibra. "We'll do our best."

"Oh, thank you! Thank you!"

"So, what exactly happened? Marvin told us your wall just… disappeared?"

"Exactly that. Not much to tell really. I woke up as usual, got out of bed – and there I was looking straight out at the garden!"

"Did you notice anything else unusual?"

Walar scratched his head. "Not really."

"Nothing at all?"

"I did have a very peculiar dream."

"What was it about?"

"There was a raven, a giant raven, the size of a house. It was wearing a crown. It flew back and forth across the sky, as if it was looking for something. It cawed and cawed until it was hoarse. It made me feel very sad."

"Do you think it's related to the wall?"

"I don't know… but it left me feeling very strange. It felt real."

"Has anything happened since?"

He shrugged. "Not really."

"Can we take a look?"

"Of course! Come in." He motioned in a friendly way and held the door open. "Oh," he said, "would you mind leaving your boots at the door?"

They all did, except for Rose. They crowded in the living room, and Walar reached up to pull down the sheets. Sure enough, there was nothing to see. Ibra reached out to where the wall should be, and his hand passed straight through. He wasn't sure what he was expecting to happen, but it still caught him by surprise a little.

"There was definitely a wall here before?"

"Yep."

"You're sure?"

"Pretty sure."

"A hundred percent?"

"Yes!" said Walar, exasperated. "A hundred percent!"

"There doesn't seem to be any signs of... well, anything really," said Willem, who was crouched down, looking at the ground. "The foundations are still there."

"Right," said Ibra, clasping his hands together. "I think we should split up. Polk, Shae, you go speak to the house that lost its chimney. Willem, Mara, you take the house with the missing fence. Rose, you and I can take a closer look around here. That's all we can do for the moment, I'm afraid, Mr Goll. I really have no idea how this happened."

"Well, gods bless you for trying," he said. "Thank you." He couldn't hide his disappointment.

"All right, let's meet up back at the inn by nightfall. Good luck."

"Good luck, captain," said Polk.

"Good luck!" said Willem.

Ibra and Rose went out through the door and back round to the outside. Ibra made awkward eye contact with Walar, who was sat inside on a chair. He smiled and nodded, before quickly averting his eyes.

He knelt down on the outside of the wall-hole. "There really is no sign of disturbance," he muttered to himself. "Nothing at all." There wasn't even a footstep in the dirt. He stood back up and looked all around. A small ridge overlooking the house caught his eye. "Let's climb up there, Rose. See if we can see anything."

Rose rolled her eyes but followed him as he turned to walk.

"So, what do you think?" asked Ibra, once they were out of earshot. "It's quite the mystery."

"Mystery? I think this is some kind of joke."

"What do you mean?"

"Well, it doesn't make any sense. There was probably never a wall there."

"Why would they lie?"

"Because they don't like us. They want to waste our time and make us look like fools."

"They've never given any indication they don't like us," Ibra pointed out.

"You can't trust them."

"I do trust them."

"Then you're naive."

"You think an entire village, that didn't even know we were coming, all agreed on the same lie together? Just to make us, some people they've never met, look stupid?"

"Well, what do you think happened?"

"I don't know, but I'll do my best to find out." They walked for a bit in silence. "There's only one thing I can think of at the moment."

"And what's that?"

"Magic."

"Because that makes so much sense?" Rose asked. "Instead of believing someone is lying to you, you believe in magic?"

"You must have heard the stories, the rumours."

"Of course I have, but that's all they are – stories and rumours. This sounds like wishful thinking, Ibra."

"If we act upon the assumption that they are telling the truth, which I am, it's the only answer I can think of. You can't just take someone's wall. That's absurd."

"Not as absurd as magic! I thought you were smarter than this, Ibra. You're starting to sound like the general. I thought you were your own man, not some puppet."

"What is your problem, Rose? Why are you so hostile to the people who live outside of the capital? Why are you—"

"It's none of your business!" she almost shouted.

"I think it's pretty relevant!" cried Ibra.

"It's none of your business," she said. She said it so bluntly, Ibra didn't dare reply. Another, very prickly, silence.

"Rose."

"Yes?"

"Can I ask you a favour? For the next few days – just for the next few days – can you operate under the assumption that they're telling us the truth? You're a very bright person, and I'd appreciate your help."

"Is that an order, captain?"

"No. I'm asking you as your friend, not as your commander."

"Why should I?"

"Please?"

"Do you have the authority to send me home?"

"No, only the general does."

"I'll play along if, when we regroup, you get her to send me home."

"I can't promise she'll allow it."

"She listens to you."

"I'll ask."

Rose held out her hand. "Deal?"

Ibra shook it. "Deal."

They were almost to the top of the ridge by now. Ibra looked back and could clearly see the house. There were wheat fields behind. On the outer side, there was a vegetable garden, a flower garden, and a path leading from the village to the wider world. It all looked very tranquil and, pertinently, completely undisturbed.

"So, what do you think has happened, then?" asked Ibra.

"Assuming the wall really has disappeared? I don't know. Not even a team of the most skilled masons from the capital could disassemble an entire wall overnight without leaving any trace or waking up the sleeping man that was just on the other side of it."

"I agree."

"And did you notice, at the corners where the missing wall would have met the other walls?" asked Rose.

"It was completely smooth," replied Ibra.

"Yes, I've seen stone cut that smooth before. But it takes a lot of time and skilled craftsmanship. I don't think it could have been done overnight. It would take at least a couple of days."

"But wouldn't Mr Goll have noticed?"

"He's old." Rose shrugged. "He frequents the tavern, and he doesn't strike me as overly observant."

"Sure, but do you really think he wouldn't have noticed a fraction of his wall was gone?"

"It seems unlikely."

"And what about the others? He isn't the only victim, remember."

"And so, if it wasn't done by a team of skilled labourers over the course of a few days, then what happened?" asked Rose.

"I don't know," admitted Ibra.

"You see how them lying to you makes the most sense?"

"Rose…"

"Okay, okay. Fine. Maybe when we meet up with the others later, they'll shed some light on it."

As they reached the top of the ridge, Ibra's eyes grew wide. He saw the remains of a crudely built fire and footprints in the mud. "Now this is a clue!" he cried. "See, we don't need the others," he said enthusiastically. "Someone camped here, not too recently. It could easily have been the night in question."

"That doesn't tell us anything about how it could have happened."

Ibra turned around and surveyed the area. "You can see the house from here, and the wall in question."

"So? You can't make a wall disappear by looking at it, Ibra."

He gave her a curious look.

"And don't you dare say magic. Since when do you believe in magic anyway?"

"I'm just keeping an open mind," he said. "Come on."

They followed the footprints. It hadn't rained recently, but it obviously had the night before the incident. The culprit had walked through at-the-time-wet mud which had dried solid since. It was the easiest tracking job they'd ever had. The person hadn't taken any care to be hidden or to even show any respect for nature. It was like a well-worn game trail. The footprints seemed to drag a bit. The perpetrator had a weird gait. The track took them over the other side of the ridge, across some fields, and straight towards a wide river.

"Of course," said Ibra. "Of course."

Rose smiled. "The world's dumbest criminal is going to get away from the great Captain Ibra."

"Not if I can help it. You wait here."

"You don't have to tell me that twice," replied Rose, taking a seat near the bank.

Ibra stuck his hand in the water. It wasn't very deep or very cold. He took off his boots and socks, rolled up his trousers, and began to wade across. It was shallow but murky, and you couldn't see the bottom. He took cautious step after cautious step. Luckily, it never got above knee height, and he made it to the other side unharmed.

"Loving the new style," shouted Rose from across the river.

His lower legs were caked in thick, wet mud.

"I can pull it off," he shouted back with confidence. Then, with a lot less confidence, "I think." He walked up and down the far bank, inspecting the underbrush carefully. "I can't see anything."

"Nothing?"

"Nothing." He sighed. "Let's head back. They could have left the river anywhere, so there's no point looking any more today. It'll be dark before too long."

He waded back across. He tried, quite unsuccessfully, to wash his feet in the river while sat on the bank. He dried them with his jumper, and put his boots back on, sans his socks.

"That looks uncomfortable," said Rose.

"What a shrewd observation," said Ibra. He sighed. "It is," he confirmed. "But I don't want to get my socks wet."

"We're going up and over a ridge," said Rose. "That's going to kill your feet."

"I'm not sure I thought this through that well."

"You'd better not complain."

"I won't." They weren't even to the base of the ridge when he did. He complained even more as they climbed over it. Halfway up, he decided he'd made a bad decision, so put on his socks anyway. "I'm going to have blisters."

"You're an idiot."

They climbed down and went back to the house. Ibra knocked, and Walar opened the door. He had another hopeful look on his face.

"You're back!" he said. "How did the search go?"

"We found something interesting. Is it all right if we ask you a few more questions quickly?"

"Of course! Come on in, and I'll put on some tea. Leave your shoes at the door."

Ibra paused for a moment. "I'm not sure taking off my shoes would leave things any cleaner. I appreciate the offer, but we can't stay long. The night of the incident, did you notice anything up on the ridge?"

"Nothing at all, but my eyesight's not what it used to be."

Rose gave Ibra an I-told-you-so look.

"What did you find?"

"A fire, probably from the day of. Is there any reason someone might be camping up there?"

"There's not really anything up there," Walar replied. "And the folks in the village are mighty friendly. Any traveller passing through could find shelter if they just asked."

"So, it's unlikely to be a coincidence?"

"I've never seen anyone camp there before."

Ibra steeled himself. "Mr Goll," he asked, "do you think magic might have been involved?"

"I didn't think they believed in magic where you're from." There was a hint of suspicion in his voice.

"Most people don't."

"I thought if I told you that, you'd laugh in my face."

"So, you do think it was magic?"

"Well, I'm not sure how else it could have happened."

"Would it be possible, if you were up on the ridge, to cast some sort of spell on your house?"

"I don't see why not. I don't really know much about magic though."

"Do you know someone that does?"

"There's a woman who lives in the village, Xīng Mèng. She knows things about magic and the gods. You should speak to her."

"Why haven't you?"

"She refused to speak to me – or anyone."

"Why's that?" asked Ibra.

"I don't know."

"What makes you think she'll speak to us?"

Walar shrugged. "Worth a try. She's the only person who knows anything about magic around here."

"Thank you for your help, Mr Goll," said Ibra.

"You're welcome. You sure you two don't want to stay for a cup of tea?"

"We need to head back to the inn."

"Oh, I see," he said laughing. He winked not-so-subtly. "You two young'uns have fun together."

"We're going to meet up with the rest of our squad," said Rose, sternly.

"Of course, of course," said the old man. He winked at Ibra again.

"Come on, Rose," said Ibra. "Thanks for your help, Walar."

"What was he implying?" Rose asked angrily as they made their way back.

"He was just having some fun," said Ibra. "He's old; he doesn't have anything better to do."

They rejoined the main road and came to the edge of the village.

"He believes in magic, even though he has no proof and no idea how it works. That's stupid. He's an idiot."

"Rose, can you stop? I thought we'd agreed."

"Are we really going to speak to this 'magic' woman?"

"How many times do we have to have this conversation? Just for these few days, open your mind up a little, yeah? Listen to what these people have to say. You don't have to believe it, but treat them with respect. He's a nice man. He helped us; he offered us tea, even after you tracked mud all throughout his house! Don't think I missed that."

"He's missing a wall! A bit of mud won't hurt."

"It's the principle!"

"I don't care what he thinks! And I don't care what you think, either."

"You're coming with me tomorrow. And unless you want to work with General Fatima for the rest of your life, you'll close your mouth and open your ears. We could be friends, me and you, good friends. It's a shame you're such a bigot."

"I'm not a bigot; I'm right!"

"Listen to yourself!"

Rose didn't reply. She walked straight to the inn, ignored the greetings of the rest of the squad, and went upstairs.

Ibra entered the inn shortly after.

"Is everything all right?" asked Polk cautiously.

"We had an argument." Ibra sighed.

"About what?"

"I'm sure you can guess."

"Ah," said Polk, "that."

"Let's leave her be for now. Let me tell you what we found." Ibra gave a summary, and the others listened attentively. "How about you? Willem, Mara, what did you find?"

"The next victim was a farmer. He lives about a ten-minute walk from Walar Goll," said Willem.

Mara pointed her finger at Ibra emphatically. "Along the river, I'd like to add."

"And more than that," continued Willem. "When we asked if anything weird had happened, he told us he'd had a dream."

"The exact same dream as the first guy!" exclaimed Mara. "Exactly the same! Big raven, sad feelings, and everything!"

"The woman we spoke to had that dream too," added Polk.

"All the night of the incident?" asked Ibra.

"Yep!" said Mara.

"Yes," confirmed Polk.

"Very interesting," said Ibra. "Anything else?"

"The woman we spoke to also didn't live far from the river. The missing chimney left no trace, just like with the wall. I'd be fairly confident in saying it's the same perpetrator. Although we kinda already guessed that," said Polk.

"Okay then," said Ibra. "So this is what I think. A single perpetrator is using the river to cover their tracks. Their motivation, we can only guess at, but they're going along to different houses and making things vanish. The man I spoke to believes it was done by magic, and I'm inclined to believe him. I intend to try and speak to this Xīng Mèng tomorrow, to ask her about magic and the significance of those dreams. Then tomorrow night, we'll split up and stand guard at different points along the river. This person has never hurt anyone, so I have no reason to believe we'd be in danger. Hopefully, we can catch them in the act and resolve this whole thing diplomatically."

He paused. "Now I know none of you probably believe in magic. And I'm not even sure if I do, but given the circumstances, it would make sense. So please humour me." He paused again. "Any questions?"

"I agree with you, Captain," said Mara.

"That's not a question," said Willem. "But I'm willing to give it a try too, Captain."

"I'm sceptical; I'll be honest," said Polk. She shrugged. "But you're the boss."

Shae gave an easy-going shrug, as if to say, "I don't care."

"Thank you," said Ibra. "I appreciate you all. Drinks on me tonight." That got a clamour of approving noises. *They're easily pleased,* he thought. Shae punched his arm affectionately.

"But do remember we have a job to do, so I want you all in bed at a reasonable time, right?" Another clamour of assent. This one he didn't really believe.

He waved across to Marvin at the bar, who came over. "Ibra! Good to see you again! You see I was just telling Anala over there… you see her right by the bar, drinking some beer? In the red jacket! Now she's my aunt's wife's sister's wife. We go way back, me and her! And I was just telling her what a great lot you are! You're all always welcome here! Always!"

"Thank you!" said Polk.

"We love you, Marvin!" shouted Mara.

"Why thank you very much, miss." He blushed a little. "Now, is there anything I can get you? We have beer – can't go wrong with beer. We have wine, and we have whisky. I know you're partial to some whisky, Ms. Shae." She gave a nod of approval. "And today's special is very special. We have our world famous – I'll say it again – world famous honey cake."

Ibra's ears perked up immediately. "Honey cake?"

"You heard me right, Ibra! This is a secret recipe passed down for generations! Two generations that is. My grandfather, who used to run this place, taught it to my father who taught it to me. We make it every time we can get our hands on good honey, which is getting hard these days, you know! It's expensive, very dear. Bees are getting very lazy these days. They need to put in a hard day's work like the rest of us I say. I'll tell you what, being a beekeeper must be pretty lucrative these days.

"Honey's worth every penny though. When you taste it, you'll see! Your mouth will thank your purse heartily. It's very, very good. My grandfather got the recipe from a mysterious traveller – a woman who'd come across the sea to the east, he said. Although last I heard there wasn't anything out the sea to the east, nothing but monsters I've heard. I'll keep both feet firmly on the ground, thank you very much! I won't be eaten by any sea monsters, that's for certain! No, thank you!"

"I'll have a slice of that cake please, Marvin," said Ibra.

The others gave their orders too, and Marvin went off to fulfil them. Before long he brought over a slice of the cake with some drinks. The cake was impressive. It was made of a dozen or so thin layers of cake, with honey icing piled on thick between each.

Ibra's eyes widened. "Marvin," he demanded, "tell me about this cake."

"He's a beauty, isn't he? It's very heavy on the honey, see. And all the layers? That gives you the perfect ratio of cake to icing, you see! The icing is made of cream and honey, and not any honey you know! Burnt honey. We cook it just until it just starts to smoke before we mix it in. And then the sponge is full of honey too! You can see how this one breaks the bank but boy is worth it!"

Ibra took some on his fork and put it in his mouth. His eyes widened further. His pupils dilated. It was perfect. The cake he'd been trying to find for so long, here it was! He took a moment to savour the flavour.

"He's looking at that cake the way he looks at his wife!" said Willem with a laugh.

"We're gonna have to tell her, boss," said Mara. "We have to. You can't be unfaithful to her like that."

"Shame on you!" said Willem.

"Shut up," Ibra snapped, with surprising severity. With equal intensity, he looked Marvin dead in the eye. "Marvin."

"Yes?" the barkeeper replied with no small amount of concern on his face.

Ibra took a deep breath in. "This cake is perfect."

Marvin visibly relaxed. "Thank you! I've always said it was the best thing we make here! I tell people all the time, 'You know, the best thing we sell here is our honey cake! You should try it.' And they're never disappointed. Not once. Well, actually, now I think about it, one person was, a very strange person. They said, 'Oh, I don't really like honey that much,' and I said, 'Well, I never, I've never met anyone who doesn't like honey before!' It was very strange."

"Marvin, my wife and I run a bakery in the capital. Would you like to come work for us?"

"What?" he replied, a little in disbelief. "Well, I'm flattered! I really am. But I quite like it here, you see, with my family and my friends. I don't really want to move away."

"Can I buy the recipe from you, then?" asked Ibra.

"Buy? Don't be silly. You know, I said it's a secret recipe but to be honest, it isn't really that secret. Half the village actually knows it. And for a good man like you? Free of charge, Ibra. Buy!" he chuckled to himself. "Buy! You're awfully generous."

"But if we sell it at our shop, we might make a lot of money from it."

"Good on you if you do! I don't think you'll be stealing customers from me out here! Ha! It's all the same to me."

"You're a good man, Marvin, but that just makes me want to pay you even more. How about if it's a success, I'll give you a cut of the profits?"

"Well, I suppose there are some people in the village who could use the help… Makena just adopted those two orphaned children. Terrible story, that! They lost their mother, poor things, and their father's not around. So Makena adopted them both! She's so kind, I've always said that. She never could stand by and watch as someone else struggled. But money is hard for her, see, so maybe I could help her out a bit… And then there's Alayah. She's the healer in the village, and sometimes when someone's sick… medicine is expensive to buy, you see, so she can't always help…"

"Marvin, you're a saint." Ibra stuck his hand out, offering a handshake. "You're taking half the profits."

"Well, I don't know what to say…" Under Ibra's expectant look, Marvin reluctantly shook his hand. "Thank you. It'll make a real difference to us here. To think our honey cake might make us rich!" He laughed. "But then again, I always knew it was the best around. Never doubted it, you see. Wait until I tell everyone!"

"One condition," interrupted Ibra.

"What's that?" asked Marvin tentatively.

"You have to promise to spend at least some of the money on yourself."

Marvin paused for a moment. "Well, there is this rare whiskey I like from up north…"

Ibra smiled wide. "That's the spirit, Marv!" Shae clapped him on the back.

"Thank you, Ibra." Marvin smiled back. He wrung his hands together. "Now, let me bring you all your drinks!"

Conversation flowed easily among the troops. They smiled and laughed for hours, until Ibra sent them all to bed. Rose heard it all from upstairs and hated them for it.

It was another late start for Ibra, who woke up around noon. Fatima wasn't there to get him, so he lay in bed a little longer, enjoying the comfort and the warmth. Suddenly, he remembered it was his job to be Fatima. He got dressed quickly and went round knocking on all of his squad members' rooms. He got no replies.

I'll grab breakfast and then try again, he thought. Sure enough, when he went downstairs, they were all waiting for him.

"Eyyy, he's finally up."

"We've been waiting all morning!"

"What time do you call this, Ibra?"

"The sun's starting to set!"

"Isn't that exactly what you said yesterday?" complained Ibra. They all sat around a table near the entrance except for Rose who was sitting alone on the next table. "You need to be more original."

Mara threw him a bread roll. "Come on, sleepy head, let's get cracking."

"I'm in charge here, remember," asserted Ibra.

"What are your orders?" asked Polk.

Ibra took a bite of the bread and thought for a moment. "Okay then," he said, "let's get cracking."

"Marvin gave us directions to this mystic's house," said Polk. "It's not far."

"Then lead the way." Ibra gestured to the door, and they all filed out. Rose was last, and he took her aside. "Rose…"

She looked at him, clearly unhappy with being stopped. "What?"

"How are you feeling?"

Her eyes burnt a hole in his for a moment, and then she kept walking. Ibra let out a sigh, then started walking too.

He caught up with Polk, who was in the lead. "I hope she agrees to speak with us," he said. "It's all very mysterious."

"I wonder why she's refused to speak to the villagers?" asked Polk.

"It's interesting, isn't it? The only person who might be able to help refuses to. Apparently, she's been nothing but accommodating in the past."

"Do you think she has something to do with it?"

"The thought had crossed my mind."

"Should we approach with that in mind? We could flank the house, surround her so she can't get away."

"We have no reason to be hostile. Nobody's been hurt, remember. I'd assume someone with magic powerful enough to destroy a wall has magic powerful enough to hurt someone. Even if she is responsible, we have no need to provoke her."

"So, you think she might be dangerous?"

"Potentially. But this is all speculation, remember. If magic exists, and she has it, and she's responsible for the incidents, and she has the ability to hurt us, and she decides to, then yes, she might be very dangerous." Ibra sighed. "But that's a lot of ifs."

"It is," agreed Polk.

"We won't use any sort of military tactics. We're just here for a chat, remember. We want her help, not to threaten her."

Polk nodded. "It's down here." She pointed to a well-worn path heading into the forest. They followed it for about a mile, before coming across a hut. The roof was covered in moss. The door was weathered, red, and round. The hut itself was wooden and octagonal. All sorts of herbs and mushrooms grew around it.

"Now this is a hut straight out of a fairy tale," said Mara. "I believe she's magic now."

"Because she has mushrooms in her front garden?" asked Willem.

"Yes."

"You're so simple."

"Image is important," said Mara. "Someone who looks like a witch either is a witch or is pretending to be one. Look at those mushrooms. They've been very carefully grown and harvested. That level of detail, it doesn't seem pretend."

"I didn't know you were a detective," said Willem.

"I am a detective," said Mara. "And I deduce you stink."

"Quiet you two," said Ibra. "Let me do the talking." He walked up and knocked on the door. He knocked lightly, but the sound was loud. *Louder than it should have been,* he thought. The door swung open, as if by itself.

"Goosebumps," said Mara, making no attempts to hide her excitement.

Taking that as an invitation, they entered. Rose took a moment to look closely at the door as she passed. They went down the hallway and into a small room. A strong smell of incense hit their noses. A woman sat behind a large table, around which there were six empty chairs.

"Sit," she said, motioning with her hand.

"Xīng Mèng, I presume?" asked Ibra.

"I am she."

Ibra took the seat directly opposite her. The others sat down around the table. "Could we ask you a few questions? We've been told you know about magic."

"I know of many things, Captain."

"We believe that these mysterious incidents in the village might be the work of magic."

"That belief is correct."

"How do you know?"

"The same way you do. Because there's nothing else it could possibly be."

"Your door opened by itself. Are you magic?"

"It was attached to some string," interrupted Rose. "It's a trick."

Xīng smiled. "How observant of you, dear. I don't have the gift of magic, no. In this age, it's become exceptionally rare. But" – she looked at Mara – "as you succinctly put it, presentation is important."

"So, you begin every meeting with a lie?" asked Rose.

"It's not a lie," said Xīng. "I never claimed it was magic. You only choose to believe it was."

"Come on." Rose rolled her eyes. "What do you expect?"

Xīng shrugged. "It can be hard for a woman to be taken seriously. Sometimes those short on intellect need to feel a little intimidated before they'll listen. Tricks like that make my job easier."

"Thank you for seeing us, Xīng," said Ibra, taking control of the conversation again. "Could you tell us about magic?"

"Magic was a gift given to humanity by the God of the Stars. She bestowed upon a lucky few the power to do things no one else could: manipulate the elements, foresee the future, distort time and space. An age ago, magic flourished. It was common and powerful. But for a long time, it's been in decay."

"What happened?"

Xīng smiled with sad eyes. "I'm afraid I don't know that. This is actually the first magic I've heard credible tell of in a very long time."

"Why did you refuse to help the villagers?"

"I was waiting for you."

"Why?"

"Because you're the ones who can solve this."

"We're planning on keeping watch at points along the river tonight."

"I know."

"Is this person dangerous?"

"Their magic is powerful. To make a stone wall disappear without a trace is no small feat. But I don't believe they bear us any ill will."

"Will you help us?"

"With my words."

Rose snorted contemptuously at that. Ibra gave her a dirty look, then continued.

"The night of the incidents, every victim had the same dream: a giant raven, a king, searching desperately for something."

"Ravens are prophetic. They're also mischievous. I wouldn't take anything they say at face value. The perpetrator may be searching for something, but there may be more to it. Let me research it. Come back tomorrow, and I'll tell you what I've found."

"We can't stay past tomorrow. We need to rejoin the rest of our company."

"Then I'm afraid I can't help you."

"How convenient," said Rose.

A thought crossed Ibra's mind. "Do you know anything about demons?" he asked.

Xīng's eyes darkened. "Why do you ask?"

"The reason we're out here at all is to investigate rumours of a demon. The rest of our party went ahead to the east. The reports aren't from close to here, but maybe there's some connection?"

Xīng sighed. "Together, the God of the Sun and the God of the Earth created all life we know: the grass, the trees, the fish, the birds, the smallest louse, the biggest whale. And they made us: man, woman, and everything between.

But creating all life is no small feat. While they were busy, things that don't belong here slipped in, things from the outside. These things, born from twisted nightmares, found their way here through secret paths. We call them demons. I hope for the sake of your comrades, and all of us, that those are only rumours and nothing more."

The squad looked uneasily at each other. "I hope that's the case too," said Ibra. He stood up. "Thank you for your help. We left it too late to come here, so we must be off. We need to prepare for tonight."

"Keep your wits about you," said Xīng.

Ibra nodded.

"Before you go, I'd like to speak with Rose, alone."

They all turned to look at Rose, expectantly. She said nothing, but didn't get up to leave.

"We'll leave you to it," said Ibra. "But try to be quick."

Xīng looked at Rose expectantly.

The latter was irked. "Well?"

Xīng pulled a tarot deck from beneath the table. "I'd like to read your fortune, if you'd permit it."

"Fortune telling is mumbo-jumbo."

"Humour me," said Xīng dryly.

"A deck of cards is going to tell my future?" asked Rose sarcastically.

"Maybe," said Xīng, "or maybe not. The past, the present, the future, all are forms of the self. If you can learn of the self, you can learn of them all – or maybe learn nothing at all. It depends on the hand." She began to shuffle with obvious skill. "Do you know how many ways a deck of cards can be ordered?"

Rose shook her head.

"Neither do I, exactly. That's a question for the mathematicians. What I do know is that the number is mind bogglingly large. Why do you think, Rose, the cards end up in the order they do?"

"Because of the way your hands move."

"My hands are old and weathered. I have no control over how the cards move."

"A skilled dealer can rig a deck."

Xīng stopped shuffling and handed Rose the cards. "Shuffle for yourself," she said, and Rose did. She dealt very roughly, with no skill. "The correct answer to that question," continued Xīng, "is fate."

"It's pure chance." Rose handed the cards back. "Now let's get this over with."

Xīng turned over the top card. "The ace of cups, reversed. You've felt a great loss. There's an emptiness inside you, which you don't think can ever be refilled."

"How generic."

She looked up from the card and into Rose's eyes. "A hole can always be refilled. When we cry, Rose, cry until we can't any more, the reservoir inside us runs dry. Filling it up again isn't easy. It takes much longer than emptying it, but it's always possible, even if it's one drop at a time."

Rose snorted.

"Your mother would want you to at least try."

Rose sat up straight in her chair. "What did you say?" she asked.

Xīng turned over the next card. "The high priestess."

"What did you say?" repeated Rose.

Xīng ignored her again. "The high priestess is the card of magic. But you know that already, don't you?" It was Rose's turn to ignore a question. Xīng answered for her. "You know the high priestess well. Her blood flows in your veins."

"No," said Rose through gritted teeth, "it doesn't."

"That's not what she thought."

"She was a fool."

"Was she?"

"Yes," she replied bluntly. "It was thinking that way that killed her."

Xīng drew the next card. "The four of cups, reversed. Clarity, acceptance, and choosing happiness."

"You can't choose to be happy."

"Not directly, no. But you can choose to make decisions that'll make you happier."

"Like what?"

"Like forgiving."

"I was eight, Xīng," shouted Rose, furiously impassioned. "Eight! And she left me all alone!"

"It wasn't her fault."

"Yes, it was!"

"It wasn't."

"You don't know anything!"

"Tonight, Rose," said Xīng calmly, "you will see that magic is real. You can accept that it wasn't her beliefs that killed your mother. You can accept that she wasn't to blame and start to move on. That is how you choose to be happy."

Ibra, Mara, Willem, Polk, and Shae waited outside for a long time. They didn't talk much. Each was thinking about what they'd just heard. They'd all heard things of the sort before in fairy tales and myths, always presented as fictional, in times long passed – never in the here and now. Mara was completely convinced. Polk and Willem were still sceptical. Shae was indifferent.

No matter the facts, Ibra, deep in his heart, wanted it to be true. He wanted to live in the world of the stories. And so, for now at least, he was choosing to. He took every word he'd been told as fact.

The door swung open, and Rose stormed out, visibly furious.

"Rosey!" shouted Mara, apparently deciding to ignore the look on Rose's face.

Her brows furrowed and her jaw tensed. "What?" she snapped, harshly.

Mara was visibly taken aback. "I'm sorry…"

Rose turned to Ibra. "I'm going back to the inn."

Ibra nodded, knowing better than to deny her. He watched every step she took as she left. No one said anything until she was out of earshot.

"What's her problem?" asked Mara.

"You're annoying," said Willem. Shae gave a knowing nod.

"I wonder what they talked about?" asked Polk.

"Me too, Polk," mused Ibra. "Me too."

They spent the rest of the afternoon gathering information about the terrain from the locals and scouting along the river. Together they decided on five spots they wanted to watch, and a possible sixth.

"Maybe we should give her the night off," said Willem. "Seems she could use it."

Ibra sighed deeply. "We need to rejoin the general soon, remember. We only have this one night. We could use her help if we actually want to catch this sorcerer."

"So, we're suddenly sure it's a sorcerer then?" asked Polk. "Because I've been thinking about it, and to be honest, I'm not sure that woman really told us anything we didn't already know. She's good at sounding mysterious, sounding like she knows things. But what did she actually tell us?"

"We're not sure of anything yet, Polk, but hopefully we will be tonight." Ibra stood up. "I'm going to talk to Rose, then we're heading out."

He hesitated, then knocked on her door. A monotonous voice came from behind it. "It's open."

He walked in. She was lying on the bed fully dressed in her armour, staring at the ceiling. "Rose, will you stand guard tonight?" he asked.

"Yes, Captain." She didn't turn her head.

"Come downstairs when you're ready."

"Yes, Captain."

Ibra looked up to the ceiling, half-expecting to find something there. It was plain, but her eyes were fixed on it. He suddenly changed his mind. "You don't have to come, if you don't want to."

Silence.

"I'll speak to the general no matter what. It's for the best, I think."

"I'll come, Captain," she said.

"You're sure?" he asked awkwardly.

"Yes."

"Okay." His tone was warm. "Thank you. We'll be waiting downstairs."

She came down as they were making some last-minute adjustments. The map they'd borrowed from Marvin was full of pins. It was crude but served the purpose. Ibra gave Rose a nod, as did Shae.

Ibra pointed at a pin. "Polk." Then to the next. "Mara." Then to the next four. "Willem. Shae. Rose. Me." He smiled. "We all had a lie in, so staying awake shouldn't be too hard. We should keep watch until dawn. Then we'll meet back here." He gestured to a pile of torches on the table. "The moon should be bright, but take one of these anyway, just in case. Keep your wits about you. Don't take any unnecessary risks, but do approach the culprit if you see them. Diplomacy is the aim, not violence. Understood?"

Nods all around.

"Good. Good luck to you all."

Rose sat alone on the bank of the river. The sky was clear, and the moon was near full. Everything was bathed in silvery light. The farmhouse she was watching was quaint. She suddenly wished she knew how to paint. It was really quite beautiful. She wanted to be able to set up an easel and capture what she saw, not just the view but the feeling of it too. Every brush stroke transforming what would otherwise have been just a memory into a tangible, real thing. The country did have some appeal, she had to admit.

She was lost in reverie – until she heard a cough. She shot up, put her hand to the hilt of her sword, and spun around, every muscle tense. Standing in front of her was a little boy. Her hand left her sword, and she relaxed.

"Hello," she said.

He said nothing.

She looked at him more closely. His face made her feel uneasy. It didn't seem quite proportioned right, like he was wearing a badly drawn mask. He was wearing a thick cloak made of dark feathers, and boots that were visibly too big.

She put her hand back on the hilt of her sword. "Who are you?" she asked warily.

He rummaged through his pockets and brought out a small carving. He held it out to her, and she took it. As she did, her finger brushed against his, and it was like ice. She examined the carving. It was crude, in a way, but a work of no small skill. It was a raven.

"I'm trying to go home," he said. "But I can't find my way. My parents are very worried."

Rose stared at him. "Where do you live?" she asked.

"I don't know," he said. "But the way back is around here somewhere. Will you help me find it?"

"How did you get out here?"

"I found a secret path. But I don't like it here. The air is funny. It smells. Will you help me?"

Rose hesitated for a moment. Everything in her body was telling her something was off. *It's just a kid,* she thought. *It's just a kid.* She kept her guard up but forced a smile. "I'll help you."

"It was next to a tree, I think. This really funny tree. It was growing sideways."

"I passed a tree like that on my way here," said Rose.

He smiled a wide, open-mouthed smile. A cloud came across the moon, and his teeth disappeared. They were gone, just for a fraction of a second, flickered in and out of existence. Rose's conscious mind told itself it'd seen a trick of the light.

"Can you take me?" he asked sweetly.

She looked back at the farmhouse. She'd not seen anything all night. "I'll take you back to the inn. Do you know Marvin?"

"Can you take me to the tree?"

"It's on the way to the inn."

"Thank you, Rose."

She was well aware she'd never told him her name. Her grip on the sword tightened. She was prepared to use it. The boy seemed to take no notice at all. With the raven in her left hand, she led the way. The boy walked beside her.

He was wraithlike. The only part of him that felt grounded was his boots, dragging slightly along the floor as he walked. She recognised the gait from the footsteps by the campfire on the ridge. It was as if he was guessing how to walk and didn't really know. His arms didn't swing; they stayed straight down by his sides.

Looking at him made her uneasy. She walked with eyes fixed forwards. A nagging feeling in the back of her mind wanted her to look though – to stare and never look away. Rose glanced over, and his whole form blinked. She was sure of it this time. The image of the boy disappeared for a moment, then reappeared. Her instincts told her to run, that this wasn't right. This wasn't a boy. This was something taking the form of a boy, and she was scared. She told herself that wasn't possible but didn't believe her own words.

They walked in silence, along the river. It took a slight turn, gurgling as it flowed. It was the same serene scene that had held her captive earlier, but it brought her no joy now. It felt eerie; her perspective had shifted. The shadows seemed to move, and the sound the torch in her belt made as she walked was deafeningly loud. It clunked, and she began taking uneven steps in an attempt to mitigate it. She looked down in order to readjust, and suddenly she saw motion from the corner of her eye and heard a yell that made the clanking of her torch seem like a whisper.

She drew her sword in an instant and turned to the side, slashing blindly. Every muscle was full of adrenaline, and her brain was in the wild sort of panic she'd only ever felt before on the battlefield.

"Ow," said the boy. Her sword hit thin air. The boy had fallen over and was safely below the swing. He'd gone face first into the muddy grass. "Ow," he said again.

Rose held onto her sword, heart beating in her ears. Her hands were shaking. The boy lay completely defenceless on the ground. She pointed her sword at his back. She breathed in, deeply and slowly. Her mind was racing, and time seemed to slow as she considered the possibilities.

She put her sword away.

"Are you okay?" she asked the boy.

The boy lifted his head from the ground, struggled a bit, and got up to his knees. He was completely clean. He sniffled a bit, then said, "I'm okay. Just clumsy." He sniffled again.

Rose vacantly replied, "it's all right," then carried on walking more quickly this time. The boy followed behind, struggling to keep pace.

As they followed another bend in the river, they came to the tree. It was a willow, and the trunk was bent. It had started its life growing vertically but then decided that the ordinary life wasn't for it. It curved and twisted over the river until it was near horizontal.

To Rose it was just a nice tree, but the boy was excited. "Yes! Yes! This was it! This is the tree! I remember!" He turned to her. "Thank you, Rose! Thank you!" He rushed to place his hand on the trunk. "This is it!"

The boy took a few steps back. He held his hands out in front of him, facing the tree. A look of concentration came over his face. A small blue sphere came from his palms. It began moving slowly towards the tree. Rose watched in horror.

It had made it halfway when the boy winced. The sphere went haywire. It accelerated madly, stopped, changed direction, then accelerated madly again. It went into the forest and hit a spruce. The sphere disappeared completely and took the tree with it. It seemed to fold in upon itself.

The boy looked frustrated. "I've been practising, but I'm still no good at it." His voice was whiny. "It's hard."

Rose watched in silence as he took position again. He put his hands out and then brought them in again. He took a big step to his left. Then a small one back to the right. He bent his knees a little. From his point of view, the top branch of the tree was just touching the moon. This seemed to satisfy him, and he took his stance again. Another sphere left his palms, and this one kept true. It seemed to hit something invisible in front of the tree, and flattened into a disc. Like a dilating pupil, it grew. It grew in two dimensions of Rose's world and two dimensions of another, until it was just taller than the child.

"Yes!" shouted the boy. "I knew I could do it!" He spun all the way around and waved his hands awkwardly in the air. "Yes! Thank you, Rose."

She said nothing, only watched with awe and confusion and hatred in her eyes. Her emotions were lost on him.

"I'm going to go," he said. "Nice to meet you, Rose!" She held out her hand, the one holding the carving. "Keep it," he said. "It's a present."

He stepped through the circle, and it closed after him. The boots stayed behind.

Rose sat down. She sat with her back against a tree, watching the boots. She sat for a very long time. Then, she got up, threw the carving as hard as she could into the river and headed back to the inn.

She was the last back. The inn was closed, and the only light was a candle on the table the squad sat around. Everyone except for Ibra and Polk was asleep. The two were talking quietly but stopped as the door opened.

"Rose!" said Ibra in a whispered shout. "We were about to go after you. Did something happen?"

"No," she said with complete confidence. "Nothing to report; I just lost track of time. Did any of you see anything?"

Ibra looked disappointed. "We didn't see anything," Polk confirmed.

Rose smiled mockingly. "I'm not surprised."

"Leave it," said Polk.

"We're leaving later today," said Ibra, defeated. "Go get some sleep."

"I'm sorry we didn't find anything, Ibra," said Polk as Rose went upstairs. "I know you really wanted to."

"Maybe she was right all along, and they were lying to us."

"Maybe. Maybe not. We can ask around tomorrow to see if anything else has gone missing in the places we didn't watch."

"We can ask. But nothing happened last night either. Nothing has happened since we've been here."

Polk looked sympathetic. "Maybe we just scared them off?"

"Maybe," said Ibra.

Polk clapped her hand on Ibra's shoulder. "Let's go to bed too," she said.

They asked Marvin in the morning if he'd heard of any more incidents. He said that he hadn't and was very happy about it. He thanked Ibra heartily, said they must have scared off the perpetrator.

They marched for three full days without talking much before they caught up to the general. The mood all around was low, and the journey had been long. The minutes had passed as hours, but they made it eventually.

When Ibra went to speak with the general, she saw immediately that things hadn't gone to plan. "I'm guessing," she said, "by the look on your face, that you didn't solve the mystery of the disappearing wall."

"I didn't," said Ibra. "Even worse than that, I made myself look like an idiot in front of the troops."

"What happened?"

"I let myself believe in magic. I thought it was the only way it could have happened. I told the whole squad that was it. And then we didn't find any proof of anything."

"Did you prove for sure it wasn't magic?"

"No, we still have no idea how it was done. It stopped happening, though."

"So, it could have been magic?"

"I suppose so."

"Ibra?"

"Yes, General?"

"I thought it could have been magic too."

He gave her a sad, thankful smile, which faded quickly. "Rose and I argued. She got a lot worse."

"Leaving her with you was a mistake, then," General Fatima admitted. "I'm sorry."

"I promised her I'd ask you if she could transfer to another commander."

Fatima nodded. "I'll organise it when I get back," she said.

"It's sad, the way she acts."

"It is. I was really hoping she'd learn something."

"Me too," agreed Ibra. "How has it been going here?"

"We've not found anything either. Nothing out of the ordinary has happened since we arrived or for weeks prior. The report got to us late apparently."

Ibra snorted. "Why am I not surprised?"

"We'll stay here another day, so you and your squad can rest up. Then we'll go home. I'll leave behind a half dozen soldiers for a few weeks, just to keep an eye on things."

"Sensible."

"I thought so."

Ibra smiled, more genuinely this time. "So, you didn't get to add demon slayer to your list of achievements then?"

"There's still time," she said, smiling back. "'Fatima, slayer of demons' has quite the ring to it I think."

"There was one silver lining to this mission," said Ibra.

"There was?" asked Fatima.

"I found the recipe that I've been looking for, for so long."

Fatima looked impressed. "You finally got that honey cake?"

Ibra's wife took a bite and let out a very satisfied, "Mmmmm." Once her mouth was empty, she formulated that sentiment into words, not overly eloquent words but appropriately conveying the feeling anyway. "That's bloody delicious!" she said.

"I know, right," said Ibra. "It's what I was trying to make this whole time."

"It's getting hard to come by honey these days," she said. "It's expensive."

Ibra shrugged. "There's enough rich people in this city to buy it from us. We can make a pretty good margin on it I reckon. Especially if it becomes popular."

"I'm not even sure there's enough honey in the world for it if it becomes popular."

"Then we drive the price up even higher," Ibra smiled. "I want this cake to make a lot of money – for Marvin."

"You're such a softie," she said, approvingly.

"I know," he said with a smile.

It was easy for him to forget his disappointment when he was busy with the people he loved, but it kept him up at night sometimes. On occasion he'd daydream about how things might have turned out differently, about a world where the stories were true.

The Bears

The Grounds of Duke Harmire's Estate, 4583

"I kinda like it, you know," said Nita.

"It's stupid," said Ayiq.

"It's not. It's intimidating, imposing. We've got a reputation."

"We don't want a reputation. We're not doing this for fame. We're doing it to survive."

"Well, like it or not," said Orso, "we're The Bears now."

"I know a group of men from the pub called The Bears," said Dubu with a snort. "They're a little different from us. Great guys though."

"This is serious, Dubu," said Ayiq. "If people are aware of us, it makes our job a lot harder. They might even start looking for us."

"I was being serious," said Dubu with a grin. "And we're good at what we do. We don't have to worry about a couple of extra guards here and there. It'll just give me more of a chance to show off my martial arts."

"Your 'martial arts' almost got us all killed!" said Ayiq. "You're—"

"Stop squabbling," said Orso, "and listen."

The two fell quiet. There were four people sat with her around the campfire, and they were all eager to hear what she had to say.

"This will be the biggest heist yet," she said. "We're hitting the Duke."

"Yes!" squealed Nita.

"About time!" said Dubu.

"Everything we've done so far is small fry compared to this. This risk will be bigger, and the reward, bigger still. The Duke has the biggest apiary ever built, a hundred hives worth of honey."

Dubu whistled. "Sweet."

"Stop interrupting, Dubu, you imbecile," said Ayiq.

Nita giggled at Dubu's pun. He'd used it a dozen times already, but it was always entertaining to see Ayiq get wound up.

"I sent Espen out to scout yesterday," said Orso. She gestured in their direction. "Tell us what you saw."

"The apiary is near the forest. The hives are surrounded by a low wall. There's a guard post, typically manned by two guards, which has a large bell. All of the sites outside the main complex of the Duke's palace have a guard station like this. The lumber mill, the water mill, the orchard, the dock. There are smaller guard posts, each with a single soldier, at regular intervals between these places and the palace. If there's any trouble, they ring the bell. Then the next post along rings their bell, and so on in a relay until it reaches the barracks. Then, the entire guard will come rushing out. There are three of these guard posts between the apiary and the palace.

"Subduing the two guards in the apiary before one of them can ring the bell might be difficult. I suggest we split up. Two people go to the next guard post, take out the guard there, and break the chain. That way if the apiary guards do ring the bell, there'll be no one around to hear it. The rest of us can then take the apiary without trouble. We'll all reconvene, collect the honey, and be gone before anyone knows what's happened."

"Brilliant as always, Espen," said Orso with a proud smile.

They nodded. "Thank you, boss."

"Nita and Dubu, you'll subdue the lone guard. Ayiq, Espen, and I will go to the apiary. Any questions?" asked Orso.

Ayiq raised his hand. Orso nodded at him, and he spoke. "How will we know when or if, rather, those two jesters have succeeded?"

"Nita, when you're successful, do the screech of a barn owl. Three times in succession, with the first and last being long, and the middle being brief."

"Like this?" asked Nitta. She did exactly as Orso had described, in an eerily accurate impression.

"It weirds me out how good you are at screeching," said Ayiq.

"Thank you," said Nita, giving him her sweetest smile. "That's why I practise so much."

"And if they get caught?" said Ayiq.

"If at any point the bells go off, we abandon the mission."

"Well, it sounds straightforward enough," said Dubu. "When do we" – he paused to make karate chop motions with his hands – "strike?"

"The moon will be full in three days. If it isn't cloudy, then that's the best time," said Espen.

"The Bears are going hunting," said Orso.

Nita made a growling sound. Dubu followed. Orso and Espen joined in.

"I hate you all," said Ayiq. He joined in with a little 'grr' of his own.

Dubu poked his head up above the undergrowth, watching the guard at his post. He dropped back down.

"We're so good at being surreptitious," he whispered.

"Damn straight we are," Nita whispered back. They fist-bumped.

"He looks kinda bored."

"Can't blame him. His job is to sit alone in the dark."

"I might become a guard once we're done with all this," said Dubu. "I could sit about in the dark. Easy-peasy."

Nita smiled. "Not tonight, it isn't."

"Good point," Dubu conceded. "It's less easy when you have to face the wrath of Dubu and Nita."

"Considerably less easy. Very difficult in fact."

"Incredibly difficult. Nigh on impossible."

"Gruelling."

"Insurmountable."

"Unthinkable, really."

They grinned at each other.

"Should we get to it?" asked Nita.

"Yes," said Dubu.

Nita snuck through the undergrowth, so she was on the opposite side of the guard to Dubu. She started barking like a dog, a very big and angry dog – a very big and angry hungry dog.

The guard was instantly at attention and wishing he could go back to being bored. His eyes scanned the brush. He drew his sword from its sheath, eyes straight ahead. Nita barked again. This time he saw her.

"Hey!" he shouted.

But too late. Dubu was already behind him. He hit the guard's sword hand with a club, causing him to drop his weapon.

Then, he grabbed the guard from behind. Nita ran up, and between them they tied him up, and gagged him.

"Easy-peasy," said Nita. They high fived.

"Easy-peasy," said Dubu. He knelt down in front of the guard and put a hand on his shoulder. "I'm sorry, fella. I know you were only doing your job." The guard made a noise suggesting he didn't really appreciate the sympathy.

Nita sent the signal. They'd been successful.

A barn owl screeched. Once, then again briefly, and then for a third time.

"What if that is an actual owl?" asked Ayiq.

"Then we're very unlucky," said Orso. "Come on, let's go." The two of them walked straight up to the guards. "Excuse me," said Orso. "I think we've gotten a bit lost. My husband and I went out for a late-night walk, and now we don't really know where we are."

"A late-night walk?" said one of the guards, raising an eyebrow.

"Can't take two steps without walking into a child or an in-law in our house," explained Orso.

"We wanted some privacy," said Ayiq.

"Ahh, I see," said the guard, looking at his partner with a smile. "That kind of late-night walk, ey?"

"Got a bit carried away during this walk, did you? I can't imagine you have much time for 'walking' at home in such a busy house," said the second guard with a wink.

Ayiq blushed, and Orso heartily agreed.

"Where abouts are you–"

He was rudely interrupted by Espen, who grabbed him from behind. Ayiq and Orso rushed the other guard, and before they knew what hit them, both guards were bound and gagged.

"Husband and wife?" asked Espen. "Didn't expect that one."

Orso smiled. "A good way to seem non intimidating, I thought."

"Not to Ayiq."

Orso and Espen laughed, and Ayiq blushed a bit deeper.

"Let's not waste any time," he said. "We should get started."

"The other two should be along soon," said Orso. "Espen, you wait here for Nita and Dubu; we'll go grab the equipment."

"Good job, you two," said Espen, as Nita and Dubu arrived.

"Good job to you as well!" said Nita. "Looks like it's gone off without a hitch."

"We're going to be rich, babyyy," shouted Dubu quietly. "Let's get this golden gold."

"Orso and Ayiq are just bringing the equipment. We stashed it a little way back."

"Smart," said Dubu.

"This guard," said Espen, "had the key to the beekeepers' shed." They pointed to a small building just behind them. "Let's check it out."

It was a very good shed. They had bellows, for blowing smoke to pacify the bees. They had beekeeping suits. They had pots for storage.

"Looks like we didn't even need to bring our own equipment," remarked Dubu.

"And Orso and Ayiq are carrying all that stuff as we speak!" said Nita in fake outrage.

"Those poor souls!" said Dubu in fake sympathy.

"They pretended to be husband and wife, you know, when they were distracting the guards," said Espen.

"No!" said Nita.

"Really?" asked Dubu.

"It was all Orso's idea, I think," said Espen. "You should have seen Ayiq. He turned bright red."

"Now that I would have liked to see," said Dubu.

"Do you think she—" Nita stopped abruptly as she heard footsteps.

"Good job, you two," said Orso when she got a little closer.

"Thanks!" said Dubu and Nita in unison.

"Check out this shed, boss," said Espen.

Orso looked inside. "You're joking," she said. "Don't show Ayiq; he'll be furious." She glanced over her shoulder. "Shut it, quick!"

"Anything good in there?" Ayiq grunted. He couldn't see much over the tall pile of equipment he was holding in his hands.

"Nope," said Espen.

"No surprise there," he said, putting down the equipment with a huff.

"Okay, let's get started," said Orso. "Espen, you keep watch. The rest of us will start collecting."

"I'll go fetch another batch of jars," said Ayiq. "We'll need them."

"Good idea," said Nita, stealing a glance with Dubu, and hiding a smirk.

"Make that two lots," added Orso. After Ayiq left, Espen raised an eyebrow at Orso. "Hey, I can have fun sometimes too," she said, with a small blush.

"We're still in the middle of a mission," they said disapprovingly.

"Then let's stop chatting and get working," said Nita.

And they did. They'd become very good at harvesting honey. They did it quickly and efficiently. Jar after jar was filled with the stuff – the very, very valuable stuff. The initial adrenaline of the heist had worn off, and now it was just business.

Suddenly, there was a clamour of shouting. Espen came rushing back. "Run!" they screamed. There were a dozen guards on their tail, well armed, angry, and looking for glory. The Bears dropped everything and followed their comrade's order. They split off in different directions, frantically running, trying to get to the forest. The guards, in their heavy armour, were slow.

Except for one, that was. The guard on Dubu's tail ran like a champion athlete. He was closing in. Dubu made it to the treeline but stumbled. He fell hard, his face smashing into a root. The guard stood over him, weapon in hand. Dubu grabbed a large branch and got up swinging. The improvised weapon hit the guard in the temple. The branch snapped with a sickening crack, and the guard fell to the ground. Dubu kept on running. He didn't see how still the guard was lying; he just kept running.

They all met, later, at the same clearing where they'd made their plans. There was no good humour. They all knew what this meant.

"It's over," said Orso. "We can't do this anymore."

Silence. They'd discussed this eventuality before, but in the whirlwind of successes, they never thought it'd happen. "We've got to go our separate ways. We'll split up the gold straight away."

What had been fun was suddenly not. They pulled a big bag from the hollow of a tree nearby and started counting. They'd sold a lot of honey, and the counting took a few minutes. When they were done, each person had a sizeable sum.

Orso stood up, and saluted. "It's been a pleasure." It wasn't the time for a long speech.

"It has," agreed Dubu. Espen and Nita nodded. Ayiq stayed silent.

Orso turned around and left the clearing without a second glance. Espen left shortly after, in the opposite direction. Dubu and Nita left together, in a third direction.

Ayiq stayed behind. He sat down, alone in the clearing, and cried for a little bit. Then, after the tears stopped coming, he left too, in a fourth direction.

A Carriage Ride

The North Road, 4583

"So how did you die?"

"I'm not really sure. I think a branch hit my head."

"Bad way to go."

"Yes." The wheels creaked slightly as they turned. "Where are you taking me?"

"Your hometown. You're to be laid to rest."

"Good. That's what I would have wanted."

"Would have wanted?"

A long pause. "Yes. I suppose I don't really care anymore." He looked down at his hand. It was pale and seemed… ephemeral. "My body felt so real. This feels so temporary."

"Ironic, isn't it?"

"I'll stay like this forever, then?"

Maroo gave a low throaty chuckle. "I'm just a carriage driver."

The horses' hooves were loud on the cobble road. The night was silent besides.

"You don't seem surprised by me."

"Reach my age and nothing much surprises you."

"That's not much of an answer to the question I was really asking."

"You're right; it's not."

They crested a small hill. The newly deceased looked up. "I don't think I've ever seen the stars as beautiful as they are tonight."

Maroo pulled on the reins, and the horses came to a stop. He reached over to the candle-lit lamp hanging beside him and snuffed out the flame between his forefinger and his thumb. Dark and still, the two sat admiring the night sky. The light of the three stars in the sky pierced the blackness.

"You know," said the deceased, "they say the sky used to be full of stars, hundreds and thousands of them. Can you imagine?"

"It would have been quite the sight," agreed Maroo.

"Yes."

They looked at the sky a little longer, and the moment ran its course. Maroo re-lit the lamp and set the horses back to a trot.

The Princess, the Squirrel, and the Prince

Little Whistling, 4583, and a Land Far, Far Away, a Long, Long Time Ago

"Read her a story?" she snorted. "That's not like you."

"I just feel like it. You have the night off. I'll put her to bed."

"You never read her stories."

"I want to tonight."

"What's gotten into you?"

He paused for a moment. "Remember Losos?"

"As if I could forget! Your little friend. I hated him. Don't tell me he's back in town?"

"They brought back his coffin today."

"Oh, so that's what it takes for you to care about your daughter, huh?"

"Look, it's put things in perspective. I should be a better father. I spend too much time working."

"You're about nine years too late on that realisation."

"My friend has just died! Can't you give it a rest for one night?"

"Give it a rest? I won't have a day of rest till you're six feet below the ground!"

He noticed Abla stood by the door. "Hello, darling!" he said in his sweetest voice, ignoring the last comment.

"Hello, Daddy!" she shouted back. She looked worried. "Are you fighting?"

"No, baby, don't worry," said her mother, forcing a smile.

"Would you like to hear a story before bed?" asked her father.

"Uh-huh!" She nodded enthusiastically.

"Come on, let me tuck you in."

"Yay!" Abla squealed and ran to her room. Her father shot her mother an angry look before following behind her.

He tucked her into bed, got comfy, and began to read. "Here's the story of the princess, the squirrel, and the prince."

It was Abla's favourite.

***

The princess of a grand nation had decided she was to be married. Word was sent out that suitors should come to the palace.

On the first day, a man entered the throne room and introduced himself.

"My name is Herodotus, and I'm a great warrior. I have slain a dragon. I have fought in a war and won it. I have the strength of an ox and the heart of a lion. I am the greatest hero in the kingdom, and I have come to claim my prize!"

"Your prize?"

"Yes."

"And what prize would that be, oh, great and mighty hero?" replied the princess.

"You." Her sarcasm was lost on him.

"Your bravery is matched only by your arrogance! Your achievements don't entitle you to marry me. Begone."

On the second day, another man entered the throne room to introduce himself.

"My name is Richard. I'm the richest trader in the kingdom. I have a giant palace, covered in gemstones. I can buy you the most elegant dresses and the finest jewellery."

"Wealth is no drawback, to be sure, but do you offer anything besides it?"

The man looked stunned for a moment, and began to mumble an answer, when he was interrupted by the princess.

"I am not for sale. I bid you a good day."

On the third day, another man entered the throne room to introduce himself.

"My name is Cobb, and I make shoes. I'm an honest man and do my best to be compassionate. I know I'm only from a humble background, but—"

"That is no issue," interrupted the princess. "I shall marry whomever I love, prince or pauper."

Cobb smiled at that. He had a charming smile, thought the princess. They talked at length. He was handsome, she thought, and she liked him. But she didn't love him, and so she turned down the proposal.

She went to bed upset.

A squirrel climbed up to her window and saw that she was crying. "Whatever's the matter princess?" it asked.

"I have met with a great hero, and a rich man, and I hated them both. I met with a good man, who was perfectly pleasant, but I didn't love him. Who will I love?" she cried. "I shall be alone forever!"

Squirrels, of course, are magical creatures, and this one took pity on the princess. "If you do exactly as I tell you," it said to her, "you will find love."

"Anything!" cried the princess.

"You must issue a decree, saying that you'll marry whoever brings you a bird whose feathers are made of gold. But you must not, under any circumstances, actually marry that person! You'll fall in love with them, but it'll be a deception. You must delay the wedding by three whole days, whereupon your true love will arrive."

"But if I fall in love, how will I be able to resist! I desire a partner more than anything."

"Carry me in your pocket," said the squirrel, "and if you make a bad decision, I'll bite your hand. That should bring you back to reason."

The princess agreed and issued the decree the very next day. She and the squirrel soon became good friends.

In a farmhouse on the edge of the kingdom, there lived a farmer and his three sons. The eldest, having heard the decree, decided he was going to go on an adventure to find the golden bird, and marry the princess. His father gave him a horse and some supplies and sent him on his way with his blessing.

Before long, the eldest son reached a crossroads. He stood for a moment, pondering. An old woman came, seemingly out of nowhere, to ask him what he was thinking. Sensing no danger, the eldest son told all.

"So, it's the golden bird you seek?" The old woman let out a little chuckle. "It won't be easy I'm afraid. The bird is owned by a wizard. But I dislike him, so I'll help you. Take the left path, and you'll soon come across a cottage by the woods. Inside you'll find the bird. If you look inside the window and it appears to be empty, do not enter. Only go in if you can see the wizard inside."

The eldest son thanked her for her advice and went on his way. Sure enough, before long, he came upon the wizard's cottage. He peeped through the window and saw no one was in. The bird sat unguarded in its cage. Being rather brash and impatient, he forgot the old woman's words of advice and rushed inside. But alas! The window was an illusion, and the wizard was waiting. He cast a mighty spell, which turned the eldest son into stone.

After several weeks had passed, the middle son, jealous of the adventures he imagined his older brother was having, decided to also set off to find the bird. His father gave him a horse and some supplies and sent him on his way with his blessing.

Before long, he came to the same crossroads as his brother. While he was deciding which way to go, the same old woman came to ask him what he was thinking. The middle son, who was a little suspicious, reluctantly told her.

The woman gave him the same advice. This time, she emphasised the final point even more. "Remember to only go in if it looks like the wizard is there! Don't go in if the hut is empty!"

The middle son came to the cottage and peeped through the window. He saw the bird in its cage and no wizard. Thinking that the old woman only wanted to trick him, and that she was in cahoots with the wizard, he rushed inside. The wizard was waiting, and the middle son was turned to stone alongside his brother.

A few more weeks passed, and the farmer had started to worry. When the youngest son asked to follow in his brothers' footsteps, his father begged him to stay. The youngest wouldn't listen, and eventually, his father reluctantly agreed. He gave him a horse and some supplies, and sent him on his way, with his blessing.

Before long, he too was at those fateful crossroads. The old woman approached him and asked what he was thinking. Being kind and honest, the youngest son told all.

The woman told him what she'd told his brothers, and he heeded every word carefully. When the youngest son came to the cottage, he peeped through the window. Seeing that the wizard wasn't there, he went to hide behind a tree and waited. As the sun began to set, the cottage door opened, and the wizard walked out into the forest.

The youngest came from behind his tree and went to peek through the window. The wizard appeared to be in there! He realised that he'd been seeing an illusion. He went into the cottage, looking for the bird cage. As he opened the door to the back room, he was presented with an army of stone statues. At the very front were his brothers! He stood shocked, and that shock only grew as he heard the wizard returning. So soon! Determined to get his revenge, he grabbed a poker from the fire and lay in wait for the wizard.

Being very crafty, the wizard knew the moment he returned that something was amiss. Instead of going in, he spoke through the door.

"Hello there, is there anything I can do for you?"

"You evil wizard! You turned my brothers to stone. Turn them back or I'll strike you down!"

"Turned to stone? Why, my boy, I'm not a wizard; I'm a sculptor! When your brothers passed through, I felt inspired. Each stayed with me for a few days while I carved these statues in their likeness, and then they went on their way with some extra gold in their pockets."

"But what about the golden bird?"

"Golden bird? I have no golden bird, nor have I heard tell of one. Why are you looking for a golden bird?"

"The princess has decreed that whoever brings her the bird shall have her hand in marriage."

"Fascinating!" This was news to the wizard – he didn't go out much. "Well, I'm friends with the beasts of the forest. If you agree to model for a sculpture, I could ask them for help."

Being overly trusting, not the brightest, and a little vain, the youngest not only believed the wizard but was actually a little flattered. He was to be a model!

"Let's waste no time. Put down that poker, my boy, and let's go to the studio."

The youngest obliged. The moment he did, though, the wizard cast a spell, and the youngest was turned to stone.

The wizard was now obsessed with the idea of marrying the princess. He left the statue where it was and rushed to his cauldron. He concocted a powerful potion to make himself captivatingly beautiful and irresistible to the princess. He needed to disguise himself, for many at court knew his face (the wizard had committed many crimes against the kingdom).

"Heart of palm and head of cabbage, black eyed peas and ear of corn, navel orange and lady fingers," he muttered to himself as he threw ingredients into the pot. "I must be sure not to get wet, or the potion's effect will wear off."

He grabbed a thick coat as he left, with the golden bird in hand. The youngest son heard all of this through the stone. He was, however, powerless to move, and became depressed.

We return now briefly to the old lady who gave the brothers their advice. She was not an old lady at all but, in fact, a fairy. She was watching everything unfold from her magic mirror. Not wanting the princess to marry the evil wizard, she cast a spell on the youngest son who had listened so well to her. This spell slowly – oh, ever so slowly – began to restore life to him.

The wizard burst through the palace doors, with the golden bird in one hand and a red rose in the other. He strode up to the princess and knelt at her feet. He presented her with the bird and the rose. "My lady, I have done as you asked and brought you the golden bird," he said. "Will you marry me?"

The princess, who had fallen for him the moment he walked through the door, was delighted. "Yes! Yes, I shall marry you!"

Everyone was delighted. The king and queen were overjoyed at seeing a smile on the face of the princess, who had been so melancholy lately. And this man was not only beautiful but obviously brave and cunning – he'd found the golden bird!

"Let us begin preparations for the wedding immediately!" said the queen.

The princess was about to agree, meaning to marry the man as soon as possible, when suddenly she felt a sharp pain, as if she'd been bitten. That's right! She must wait three days before she could be married.

"It is cloudy today," she said. "Let us wait until the weather is better for us to be married!"

The queen assented. The wizard was incensed, but assented too, not wishing to annoy the royals before the marriage.

The next day, the rain had stopped. The wizard came to the princess and asked to be married that day.

"Yes! Yes! Let us be married!" said the princess, overjoyed. "Yeeeooowwwwww!" She screamed shortly afterwards. "Ah, I just realised! It's windy. This won't do. We shall wait for it to be still, too."

Full of rage on the inside, the wizard acted polite and dignified on the outside. "Of course, my lady, it is only fitting."

Now the princess really did believe she was in love with this man and the squirrel had bitten her harder than was needed. Even though they were friends, she thought this was too far. After her husband-to-be had left, she pulled the squirrel out of her pocket and threw it across the room.

"I never want to see you again," she shouted.

The squirrel left dejectedly. "I can only do so much," it said. "In the end she has to do this herself. I believe she has the strength to do it." Despite her harsh words, it still cared for her.

On the third day, there was not a cloud in the sky. The sun was shining bright, and the air was still. Whether this was a coincidence or the consequence of another one of the wizard's spells, who knows, but the wizard came to the palace asking to be married that day.

The princess agreed, and the preparations were made. Wanting to get it done as quickly as possible after all the delays, it was a simple wedding.

As they were stood at the altar, the princess began to have doubts. Three full days she had promised the squirrel. She felt guilty for the way she had treated it, and despite her love, she wanted to at least honour the promise. She ran from the altar, straight to her chambers, and wouldn't let anyone in.

The king and queen were concerned but put it down to pre-nuptial nerves. After speaking to the princess, they decided to postpone the wedding by another day.

The couple stood again by the altar the following day. It had now been very nearly three whole days since the man had arrived.

The princess had held her end of the bargain, and was going to marry this handsome, charming man.

As the officiator began his speech, the doors burst open. A man came rushing in with a pail of water. He squirmed past the guards and threw the water all over the groom. Instantly, the spell was undone. The princess fell out of love, and the man was revealed before the whole crowd to be the evil wizard.

"Seize him!" shouted the king, rising from his chair.

The wizard was thrown in prison. The youngest son had made it just in time. The princess fell in love with the youngest son straight away, for real this time. The two were married that same day.

The wizard, in return for his freedom, agreed to undo all of his spells and live in exile. Thus, the older brothers and all of the other statues were restored to normal. The princess found the squirrel and begged forgiveness. The squirrel, knowing she'd been under a spell, forgave her. And so they lived happily for the rest of their days – the princess, the prince, and the squirrel.

***

"Thank you, Daddy!" cried Abla.

"You're welcome."

"What's the meaning of this story again?" asked Abla.

"Um, I don't know, actually," replied her father.

"If you're kind, you'll be turned to stone?"

"No, that's not it."

"Never trust a wizard?"

"That's not it either. Wizards are actually very trustworthy," he added. "If you're ever lost, go find a wizard."

"If you want to find love, listen to a squirrel?"

Being the least harmful message so far, he decided to agree. "Yes, that's it!"

"I knew it," she said, as if it weren't her third guess. "I'm going to the forest tomorrow."

Poor squirrels, he thought. "Okay. But take your brother with you, and don't pester the squirrels if they're not interested."

Kofi and Abla

Little Whistling, 4583

"Come on Kofi!" screamed Abla. "Hurry up!"

"He's finding his shoe," said their mother, who was tying Abla's laces. "Make sure not to wander off too far, yeah?" She was speaking from experience.

Abla nodded dutifully.

"And listen to what your brother says – he's in charge."

Abla squealed with excitement as Kofi came rushing in. "Let's go exploring!" he cried.

"Don't go too far, Kofi," said their mother. "And look after your sister. If there's any hint of danger, you come right back here sharpish, got it?"

"Yep!"

"Promise?"

He held out a pinkie finger to his mother, and she wrapped hers around his. "I promise," he said.

"Now you two, go have fun!" She leaned in close to Kofi, so only he would hear. "And if she doesn't find her magical squirrel, will you do your best to cheer her up for me?"

Kofi nodded.

They're good kids, she thought.

And so off they went. The sun was just rising, and there was a slight chill in the air. It looked like it'd be a beautiful day. Perfect adventuring weather. The pair went along the well-worn path behind the house. It wiggled its way past the vegetable garden and into the wheat field.

Abla bent down to look at a bug that was crawling on an ear. She held out a stick, trying to get it to crawl on. It went in the other direction. She moved her stick in front of it again, giggling at her fun game.

This made Kofi sad. She was too young to know the significance of that bug, but it was bad. He'd heard his parents arguing one night, after they thought he and Abla were asleep. The bugs were eating the grain – and no one knew how to stop it. It was the same on the next farm over, and the next. Times were going to be hard very soon – harder than they were already.

His pessimistic thinking was interrupted as Abla let loose an "eeeee" of excitement. The bug had finally climbed onto her stick. Kofi smiled. "What are you gonna do with it now?"

She held the stick at both ends and presented it to him. "For you."

"Aww, that's so sweet of you, Abla. Thank you." He took it gratefully in one hand and took her hand in the other. They resumed walking.

"What will you wish for, Kofi," asked Abla, "when we find the squirrel?"

"I thought the squirrel found you true love?"

"Nope," she said. "Wishes."

"Okay," he said, not wanting to argue. "I'd wish for a good harvest."

"That's a bad wish."

"Yeah? And what would you wish for?"

"A million, million bits of gold."

Can't argue with that, he thought. "That's a good answer."

"I know," she replied. There was a lot of smugness in those two words. After strutting in her victorious air for a while, Abla reached the end of the field, with Kofi in tow. This was where the forest began.

"I should let this bug go home now," said Kofi.

"Okay." Abla nodded with great understanding. She was good at nodding. "Bye-bye, mister bug! I hope you have a nice day!"

Kofi knelt down to the ground. He double checked his sister wasn't looking and squashed the bug in his fist. He wiped his hand on the dirt.

Abla paid no attention – she was staring into the trees, on the lookout already. She wasn't here for leisure, oh no. She was here on business. That magical squirrel was going to get found, and those wishes were going to be redeemed. She may have completely misunderstood the fairy tale, and forgotten that it was made up, but nothing apart from that escaped her attention. Her poise was that of a hunter stalking its prey.

"What do squirrels eat?" she asked spontaneously.

"Acorns."

"Can we find an acorn tree?"

It's as good a place to start as any, he thought. "Yes, we can."

And so they searched. They scrambled under fallen trees, and over big roots. They went around great patches of nettles and through a little stream. Kofi kept note of landmarks, as they went, and of the position of the sun. He was good with directions and, anyway, he was fairly sure that stream fed into the river in the village. So even if they did get lost, they had a way back to safety.

Before long Abla was tired, and she threw herself down on an inviting patch of moss. "Ahhhhhh," she said, very contentedly.

Kofi admired her optimism. So far not a whiff of squirrel or even an oak tree, but she wasn't demotivated. As she lay there comfortably, a little woodlouse crawled onto her hand. "A roly-poly bug!"

Kofi smiled. Now this was a bug he could get behind. No one's ever had a bad word to say about a woodlouse.

"Should I show him my roly-poly?" asked Abla. She'd been practising.

"Go for it!"

She carefully put down the woodlouse. She stood up and planted her hands on the ground in front of her. With her head tucked in, she pushed off with her feet. She went awkwardly over, in a slow sort of roll, and landed on her back. Kofi heard a little sound escaping, best described as 'ehhhhhyaahhh'.

"Impressive," said Kofi.

"Very impressive" said a voice that Kofi didn't recognise.

He turned around, instantly on edge. He didn't see anyone.

"I think the roly-poly bug is jealous," said the voice. "You have a thing or two to teach her."

"Thank you very much, miss," said Abla.

Next to where she'd landed, on a red and white toadstool, sat a fairy.

Kofi was nervous. He was sceptical of magic and didn't trust fairies. He'd grown up on stories of them kidnapping children and doing spells.

"Those are rude things to think about someone," said the fairy, looking straight at Kofi.

He turned a little red in the cheek. How did she know?

"I don't kidnap children. Not unless they're rude to me and treat me with disrespect." Her voice suddenly became loud, and it was as if it echoed in his mind. He heard it coming from every direction at once. "I am a powerful creature, little farm boy, and you're out of your depth. You'd better lose that prejudice before I lose my temper."

Her gaze was strong, and he broke eye contact. There was real power in those eyes, and it was unlike anything he'd ever seen. It was alien to him, and he felt threatened.

"Just kidding," she said, with an innocent laugh. Her voice returned to normal. "You should have seen your face!"

She laughed again, and Abla joined in. Kofi sneered, angry and embarrassed. He looked back at the fairy, and all he saw was a very small girl with a pair of butterfly wings. Her eyes looked human. Was that just an illusion? It had felt, to him, so real.

"What brings you to the forest today, little lady?" the fairy asked Abla, who seemed completely unfazed.

"We're looking for acorns!" she said with excitement, then her face turned sad. "But we haven't found any."

"Well, that's because you're looking in the wrong place, silly! You see that hill, over there?" She pointed. "Just the other side of it, you'll find your acorn tree."

"Really?" asked Abla. Her face lit up.

"Really," confirmed the fairy.

"That's where we came from," said Kofi. "There were no oak trees there."

"Well, maybe it's worth a second look, mister."

"I don't trust you."

"I know," replied the fairy. "But Abla does."

"How do you know her name?"

"I like her," said the fairy, completely ignoring the question. "She's sweet. I'm telling the truth; you'll find a tree."

Try as he might, Kofi couldn't seem to believe she was lying. She obviously perceived his concession and smiled. "Good luck

Kofi. And you, Abla. I'll see you soon!" She giggled, and waved goodbye. There was a quick burst of light, and she disappeared.

"She's tricksy," said Kofi instantly. "She's obviously a troublemaker. And that hill had no oak trees near it, I'm sure. I think we should go home."

"But the acorns," said Abla, with tears starting to form in her eyes. "The acorns…"

She doesn't seem to care that we hadn't found any a few minutes ago, he thought. *But I can't say no to her like that. She knows exactly how to get what she wants.* He sighed. "Okay, but no further than that, got it?"

Abla nodded her assent. "Can you carry me?" she said, sniffling.

Kofi caved and lifted her up onto his shoulders. She smiled at that. As he trudged up the hill, she had great fun reaching for branches and touching the leaves. But for Kofi, the light-hearted mood had faded away. He was uneasy. He decided to remain vigilant and was prepared to run home at the slightest whiff of foul play, or magic. But a small part of him, a part which remained untouched by scepticism, was excited. This could turn into a proper adventure.

The top of the hill poked above the treeline. They could see for miles, and Kofi audibly gasped. Straight ahead of them, a mile or so away, stood the largest tree that had ever grown. It towered above the rest of the forest and even dwarfed the hill they stood on. It was gnarled and ancient, but so obviously strong, powerful, and full of life.

All around them, in every direction, all they could see was forest. Kofi's stomach dropped. They must have gone further in than he thought. They should be able to see home from here. He suddenly felt a little panicked. His heart rate shot up. The promise he'd made to his mother was at the front of his mind. As he squinted his eyes a little, to look closer at the giant tree, he realised it was... of course it was. It was an oak tree.

He weighed up the options in his mind, trying to think rationally. *We should try to go home,* he thought. *But where is home? To the east.* He looked up at the sun. It was about noon, which made that direction south. That placed east right in the direction of the tree.

The fairy had played some kind of trick on them. He was sure of it. What were her intentions? He looked around again. Nothing but forest. Seeing no other option, he decided to play along.

He said to Abla "You see that tree over there?" She nodded. "It's an acorn tree!"

Her face lit up, and her eyes sparkled. "It's so big!" she said, as if only just releasing the fact.

"It is!" confirmed Kofi.

"Will there be squirrels there?" she asked tentatively, eyes full of hope.

"Well, if there are squirrels anywhere, it's probably there." He was starting to think maybe magic squirrels weren't so far-fetched. Maybe if they found one, it could take them home – them and their million, million pieces of gold.

The walk was pleasant, and Kofi's anxieties faded away. They were replaced by wonder. The forest was lush beyond anything he'd ever seen. There were flowers everywhere. He recognised enchanter's nightshade, and butterfly orchids, and star of Bethlehem. Honeysuckle, lily of the valley, bluebells, foxgloves, holly berries, everything was in bloom, as if all four seasons had reached their peak at once, in a great crescendo of colour.

The air was fragrant, and the sunlight peering through the canopy seemed alive. It jumped, and smiled, and spun, obviously happy to be there. There was light for the trees, light for the flowers, light for the undergrowth. Every layer of the forest was radiant, and every hue was represented. It was absolutely enchanting.

The wonder wasn't lost on Abla either. "It's so pretty!" she said. She put her face in the honeysuckle and took a long and loud in-breath through her nose. "It smells pretty too!"

"It's amazing, isn't it, Abla?" asked Kofi.

She wasn't listening. She'd seen a butterfly and was enthralled. She watched it feeding from a flower she didn't recognise. It had bright white petals, with a corona of blue and purple, and eight yellow stamens in the shape of a star. It seemed to notice her and flew up to her face. She stayed perfectly still, and it landed, very gently, on her nose. It stood there, and Abla almost went cross eyed trying to get a good look. She let out a little gasp, and the butterfly took flight again. A wonderful moment.

They felt drawn to the giant oak. The closer they got to it, the more wonderful and surreal the forest seemed. Abla took Kofi's hand as they walked together, in bliss. All too soon they reached the clearing which housed the tree. Up close it seemed even more impossible. Its trunk was thicker than a house and was home to a symphony of songbirds.

"You made it!" shouted the fairy happily, floating beside them.

"What is this place?" asked Kofi, not surprised in the slightest.

"The forest behind your farm."

"No, it's not."

"It is." She giggled. "'Where' isn't the right question to ask."

"Is this some kind of illusion?"

She giggled again. "Why don't you try and find those acorns you were looking for?"

"Yeah!" shouted Abla. "Yeah!" She started towards the tree.

Kofi followed with a wary glance at the fairy. His scepticism had returned. As they got closer to the base of the tree, he noticed something. Slowly, and rhythmically, it was rising up and down, ever so slightly. A chill went down his spine. It looked as if the tree was breathing.

"Hang on a second, Abla," he called.

She didn't listen; she kept running.

"Abla!" he called, with a hint of panic in his voice.

She didn't listen.

"ABLA!"

She didn't listen. She ran right up to the base of the tree and touched it.

There was an uproar. There was a desperate flapping of wings as the birds scrambled to escape. Leaves rustled, wood creaked, and wind blew. The base of the tree seemed to come alive. It writhed, contorting and unfurling. It revealed its form and became separate from the tree, standing proud on four strong legs. As quickly as the uproar had happened, it gave way to silence. Muddy scales, covered in moss and fungi, had served as excellent camouflage. It unfurled two great wings and spread them wide.

Abla screamed and ran back to Kofi as fast as she could, tears flowing. It looked, like the tree, impossibly ancient and impossibly full of life. Its eyes were large, and bright, and shrewd. There was no mistaking it.

This was a dragon. This was the God of the Earth.

The children were paralysed with fear. Abla held Kofi as tight as she could, and Kofi held her back. The God of the Earth looked around, as if wondering what had awoken it. It looked straight at Kofi and Abla for a moment but seemed to see straight through them. It looked around a second time, made a sort of hmphing sound, and curled up again at the base of the tree.

The siblings still didn't dare to move. They stood there for what seemed like hours.

Slowly, the light began to fade. The tree's lustre diminished, and it began to lose its height. The everblooming forest began to wither. The zenith of every season became its nadir. Suddenly, everything seemed grey and monotonous. Instead of a great tree, all that remained was a stump.

"What's happening?" said Kofi "I–"

"You're being brought back to your own time," said the fairy.

It was so dull and small. Kofi had wanted to go home, but now he was deeply saddened by the change. He wished he could have stayed longer. He looked away from the fairy and towards the remains of the tree and noticed something horrifying. Wrapped around the stump was a skeleton – old, and massive, and illuminated by a warm sunlight that had no real right to be there. He felt tears come to his eyes and saw that Abla was crying too.

"Why would you show us paradise, just to take it away?" shouted Kofi.

The fairy didn't answer.

"You're cruel!" Kofi's tears were flowing freely now. He held Abla close.

Suddenly serious, the fairy replied. "These bones are ancient beyond belief. They've lain here for an age, hidden deep in a forest few people know and even fewer enter. The world outside has forgotten. Fact has become myth. It's time, Kofi, Abla, time for the world to remember."

Kofi looked at her for a long time. He felt like he'd been used. He hated the feeling, and he hated the fairy. Despite that, he knew that he'd do what she said. He'd tell everyone what he'd seen today and show them all this cursed place.

"It's dark." Abla sniffled.

"I know," said Kofi, patting her head.

"Can we go home?" she asked.

"Yes, we can," he said. "I'm really sorry we didn't find any squirrels."

"It's okay." She snuffled, hugging him tighter.

"Where are we?" asked Kofi.

"Not too far from home. Here, take this," said the fairy. She threw Kofi a small ball, which glowed brightly. She pointed behind her. "Head that way. Before long you'll find the stream you saw this morning. Remember the way here."

"Let's go, Abla," said Kofi, and turned to leave.

"No human alive has seen what you two saw today," the fairy shouted after him.

Kofi paused for a moment. *She's right,* he thought. *In a way I'm lucky.* But now how could his world ever compare? Nothing ever could. Did she really expect gratitude? He didn't reply to her shout and squeezed Abla's hand tightly.

They began the journey home.

The Diary of Martha Briggs

23/6/4585

My name is Captain Martha Briggs. What am I the captain of? Of the good ship Vitus, one of the most impressive airships ever built. We're on a pretty interesting mission this time. We're hunting a dragon. Since the bones of the God of the Earth were discovered, people are taking the rumours about this 'sea dragon' a lot more seriously. So seriously, in fact, that a very wealthy man (who naturally wishes to remain anonymous) has paid us a very large sum of money to kill it. Whether he believes its scales really hold some ancient magical power, or he just wants a trophy for his wall, I'm not sure. Nor do I really care. It doesn't matter. I get a hefty sum of gold and a grand old adventure. I'm happy.

We left the capital to much fanfare: banners, cheering crowds, handsome men, handsome women. And a literal fanfare. I enjoyed it very much. Skyle, my first mate, did not. He's a man who shies away from the limelight. If he wanted to, he could be one of the most famous people in the world – and would have earned it, too. I don't understand him.

We headed west, stopping off at some major towns along the way. Smaller celebrations awaited us at each one. The nation really seems to be behind us. That, or they just have nothing better to do. I think the latter is more likely.

As I'm writing this, we're moored at Pysgod Port, the last stop before the open ocean. If I look west, I can see nothing but blue. I'm going to spend the rest of the stay looking east at the land. This voyage might be very long. We have a half year's worth of food and will have the ocean's bounty beneath our feet.

We're going to take a day to talk to the locals and try to get as many details as we can. This is where the rumours first started.

24/6/4585

The first place we went, of course, was the pub. The barman was friendly and, when we asked about the rumours, pointed us towards an old sailor sat alone in the corner smoking his pipe. "That sounds like his old ramblings," he'd said, and right he was. The old sailor spun quite the yarn. Here's (as best as I can remember) what he told us:

"You, city folk, may believe in the gods now, now you have yer 'proof', but we've been belie'ing our 'ole lives. We know things you don't know. The God of the Stars, she lives, aye, out there, among the waves. Ye seek to kill her? Then ye be fools."

We asked why, and he laughed at us.

"'Cause she's a God, and ye're just men. And, er, women, of course," he said, nodding towards me. "Men or women, it don't matter. If yer lucky, you'll never find her. If yer unlucky, you will, and she'll kill you all."

We asked if she had any weaknesses; he said none. We asked about how she might attack; he said even if we knew, it'd be no use. Answers continued in that fashion, which wasn't particularly helpful, so we thanked him and said goodbye. He said a prayer for us as we left.

We didn't hear much else that was helpful after that, so I'm going to use the lack of news as an excuse to talk about Flotsam.

Flotsam's my new pet, a moon gecko. A shop owner back home had wanted to rid of him on account of the fact he's missing a leg. And an eye. And an ear. And a good chunk of his tail too.

The rich folk that shop there like everything to be perfect. Unspoiled. Wasn't worth the cost of feed, so I got him for the very reasonable price of free. I named him, quite cleverly I thought, Flotsam. I like him a lot. He's charming.

26/6/4585

We are well and truly into the ocean now, and last night we saw something beautiful. After the sun had set, and darkness had well and truly fallen, the waters beneath us lit up. The ocean at night is a sombre place when the moon isn't out. Deep black in every direction, for miles and miles and miles. So when we heard the lookout shouting about a bright glow coming from below, some of the crew thought he might have gone a bit mad, or that maybe he was pulling some kind of practical joke. But he wasn't. We rushed out and saw the lights, every colour you could imagine: the deepest of purple and the brightest of yellow, a forest green, a muddy brown, and all the dancing shades of fire. It was a sight to behold. And behold it we did. We must have been an equally impressive sight, hanging over the edge of the ship slack-jawed, with faces lit up like an artist's palette that's never been washed.

I was informed by Markus, our resident knower of things, that they were luminous jellyfish coming up from the depths to breed – a very rare phenomenon. Mating with a jellyfish on the opposite side of the colour wheel ensures genetic diversity. It's pretty clever really, in some way. But not that clever in others. The show attracted quite a lot of predators.

He's an invaluable member of the crew, Markus. His knowledge is broad. He knows about zoology, medicine, mechanics, mathematics, astrology, and history – anything we could need, really. He's brought hundreds of books with him. His quarters are bigger than mine and house a full library. I imagine his diary will be highly valued by scholars when we get back. Mine maybe not so much.

The jellyfish disappeared as quickly as they'd appeared, and the darkness returned. We all lumbred back to our beds, a little disappointed it hadn't lasted longer, but in awe nonetheless. I had very vivid dreams that night.

28/6/4585

We're at that stage where not much is really happening. We're headed for some very small, very remote islands right at the edge of the map – if they even exist that is. They seem to have a semi-mythical sort of aura around them. Some very reputable sailors swear their existence. Other equally reputable sailors swear that there's nothing there but open ocean. That's how these things usually go though, really. The deniers were either lost, or the believers were drunk. Despite the uncertainty, it'll be our first point of call. It's there that strange things have been said.

The journey there will take a few more days and should be plain sailing. So, while there's not much to report, I'll write about the ship and her crew.

The good ship Vitus is a marvel. Forty metres long, crewed by over three hundred fine people, it resembles the seafaring crafts of old, but soaring above the earth and the oceans, powered by steam. Instead of a mast, it has a dozen thick cables, attached to a zeppelin. Six boilers run around the clock, heating air so the ship can stay airborne. There are three propellers at the back, a large one in the centre, with smaller ones to the right and left. We also have a propeller on each side. These five combine for incredible manoeuvrability.

It's armed to the teeth, too. We have twenty cannons on each side, specifically designed to pierce armour. We have stacks of hydraulically boosted harpoons and hunters who know how to use them. We have swords. We have poison. We have gunpowder. People say the dragon is strong. Powerful. Unkillable even. But that was said a long time ago. We have weapons now that can kill it.

The crew are experienced. This is far from our first voyage. For years, we've hunted. I've already mentioned my first mate, Skyle, and the man who knows things, Markus. There's Ellham, the chief harpooner. My word is she strong! And there's Sage, the chef. My word is he good at cooking! John is the quartermaster, and my word— actually he's just okay at his job. I mean, I have no complaints. He's just not much to write home about.

29/6/4585

I've been trying to teach Flotsam some tricks. I've not been very successful. He's either very stupid, or very smart and mocking me. My money is on the latter. He has this sort of look in his eye, just sometimes, that makes me think. Moon geckos are mostly nocturnal. His eye is very reflective and glows like a little moon in the dark. That's where the name came from, I suppose. Despite my recent failures, I think he likes me. And I like him.

Ellham has been fishing. She caught a gigantic tuna. As she was hauling it in, a shark took a bite. Before long, she'd caught a shark as well. She called me over and offered me the prime cuts. It was really sweet of her. Sage prepared it beautifully, and we ate well. None of us are sick of seafood yet.

I stood for a time at the bow, looking out over the ocean. It's been calm so far. It never stays that way for long though. I feel it starting to change, and I'm not often wrong about things like this. We'll reach where the islands should be by tomorrow. Let's hope they're there and we can wait out the storm on the ground. Skyle believes it, and he has good instincts.

30/6/4585

Well, what do you know? The islands are real. Real but bizarre. We reached them early in the morning. We're lucky Markus is such a good navigator, or we might have missed them in the fog. Visibility is poor. The good ship Vitus touched solid ground before the winds got too strong.

There are two islands, each no more than eighty metres or so in diameter, and somewhat oblong. We landed on the left one. The islands are made of what looks like some sort of volcanic rock. Nothing I've seen before, though. They're not just black; they seem to absorb every single ray of light that touches them. It's a little unsettling. There's no sign of any life at all except for a few barnacles. I guess even the sea birds find this place weird.

The storm is really getting underway as I'm writing this (in the evening), and it might last a while.

31/6/4585

We didn't go outside today. There's thunder and lightning, and ferocious winds. Even though we've landed, the ship is swaying, which is a little unusual even in winds this strong. It's designed to cut through the wind. But so long as we don't topple, it's no big deal.

Determined to not let the day go fully to waste, I held a meeting to discuss what we know about this dragon. The long and short of it is this: in ancient times, during The Age of the Dragons, there were four divine dragons (some even claimed the Dragon King was a literal dragon, which would make five, but I think that's a little far-fetched). Each of these four dragons was a god, representing the Sun, the Moon, the Stars, and the Earth. The one we're after is Stars. The story goes that during that age, the night sky was covered in stars, and that they've been slowly fading ever since. A load of rubbish if you ask me – there's only ever been one star in the sky.

The God of the Stars is said to be covered in dazzlingly bright spots, hard scales, strong legs, vastly intelligent, master of magic. Sounds like quite the opponent. There's a lot we don't really know. How big is it? Does it breathe fire? Does it really have magical powers? Where does it live? Some remote island or in the ocean itself? That's what some of the rumours suggest. Markus thinks this might be a different creature, some sort of sea monster. Or, perhaps, he says, the dragon has evolved in some way and has learned to breathe underwater. It has been thousands of years after all.

Is it even still alive? That's perhaps the most important question. We have no idea. The smart answer might be no. The God of Earth had been dead for a very long time, a very, very long time. We don't know what killed it. Old age? Surely nothing can live forever. If so, Stars is likely long dead too.

If it was killed in combat, that's good. It means it can be done. We did, through not-entirely-legitimate means, get our hands on one of the bones. A rib. We tested our weapons against it, and they worked a charm. A couple of cannon blasts and it was dust. Granted, they're old, but it bodes well.

So really, there's a lot of speculation. The reality of it is that we now know these dragons were real. We don't know their exact nature – whether they were really gods or just animals. My money is on the latter. There have been sightings of some big mysterious beast in the western ocean. We don't know what this creature is, but it's our best lead. We plan on using these islands as a base and scouring the nearby waters for any signs. Even if it's not a dragon, a sea monster would be quite the prize. Skyle suggested we start by heading even further west, before turning to the north, and circling back around.

Afterwards we played cards. Over the years me and Ellham have built up a collection of secret signals to communicate with each other. Used, almost exclusively, of course, to cheat. We cleaned up, which is ironic, because the losers were covering the winner's cleaning shifts. I usually do them, even as captain. Something has to keep me humble. Ellham told me she enjoyed it and gave me a wink as we left. She's a good friend.

1/7/4585

The storm cleared up, finally! We took to the air early in the morning. We headed due west for hours, and we saw... absolutely nothing. A few dolphins, that was it.

It seems Flotsam has discovered the pantry. Whenever I take my eyes off him, he seems to slip away and end up in there. How is a big lizard with only three legs so fast and stealthy? Sage'll have his head if he's not careful. I want to tie a bell around his neck. The only problem there being I don't have a bell. I tried tying together two bottle caps so they'd jangle, but that went quite poorly. If he wasn't busy with actual work, I'd ask Markus for help.

There weren't many orders to give, or much steering to do, so I left Skyle at the helm and climbed up to one of the lookout posts. This one was at the very back of the ship and involved a somewhat treacherous climb. I told the woman on duty she could have a few hours off, and kept watch myself.

The sun had come out, and it was really quite beautiful. The waters were clear and a lovely shade of blue. For the first time since we set out, I had some serious doubts. How can we possibly hope to find it? Even if it is alive, the ocean is so vast and deep. I did my best to keep these doubts out of mind. No matter what, we'd been paid a portion of the fee upfront. And it was a beautiful day! Why was I sad? I was sad because I really want to catch this dragon.

A bell rang before too long, which signalled the end of the shift. The next lookout came up to take my place. If only that bell was smaller, I thought, and not an important part of running the ship.

As night began to fall, I spoke with Skyle, and we decided not to anchor overnight. Let the wind take us where it may. Who knows, maybe we'll end up somewhere interesting. Markus can find our position just by looking at the moon and the star, so I wasn't worried about getting lost.

7/7/4585

We've spent the past week hunting and have nothing important to report. Flotsam managed to steal an entire ham one day. It was one of our last, and I swear I saw Sage turn the colour of said ham. It's definitely caused some tension between me and him. I said that if he lays one finger on Flotsam, I will tie rocks to his feet and throw him overboard. I've taken to sitting up in that lookout spot in the evening and watching the waves as the sun starts to set. Flotsam keeps me company. His presence and his glow comfort me. I swear that if that dam cook even thinks about doing anything… Flotsam is crippled and half blind! It's not my fault Sage isn't smart enough to keep a little disabled lizard out of his stocks.

We let ourselves drift for several nights because I was feeling lucky. I wasn't lucky it turns out. It got us absolutely nowhere, so we've gone back to a more methodical approach.

The crew came up with a game they very wittily called 'dice punch'. It's played like this: You roll two dice, and look at the outcome, say it's a 5 and a 2. You then each take turns rolling the dice, and first person to roll a 5 and a 2, you guessed it, everyone punches them.

As dumb as it sounds, it was actually kinda fun. Until it was my turn to be punched that is. Not because it hurt – but because it didn't. Everyone held back because I'm the captain. I do my very best to be down to earth and to be just like them. I guess I'm not quite there yet though, even after all this time. It makes me sad.

14/7/4585

Another week of looking… and nothing. We anchored for a bit, and one of the harpooners, Linh, went diving using the breathing apparatus. They brought back up with them all sorts of things from the ocean floor. There was absolutely nothing relevant to the mission. So why am I making note of this? Because one of the things they brought back was a hermit crab. Ellham evicted said crab and used his house and some metal to build a basic sort of bell. A bell! She is honestly the sweetest. I put it around Flotsam's neck, and he now does a sort of nautical jingle whenever he walks. She's so thoughtful.

We decided to head back towards the islands and discuss what we want to do next. We've been going east and west all along different latitudes, so we're only actually two days away.

15/7/4585

I heard a few members of the crew telling stories. One man was telling the story of how he'd killed a vodyanoy with his bare hands. A vodyanoy is an immensely powerful water spirit, so I very much doubt it. Markus suggested that maybe he'd slipped and hit his head while bathing. Skyle cracked a rare smile at that, and the audience laughed.

I've heard reports that this man has been shirking his duties. The words 'lazy' and 'incompetent' have been thrown around, and he's yet to prove himself. So of course he has the most to say. It's always like that. Fools. I hope that he can prove his mettle when the time comes.

As we get nearer the islands, it looks more and more like a storm is coming. Hopefully, we can land in time, like we did before.

"And that's where the original diary stops, I'm afraid." Martha sighed, putting down her glass. "But I've finished it since. It's written with hindsight, so maybe it's not so accurate. But hey, you take what you can get. It goes like this…"

16/7/4585

The storm was really in full force now. The rain was falling heavily, and even though it was midday, the sky was black as pitch. Thunder boomed, and lightning crashed. That was the only time we could see more than a few feet ahead of us. I was barking constant orders. We HAD to keep on course and reach those islands. Using all of the ship's propellers to keep us steady, and praying that the compass was right, we kept going.

It was a hard fought few hours. Muscles strained, voices were hoarse, the ship rocked, but we kept going. We kept going until we reached where Markus told me the islands were.

And the islands weren't there. Markus, the man who knew things, had failed me. I relied on him, and he'd failed me. We'd have to weather this storm in the air, and it could cost us our lives.

Lightning split the heavens, and for a moment, as the whole ocean was lit in that harsh light, it appeared as though a dark shadow lay just beneath the waves. Was the storm violent enough to drown the islands? There was no time to think about it as I got thrown off my feet. Two of the cables connecting us to the zeppelin had snapped, and the ship was no longer level. That wasn't supposed to happen.

A deep rumbling was heard all throughout the ship. So deep and so loud that I felt it in my bones, in my teeth. It almost brought me back to my knees. Lightning flashed again, and I saw the water part.

A creature came bursting out of the waves, and I knew straight away what it was. It might have been noble, once, but for thousands of years it had lived in the deep, alone. It had grown, and adapted, and become unrecognisable.

I shouted to Ellham to prepare the weapons, unsure if she could even hear me over the pounding of the rain. We didn't have much crew spare to man the cannons or to launch the harpoons.

Another flash, and the creature was in the air. You could only tell from the absence of light. Even in the lightning, it was only a silhouette. I thought at the time I must have been judging it wrong. It must have been farther away. It couldn't be that big.

But it was. This was the power of a god. Any light that had been there was long gone. It was mighty and terrible and dark – the God of the Stars.

Someone somewhere launched a cannon. The gunpowder sent the heavy ball launching at a hundred metres per second, crashing straight into the side of the creature. Another cannon went off, and then two more, and then another. We were making our own thunder.

In a few quick flaps of its wings, it was upon us. How could something so large possibly fly? And fly so quickly? I saw Ellham beside me. She threw her harpoon with all of her might. It glanced off a scale and fell into the ocean. I saw that she was scared.

It was like a soldier's boot on a child's sandcastle when it happened. The God of the Stars broke the ship into pieces with no more effort than it took me to breathe. I was one of the lucky ones; I died on impact. Others fell into the sea. No one survived.

The dragon screamed, a scream of victory, I suppose. But it was hollow, painful. Any wisdom it may have had once had been replaced by a bestial madness. The storm hit a new frenzy, as if in response. The dragon hovered in the air for a moment, looking around, making sure the threat had been dealt with. As it hung there, in the dark storm, there was one small but bright light to be seen, near the base of its tail. Maybe, just maybe, the God still lived inside the monster.

It flew back into the sea, creating a wave even taller than itself. The gale slowly turned into a breeze, and the torrent became a drizzle. Soon, it went back to sleep, floating just below the surface, and two dark islands reappeared where they were rumoured to be.

"And so that's how it went, the great Martha Briggs, food for the fishes. It's a shame really because I had a lot more adventures planned. And I never got to retire."

"That's how it goes with you adventurer types," said the spirit sat opposite her. "You never know when to call it a day."

"Sure, but I lived twice as much in twenty-five years than you did in seventy. And I died in a really cool way, fighting a dragon. How did you die again?"

"I fell from a ladder."

"I rest my case."

"A mundane end to life, I must agree. But there's more to it than it seems…"

Cool Party, Man

Unknown, 4585

"…I was a very successful businessman, you know."

Martha rolled her eyes and said, in a completely deadpan voice, "Why am I not surprised to hear you say that?"

He looked a little confused for a moment, then decided it could be nothing but a compliment, and smiled. "Why, thank you, I do strike quite the figure. Coal was my business. I was the first, you know, to start selling the stuff in bulk. I had fourteen mines. I'd carry the stuff across the country and into the capital, feeding the fires of industry!"

"Carry it yourself, did you?"

He looked outraged at that thought. "Of course not! Filthy stuff. I had people transport it for me."

"Ah, of course! Silly me."

He wondered if perhaps she was a little slow. He then decided that he didn't really care and would take any opportunity to tell his story to someone who would listen. "I became fabulously wealthy, you see. I lived in a mansion on the outskirts of the capital. Twenty-eight bedrooms it had, grand pillars by the door, and a beautiful stately garden! They say that money can't buy taste, but it bought me taste. The taste of caviar!" He took a break from speaking to laugh, heartily, at his own joke.

Martha smiled politely and let out an awkward chuckle.

"That adventuring life isn't for me, you know, Captain. I was made for a life of comfort, and that's the life I led. I had everything I ever wanted, but one thing stood out amongst the rest."

"What was that?"

He held up his hand and pointed to the wedding ring on his finger. "My Farishta. The love of my life."

Matha smiled, genuinely this time. "That's sweet."

Ochir smiled too. "We were childhood sweethearts, she and I. She was a tremendous woman. Twenty-six years we were married, and that's no small feat let me tell you!" He chuckled to himself, and then his tone changed, to one of melancholy. "But alas! Every beginning has its end, every symphony its coda. She passed on my forty-second birthday."

"I'm sorry," said Martha. She was sympathetic, and meant it. "That must have been hard."

"It was." His tone lifted, back to the boisterous one he'd been using earlier. "Every year, I throw the most fantastic party, in her honour. It's what she would have wanted, you see. And to celebrate my birthday, of course! No point languishing like a beaten dog!"

"I'm not sure I agree with how you phrased it, but I do agree with the message. Celebrate the dead, don't mourn them. If my crew don't celebrate me, I'll find a way to go back and haunt them."

"Didn't your entire crew die as well?"

Martha cocked her head, narrowed her eyes, and thought for a second. "Good point," she admitted. "They did."

"Well, I'm sure someone is celebrating you! You're a fine woman! Not as fine as my Farishta, though of course. Now, these parties we threw her were grand! She always preached temperance, you see. But with her gone, I could be truly extravagant, each year more fantastic than the last! And this last one was truly something. They'll be talking about it for years to come!

"The decorations were resplendent! Banners of gold hanging from every surface – and not gold coloured, no, no, no – real gold! There were once-in-a-lifetime floral arrangements: only the rarest of flowers, from the most remote mountaintops, from the most hidden valleys, from the lushest meadows. Diaphanous petals shone like the Sun and the Moon themselves – a fantastic sight!

"And the menagerie! The menagerie! We brought in all manner of exotic creatures. A snow bear from the far north with his mighty paws! An elephant from the south with his mighty tusks! A peacock with his beautiful tail! Even some disgusting creature from the depths of the ocean. It was caught by a fisherman and was the only one of its kind ever seen, an absolute freak! It slithered and squirmed and played its role to a tee. The guests were horrified! I must admit, I was very glad to have it disposed of afterwards."

"You killed it?" asked Martha.

"Of course! As I said, it was an absolute freak! It has no place in the civilised world, I'm sure you'd agree. And good riddance to it too! We took it out of its pool and threw it in the fire."

"That's cruel."

"Cruel? My lady, you are a hunter by trade! You kill as a profession!"

"That's different! I kill with respect, and I don't kill something because I think it's disgusting."

"No, you kill for adventure, my dear." Martha began to speak, but Ochir held up a hand to silence her. "And I don't blame you for that in the slightest. But let's leave this unsavoury topic behind us. Let me tell you about this wonderful technology I procured!" Nothing was going to stop him talking about the party for more than a few sentences. He spoke quickly and didn't give Martha a chance to interrupt.

"I funded the research myself! That marvellous creation was my pride and joy! I called it the thermo-cabinet! It keeps food and drinks cold, even on the hottest day! And the day of the party was just that. It was blistering, but every drink served was cool as ice, without needing any ice! The elements themselves were defeated! Nature had become my plaything!" He paused for dramatic effect here, obviously hoping for some comment of admiration from Martha.

Instead, she just looked at him incredulously. "Tell that to the massive dragon that killed me."

"It's a metaphor my dear! Don't you see?" he cried, again wondering if she was a bit slow.

Martha muttered something under her breath about how he should be glad he was already dead. Then, she said more loudly, "Can you get to the point of this story? I get it, you spent a lot of money on a party. I'm really impressed." She wasn't. "What does this have to do with how you died?"

"It is impressive, isn't it? Well, the party was fantastic! Unrivalled! But alas, it had to come to an end. The guests left, and I was left alone. I sat watching the servants clean up the mess, and it was clear that the festivities were over. The celebration of Farishta's life had come to an end, and I couldn't help but mourn. Alas! Mirth was usurped by sorrow, and I wept. It must have been a poignant sight. A perfect outfit, not a crease on the jacket or a scuff on the boots, but the man inside it was crumpled.

"One of the servants must have taken pity, as she sat down next to me, and handed me a handkerchief. She put her arm around me as I cried, abandoned in this world. And then I remembered something Farishta did sometimes. She offered to help with the tidying up! Can you imagine it? She never forgot her humble roots, such a selfless soul. I was moved, and so I decided to help, too. I swept up broken bottles, and I mopped the floor! Back-breaking work, let me tell you!"

"I can't imagine how difficult that was!" cried Martha. The sarcasm was completely lost on him.

"It was! Let me tell you. And after that, I went to take down some of the banners. I placed the ladder against the wall and began to climb. But it slipped! I fell, hit my head, and died on the spot! That's what I get, you see, for doing something I wasn't meant to do."

"You didn't get someone to hold the ladder for you?"

"Whatever do you mean?"

"Never mind. You're right, it was doing the work of a servant when you were born to rule that killed you."

"My thoughts exactly! The weaver of fate has a peculiar sense of humour, doesn't she?"

"She does," agreed Martha. She had an interesting thought and didn't really care if the question was improper. "Who got all your stuff when you died?"

"My daughter, Cassia. We weren't close; we never really did see quite eye to eye. But she's the only family I have left." He huffed. "I suspect by now my beautiful mansion will be full of filthy homeless peasants. She always had a soft spot for people like that. She's so naive. They need to pick themselves up by the bootstraps, not get handouts!"

"Right," replied Martha. She thought she was probably speaking to the wrong family member, then remembered where she was, and thought it was probably for the best. "Have you thought about trying to find your wife here?"

"This place is enormous, my dear! I don't know how I'd find her."

"Isn't she worth the journey?"

"Of course she is!"

"Then go! Go find your love!"

Ochir stood up dramatically. "Why, you're right!"

"Then go!"

"Why am I sitting around?" he cried. He was inspired. "I'll start at once! Best of luck to you, my lady! I hope our paths cross again someday, but I haven't another moment to waste!"

"Good luck, Ochir!"

He began walking off, somewhat unsteadily. Martha breathed a sigh of relief. She wasn't so keen on the reunion and was glad to be rid of him. She hoped he'd succeed, though. He didn't look at all prepared for a long adventure, but the rules in the afterlife were different. Maybe he'd find her.

Martha wondered if maybe she should try and find someone. She'd said a lot of goodbyes in her time but wasn't quite sure if she was ready for them to turn back into hellos yet. She sighed heavily and reached for the bottle of rum. When you have forever in front of you, there's no rush.

Cassia & Emmeline

Toormoor Manor, 4587

Emmeline sat on the stool, a dark silhouette in the white light. Her fingers gently and purposefully moved from key to key. There was no wasted movement. Every finger was exactly where she wanted it to be, exactly when she wanted it there. The notes rang out perfectly.

"What are you doing out here?" asked Cassia. "It's cold."

The playing paused.

"I'm keeping the moon company," replied Emmeline. "It seemed lonely."

"It would seem you're moon-stricken," said Cassia, smiling.

Emmeline laughed. "What are you playing? It sounds familiar."

"It's a suite my father taught me a long time ago. This movement is called 'moonlight'."

"Fitting." Cassia smiled. "Please, do continue."

She went to lean on the balcony, looking up at the moon. It shone full in the sky, opposite a lone, dim star. The piece was slow, and simple, and beautiful beyond words. It brought to the moon an uncharacteristically warm light.

Emmeline picked up the tempo. The melody grew with every key press and soon came to rival the finest works of the songbirds – a night-time contrast to the goldfinches' song that was so full of sunshine. It built to a crescendo, before slowing down again, and returning the original theme. Arpeggios ran up and down, and the world seemed entirely at peace to Cassia, as she looked out over the gardens. Not quite ready for the moment to be over, as the piece came to a close, she asked for an encore.

Cassia stopped watching the moon and went to sit beside Emmeline, watching her play instead. She sat in silent reverie for the length of the encore and for some time after it had finished.

"The moon is lucky to have you," she finally said. Emmeline smiled at that. "You make good company."

"As do you, my dear."

They sat together looking out.

"It does look lonely up there, doesn't it?" mused Cassia.

"It does."

"I wonder if anyone has ever tried to visit?"

"It would be quite the journey."

"You and I should go together one day – just the two of us."

"That would be nice," said Emmeline. She gestured vaguely around her. "We could leave all of this behind us."

"And live with not a care in the world!"

"So, Cassia," said Emmeline, with genuine interest, "how would we get there?"

"Hmmm. That's a tricky question." She thought for a moment. "Ah, of course! We take a ride on an aerophorius!"

"An aerophorius? What on earth is that?"

"Half horse, half eagle, and half bat. Our noble steed!"

"Ah! Of course. How could I have forgotten!" feigned Emmeline. "We shall name her Luna, in honour of our quest."

"And we shall fly, you and I and Luna, all the way up!"

"And we'll meet the dragon on the moon!"

"And he'll say," Cassia put on a deep, gruff voice, "'Why Emmeline, I do so love your playing. Thank you for keeping me company all those lonely nights.' And in return for your kindness, he'll gift us a palace."

"A palace?"

"Yes."

"My, my, that's mighty generous of him."

"He's fabulously wealthy."

"Oh, is he? Fabulously wealthy and a flatterer? He sounds like quite the catch."

Cassia played at outrage. She let loose a dramatic gasp. "After Luna and I took you all the way to the moon? Alas! The heart of this lady is cold! It'll be just the two of us now, Luna."

Emmeline surpassed Cassia's play-shock with a gasp of her own, even larger, and even more dramatic. "You're taking Luna in the divorce?"

"I raised her," shouted Cassia, "since she was a foal!"

"Can I at least visit her?" asked Emmeline gingerly.

"You can visit," conceded Cassia.

"Thank you."

"You're welcome."

They sat daydreaming for a while.

"I wonder what the earth looks like from up there," asked Cassia eventually.

"I bet it's beautiful."

"You're beautiful, Emmeline," said Cassia.

"Am I?"

"You are. You're like a… like a…" Cassia stammered. "Oh, I don't know!"

Emmeline smiled. "That's okay, I know what you're trying to say."

The words that Cassia wanted came to her suddenly, and excitedly, she burst out, "You're like a flower in the winter, like one small splash of vivid red in a world of monotonous white." Emmeline hugged her tightly. Cassia's tone softened, and became slow, quiet, and sincere. "You make me believe that spring will come. In this… this soiled world, you give me hope."

"I love you, Cassia."

"And I love you, Emmeline."

They hugged tightly, as tears rolled down their cheeks. In their duality they found solace, and in a way unique to love, their worries faded away – for the time being, at least.

Emmeline wiped away Cassia's tears, and then her own.

"Come on, let's go to bed," said Emmeline, looking up. "We won't outstay our welcome in Mr Moon's back garden."

"We'll call again, Mr Moon," said Cassia, a little nasally. "It's been a pleasure."

Her dreams that night came in stark contrast to the peace of the night.

Red Dream

Red wastelands stretch as far as the eye can see. The woman is wearing red, a practical red dress down to her knees. Underneath, tights, with black and red stripes. She holds out an open hand, and a red bird flies over to eat the red seeds she's placed there.

The doll sat next to her on the tree stump is dressed the same as she is.

Without even so much as a nod of thanks, the bird flies away. Her hand is empty now. She closes it and brings it to her lap.

A slight breeze blows, a silent breeze. The air is dry.

The doll turns its head towards the woman. The woman looks at it and then looks away. Her red lips form a grimace. She turns and opens the pack next to her. She picks up the doll, gently, and puts it inside.

The woman sits, and stares straight ahead.

Watching, from behind, is a giant. It raises to above its eye an open hand. Its metal armour clinks. The red sun is bright. The woman is far away, but its eyes are sharp. She won't see it if she turns around, but it sees her perfectly.

It sees her put away the doll, and it grimaces along with her. A lost cause. It turns around and leaves, retracing the enormous footprints left in the red dust.

The sun stays still in the sky. There is nothing to show the woman that time is passing. She glances down at the bag. She looks back up, and the tower is there, dark stone stretching to the sky. On the balcony stands a man. He wears a red hat on his head. He wears a long, red, button-down shirt, with all of the buttons undone. He wears nothing else.

A fishing rod dangles down. The man is holding it tightly, ready to react at any moment. The hook hangs well above the ground.

The woman looks at him, now. He takes no notice and remains perfectly still. There is once again nothing to show the woman that time is passing.

A buzzing comes. As the insect changes its direction, the pitch of the buzzing changes slightly. The woman turns her head, and watches it flit. For a split second, reflected in its eyes, she sees a memory, a blue memory – one she'd forgotten a long time ago. It flies towards her and hovers in front of her face. It's as big as she is, and red. The memory plays out in full then it flies away towards the tower.

The hook catches the insect, and the man leaps to action. Struggling wildly, the insect lets loose a scream. The contest is short. The man reels it in and grabs it in his arms. Behind, a door opens, and he takes it inside.

After some time, another door opens. This one on the ground. He walks purposefully out, with closed, empty hands, and comes before the woman. He holds his right hand out and opens it. She stands, puts the pack over her shoulder, and reaches out her own hand. They walk together into the tower.

As they cross the threshold, she turns into red dust. The man keeps walking, fetching a red broom. He sweeps the dust outside and shuts the door behind him. The last star in the sky goes out.

Epilogue

Unknown, Unknown

The God of the Sun and the Dragon King stood side by side, and it was cold. They looked at each other, solemnly.

The Sun spoke first. "I don't know if we have the strength for this anymore."

The two watched, as the barrier around the world strained.

"I'm glad you woke up in time, though," she said. "Wouldn't fancy doing it all by myself."

"Of course. I wouldn't miss it for the world," replied the king. "Admittedly, it was a rather long metamorphosis. I'd become quite attached."

"I like you dressed like this. It takes me back."

The king chuckled. He'd shed the form of a dragon. He appeared now as he truly was, in a form not quite comprehensible to the human mind, a form which exuded majesty – he was not just king of the nation, but King of the Gods.

"Those humans you made," said the Sun, "they were quite entertaining. Good work."

"Thank you," replied the king. "I think it was my finest."

"I know we've bickered," started the Sun.

The king laughed heartily at that.

The Sun smiled her characteristically toothy grin and continued. "I know we've bickered, but this has been a wonderful few years."

"It has."

"But all good things must come to an end."

"All good things must come to an end," agreed the king. "But not without a good fight, ey?"

"Not without a good fight," agreed the Sun.

The last star in the sky went out, and the God of the Stars' barrier failed.